# SO THE SIGN SAID

## NATASHA OSTEEN

*SO THE SIGN SAID*
NATASHA OSTEEN

**Moonshine Cove Publishing, LLC**
**Willow Point, Abbeville, SC 29620**
*Books that Beckon*

This book is a work of fiction. Names, characters, places and incidents are products of the author's imagination or are used fictitiously. Any resemblance to actual events, locals or persons, living or dead, is entirely coincidental.

ISBN: 978-1-9373270-7-1

Library of Congress Control Number: 2012940924

Manufactured in the United States of America.

Also available in Kindle, Nook, and ePub formats.

Book cover by Mara Page; church and sign images iStockphoto.

For my mother, Elaine,
and my most awesome miracle,
Micah Rose

*Miracles are like pimples,*
*because once you start looking for them*
*you find more than you*
*ever dreamed you'd see.*
—LEMONY SNICKET, *THE LUMP OF COAL*

# Chapter 1

The city smelled so bad, I wished I were congested. But that's what happens after a warm rain in New York. The air takes on the stench of car exhaust, hot garbage, and all the people flooding the streets carrying cappuccinos. The smell just hovers there—like the city has body odor.

Don't get me wrong, I loved New York. But use a little soap in that shower.

If the urban bouquet wasn't bad enough, the crowd of classmates behind me echoing their exciting summer plans was enough to induce stomach pains. Searching for a distraction, I stared at a soggy page of Virginia Woolf and wrinkled my nose.

*Now, where was I?*

I squinted, trying hard to finish a sentence I'd read before, when a particularly strong gust of wind lifted my hat into the city traffic. All I could do was watch as a city bus flattened my favorite black fedora against the slick asphalt. The hat's lone brown feather struggled to perk up above the sludge.

A loud laugh boomed behind me.

"Hey, Curly Fry!" It was a voice I knew all too well. I set down *Three Guineas* as my boyfriend, Stryder, plopped beside me, laying his pinstripe umbrella on the sidewalk.

"Hello, Sitzpinkler," I responded, with a cheesy grin.

Stryder winked before he kissed me—clueless that *sitzpinkler* means "one who sits down to pee" in German.

"Get out of here," I puffed. "No groping in public, remember?"

I always thought Sloan or Brianna would be a better match for Stryder. They were more his type: uber-rich, beautiful, and always absorbed in some kind of self-induced drama.

"Fine." He smiled, glancing around to see who was watching us, or more likely, watching him—the one and only Stryder Wendell-Vaughn.

"You're definitely down for the beach next weekend, right?" he asked. "The first party's always sick."

It had been pouring rain for nine days straight. Every now and then, the clouds would break long enough for me to camp outdoors and soak in a few pages of my book, but that was it.

"I hate to rain on your parade . . ." I started as Stryder let out a groan, "but this weather is going to ruin the weekend." As though following a script, a stray raindrop fell onto my head.

"No way," Stryder said, checking his phone. "This weather rocks. It's warm enough to wear skimpy bathing suits, but cool enough to get cozy."

I raised an eyebrow skeptically.

One of the best things about Stryder was that I never had to worry about him displacing my class rank. In our very first conversation, he assured me that Don Quixote was a type of tequila. But his loyalty as a boyfriend? That was still to be determined.

"Great observation," I said. "Speaking of, we're wearing our matching jaguar bikinis, right?"

Stryder laughed. "No, your dad borrowed mine."

Dad. Thanks for reminding me. As I started to calculate how late he was, I remembered an article from *The New York Times*. It said there were fewer homicides when it rained.

*I might have to skew that statistic.*

He was always late picking me up from school—even on this, the last day of junior year. And while some parents might have valid excuses, there was no reason to assume my father was anything other than chronically late. It was one of the perks of being Professor Eli Klein, the unapologetic eccentric. Like how he insisted on picking me up when I could just as easily take the subway.

Stryder looked to the street as a black Mercedes pulled up next to the curb. He hesitated. "Do you need a ride?"

"No," I lied. "My dad just called. He's on his way."

"Maybe I'll wait with you 'til he comes?"

I forced a smile. "Get out of here. I'm fine."

Stryder played the concerned boyfriend well, but I had a creeping suspicion he planned on a summer of hot tub hookups. Despite his promises of "hopeless devotion" every time a rumor swirled, I could easily imagine him drunk and stumbling from one girl to the next.

"Talk to you tomorrow?"

"You'd better," I said, quickly kissing him good-bye before he jumped into his father's car. In seconds, the black sedan disappeared in a sea of yellow taxis.

As if waiting for Stryder to leave, two girls clad in Burberry strutted up to me: Sloan and Brianna—thorns in my side since ninth grade.

Sloan took one look at my hat-hair and rolled her eyes. "Nice 'do, Jordan."

Brianna flicked her perfect blonde braids in my direction. "Yeah, nice hair, *freak*."

How droll. I'd never been what you'd call "popular" with my female counterparts—and the fact that Stryder, the most revered boy in school, found me worthy of his affection didn't help. Oh, sure, while Stryder Wendell-Vaughn was around, everyone was sugary sweet, but the minute he turned his back, I morphed into the girl who smelled like unwashed armpit. In the cafeteria, when I showed up Stryder-less, every seat was "taken."

That was my life story. I liked to consider myself a "dipper," someone who dipped in and out of cliques. And, truth be told, I was more a little dipper than a big one. I wasn't catty enough for the gossip girls. I wasn't angry or tough, so I felt out of place with the juvenile delinquents. My grandfather had been Jewish, so you'd think I'd have an in with the Hebrews, but my father had converted to Protestantism long ago, so "Oy vey!" I was neither tall nor short, neither the life of the party nor wallflower. Neither painfully shy nor bluntly forthright. I was, quite simply, stuck somewhere in between.

The only things that set me apart from my peers were my green eyes and my hair—an abundance of unmanageable amber-colored waves. Naturally, I took every opportunity to cover my mop. And alas, one of my trusted disguises, the vintage fedora, was no more.

Turning my back to the girls, who'd lost interest in me anyway, I took out my cell.

"Hello, you have reached the voicemail of Dr. Eli Klein, Professor of Divinity. I wish I were available to take your important call but I'm trying to do a lot of things that cannot get done while—Yes, thank you, Miss Collins, you can put it over there. Please leave your name and number, uh, over there, Miss Collins." *BEEP!*

"Errrrrrww," I growled into the phone. He'd know my deranged, irritated howl anywhere. I called again, only to get the same result. I waited a few moments before calling again—*BEEP!*

"Eli, it's your daughter, Jordan. Remember me? In case you forgot, we live in the same house. You pick me up from school because you won't let me ride the subway. Ring a bell?"

I was going to call again, but one of his numerous "daily lessons" came to mind. *The definition of insanity is repeating the same action and expecting a different result.* For once, his lesson (stolen from Albert Einstein) actually applied to real life. I looked down at my watch—school had let out forty-five minutes ago.

Growing up, I had idolized my father—an established author, professor, and public intellectual. But somewhere along the way, that had changed. I started calling him by his first name, wondering if he would come from behind his desk amongst piles and piles of paperwork to scold me. He never did.

Resigned to the fact that my father had forsaken me, I dug through my faded backpack and found the small digital camera at the bottom of my bag. Other than reading, photographing the city at unusual angles was another favorite preoccupation. I hopped off the ledge and strolled down the street, looking for inspiration—for color, for life, for anything that popped out of the shadowy gray of the buildings and the overcast sky.

A couture shop caught my attention. The sign in the window espoused a callous philosophy: "I Shop, Therefore I Am." The silvery letters were set against a glowing stage decorated with bright yellow summer clothes and heartbreakingly high heels. A homeless man in front of the store clashed with the textures of consumerism, the tactile sheers and silks. *Snap-Snap.* He grinned as I showed him his picture and handed him a pack of Fruit Stripe gum.

I raised my camera toward a duo of billboards. The first advertisement featured a doctor with a resigned look, and the caption read, "Childhood Obesity, Don't Take It Lightly." Next to it in another ad, a teenager held up two McDonald's bags, with a thought bubble floating above his head—"My Kinda Shoppin' Spree!" *Snap-Snap.*

I figured I'd killed enough time, so I headed back, hoping to find my father waiting on me this time. But no such luck. I twiddled my thumbs for another twenty minutes before he finally pulled up in his Volvo station wagon. He attempted to parallel park, and I pretended to ignore him. After three false starts, he gave up and honked the horn. He leaned across the front seat to open the passenger door.

"Wow, you're early," I said facetiously.

"Am I?"

"No. You're an hour late."

"I'm sorry."

"On the last day of school, no less."

I guess he hadn't gotten my messages.

A taxi driver yelled at us to move. Dad checked his mirrors half a dozen times before pulling the station wagon into traffic. He swayed in and out of the middle lane. I was used to him being distracted, but today he seemed even more so than usual.

"Are you okay?" I asked, slightly concerned.

He turned from the window and looked at me, deciding to join me on planet Earth. "What? Of course, sweetheart. It's been a long day."

I eyed him suspiciously. Maybe I could take advantage of his state of mind. "You know—if you got me a car, you could play all day without hearing a single peep from me." He'd never go for the car idea. *But if I aim high, maybe he'll at least let me take the subway.*

"Believe me, Jordan; having a car would make life harder, not easier. And, anyway, only crazy people drive in the city." He sailed through a red light, almost clipping a pedestrian.

"Obviously," I muttered.

"Let's talk about something else. You had an enlightening school year, I take it?"

"Sure."

"Excellent!" he said, with an anxious whistle at the next stop. "If you had to pick one thing, what was the most valuable thing you learned?"

I'd come to expect questions like this over the years. Our father-daughter talks were not conversations; they were interviews.

"Punctuality," I said with a straight face.

We sat in silence as we passed apartment buildings and ads for cosmetics and clothing.

"Actually, we did learn something new today that you may be able to teach your seminary students," I volunteered.

"Really? What's that?"

"We learned why Jesus wasn't born in America."

Instantly cautious, he replied, "Okay, I'll bite."

I let out a long sigh. "God couldn't find three wise men and a virgin."

"Very funny."

I smiled and stared out the window. Next to us was a wispy-thin man in a Hawaiian shirt. He was riding a bike while holding a cello in one hand and balancing a six-pack of Heineken over the handlebars.

*Man, I love this smelly city!*

Out of the corner of my eye, I saw my father shift uncomfortably.

"Oh y-e-s," he said, dragging "yes" out into a three-syllable word, which always meant trouble. I braced myself for the worst.

"I forgot to mention. We're going to have a Klein family conference this evening. Six thirty sharp."

# Chapter 2

I sat next to my mother on the sofa, watching my father sitting across from us hunched over in his favorite plush armchair lost in thought. Absentmindedly, he rearranged the coasters on the coffee table. My father was an academic elite, an avid wearer of plaid, and . . . many times, a dipsy-doodling disaster.

*And I am his spawn.*

I looked at the clock: 6:30 sharp.

Sitting next to me, Mom cut an intimidating figure. She looked dignified in her black pencil dress and Italian black leather pumps. Her honey-colored hair was pulled back in a ponytail, showing off the sparkling diamond studs my father bought her after she became partner at the law firm. That was five years ago.

"Eli?" She waved a hand in front of his face, careful not to spill her gin and tonic on the black leather couch. "You do realize I came home early because Byron is coming for dinner, don't you?"

Finally, my father pulled himself away from the coasters.

"Yes. Of course." His face was strained, and he spoke hurriedly, in one long word without any spaces. "I've called this meeting to tell you that Jacob was detained while trying to sneak contraband into China."

We both looked a little perplexed as he simply stared at us.

*That's it? Really?* It had to be something more than my uncle's latest shenanigans, and it wasn't like him to peddle drugs. To the entire Klein family, Uncle Jacob was forty going on sixteen—the consummate dreamer, always trying to save the world.

I shook my head. "Crazy Uncle Jacob is a dope pusher? No way."

Dad stood up and paced around the living room. "It wasn't narcotics, Jordan," he huffed. "It was religious contraband. Bibles."

My mother and I looked at each other. We weren't surprised.

At least twice a year Uncle Jacob came to visit us in New York City. He'd blow in like a breath of fresh air to a place where rich young traders impressed their girlfriends by refusing tap water at restaurants. Jacob was a small-town pastor, living an anti-materialistic lifestyle, and it suited him. Plus, he always got cool points for bringing me campy knickknacks from Texas, like pink cowboy boot saltshakers, a potato gun, or a miniature Alamo.

I truly enjoyed his visits; that is, until he and my father butted heads. While Dad was usually blithely optimistic, when his little brother came to town, he turned into an arguing machine. They'd debate topics like nuclear power, woolly sweaters versus polyester-blend Lycra, and, most recently, the evidence of modern-day miracles. Sometimes they'd wait until after nightfall to bicker but, in most cases, the debate raged early at the dinner table, despite my mother's pleas for "normal conversation." She wanted to talk about new case law, or discuss the latest additions to our wine cellar, or rib my father for something wacky he did—like slipping on some ice and landing on our neighbor's shih tzu, Wookie.

I remember, just last winter, we were out to dinner at one of those velvet booth type restaurants when one of their arguments erupted.

"And what about those who believe God doesn't use magic tricks to entertain the masses?" my father asked Jacob.

"That's the problem with you ivory tower types, Eli," Jacob said, scooping a robust portion of Eggplant Napoleon onto his plate. "You're too far removed to see what takes place all around us."

"Will you pass the asparagus?" I asked my father, who set his knife and fork on the edge of his plate, lifted his white linen napkin from his lap, and dabbed the corners of his mouth. He didn't pass the asparagus. Instead, he took off his black-framed glasses to respond to Jacob's challenge.

"While *naive* people accept stories of supernatural occurrences, rational scholars understand that these are just stories. They're parables, told to make a point."

Even without his glasses, my father looked much older than his younger brother—especially with tomato sauce on his nose.

"Will you pass the asparagus?" I asked Uncle Jacob, who looked at my father and crooked an eyebrow. He didn't pass the asparagus. Instead, he picked up the small green pear from the ornamental bowl in the middle of the table and bit into it.

"Will you pass the asparagus?" I asked my mother.

"That was a decorative pear, Jacob," Mom said, tipping her wine glass toward him and rolling her eyes.

It was obvious that no one planned to pass the asparagus. I tore off the end of the French bread and placed a fat piece on my tongue, letting it rest for a moment. Leaning back in my chair, I looked up at the ceiling, trying to block out their conversation with the sound of my teeth crunching into the crust. It didn't work.

I fought back the urge to jump on top of the table and dance a jig. "What about passing a peppermint stick and a sour pickle?"

"Oh, never mind," said Uncle Jacob as he placed his napkin on the table. "You wouldn't believe in airplanes if you didn't see them flying overhead."

"You should check your eggplant, Jacob," Dad said, pointing with his fork. "Perhaps you'll see the face of Mary etched in the ricotta."

Uncle Jacob gripped the stem of his wine glass and smirked at my father, but his cell phone ended any further dispute. He rose from the table and answered, determined not to let my father set him off.

"Hello?"

We sat silent as my uncle's hand pressed upon his forehead and he closed his eyes while listening to the caller.

"No. That can't be right. Are you sure?" After a minute, his mouth fell open. "It said what?"

Hurriedly, Uncle Jacob grabbed his coat and walked out of the restaurant and onto the city sidewalk. I watched him pace in front of the restaurant's windows, disrupting the packs of pedestrians racing to get out of the cold.

Oblivious to Jacob's exchange or absence, my parents continued their normal dinnertime tête-à-tête.

"So today's CNN.com poll asked people their opinion, 'Does Viagra cause blindness?'" Mom complained. "Is this news now?"

My eyes darted outside again. Uncle Jacob still paced, his hands making broad and deliberate sweeps through the air. It was unusual to see him so flustered. That space was usually reserved for my zany family. Jacob always carried himself with confidence, as if he had life completely figured out. It was easy for him—not because he had a lot of money, not because he had a perfect love life, but because . . . well, I hadn't gotten to that part yet. But when he returned to the table, running his hand through his hair, he looked tired in an unfamiliar way, and I was curious.

"Is everything okay?" I asked.

"No." Jacob smiled faintly. His hand touched my shoulder. It was heavier than I expected. He tried to sound calm, but his voice cracked. "There's been an accident involving one of my parishioners. I need to get back to Ashworth."

"That's unfortunate," Dad said, the last Brussels sprout rolling around his mouth. "Make sure they know our prayers are with them. . . . Oh, and I'd take you to the airport in the morning, but I have a lecture. You'll have to take a cab."

Uncle Jacob took a deep breath and closed his eyes. Right before he left, he passed me the asparagus.

That dinner in January was the last time we'd heard from Jacob—other than a short letter written from a small village in Guatemala. Apparently, he'd joined some group building water wells. Jacob vacationed a little bit differently than we did.

"You see, it's still illegal in some parts of the world to transport printed religious materials," my father explained. "Well, technically, it's only illegal to bring them in if they exceed the amount for personal use, but—"

He wore down the Persian rug in front of us and chattered with animation. "Smuggling them into the country wasn't the brightest idea. Fortunately for Jacob, the authorities have released him, but he's been advised not to leave until the charges are officially dropped."

"How long will that be?" Mom asked, shifting in her chair.

"About three months." He paused. "Which brings me to the main reason for our Klein family conference."

"Uh-oh," I said. "Are we going to China to break him out?" *China might be fun.*

"No, Jordan," he said with impatience. "Jacob called to ask if I would . . ." He took a deep breath. "Jacob asked if I would take over his church."

Mom took a deep drink. I sat still, incredulous.

"What?" I finally stammered, swallowing hard and peering up at him. I'd been blindsided.

My father stopped pacing and looked at me reassuringly. "Just until he gets through this little international incident. No more than three months."

"I thought he was at some church in the middle of nowhere," I said, dumbfounded.

"Yes," Mom added, barely coming out of shock. "Ashworth, Texas."

My father once explained that Jacob had landed in Ashworth after dropping out of seminary, due to his "inability to accept proven philosophical principles." Mom had made it sound like a prison, like Siberia. But Ashworth was in Texas. It wasn't cold there; it was unbearably hot.

Hot like *Hell.*

"What would *we* do in Ashworth?" I asked.

"I'd do some weddings, Sunday sermons, hopefully no funerals—"

"—Not *you*, Eli. What would *we* do in Ashworth?"

Mom had been uncharacteristically quiet, until she realized how serious her husband was. "*You* would do the sermons? You've never given a sermon in your life! How could you even think of such a thing," she said tersely, her grip tightening on her glass.

"I do have a Ph.D. in Biblical studies, Rachel, and I lecture four times a week at Columbia," he said, looking hurt. "And I didn't ask you because I knew you'd say no."

"You're dreaming if you think Byron will let me leave the firm for three months," she said. "I would kiss my career good-bye!"

My mother's career meant everything to her. She'd fought for years to become a partner at her firm. She was a struggling law student when she met my father, who was in his first year of seminary.

And while Grandfather Klein had acted as a safety net for all of Dad's endeavors—most of them harebrained—Mom hadn't grown up with money.

I never met my mom's parents, and she rarely talked about her childhood. In fact, from the snippets of information I gathered (from photographs and odd comments here and there), I got the distinct impression that her father had been a deadbeat and her mother had disappeared for days at a time, smelling like Wild Turkey and musky cologne when she crawled back through the door. Mostly, due to sheer force of will rather than natural intellect, Mom excelled in school. It was her only ticket to a better life. She had no family name, no connections, and no cash to fall back on. But she did have street smarts, a beautiful smile, and unrelenting determination.

"There will always be someone smarter than you, prettier than you, richer than you," she often told me, "but you can always work harder than everyone else. That's how you make it to the top."

Tenacity was why she got into the *right* law school. Persistence was how she found the *right* law firm. And, if my calculations were correct, her only misstep was the main reason she married my father:

Me.

"You could talk to Byron tonight," Dad begged.

Mom gasped, choking on her drink and spraying it all over the Persian rug. But she didn't say no. *Surely not.* With the request on the table, my father settled back into his chair and sighed. Did he really think he'd get away with this?

I started pacing the room, just as he had. "Seriously? I'm supposed to go to the Hamptons next weekend with Stryder. Next weekend! This is beyond wrong."

"What's a 'Stryder'?" He looked at Mom for help.

"Her boyfriend," she said, as she knelt on the floor, dabbing the fresh stain off the rug. Wait—I thought she and I were in this together. Was she caving already?

"Look, a boyfriend is not your strongest argument. You'll have the rest of your life to date," he said firmly.

"Yeah, you're right! What was I thinking?! I'll hang out at the Dairy Queen in Ashworth and listen to some hick's aspirations of owning a fireworks stand! For all that is *holy*!" My blood was boiling—my head spinning. I stared at my father with narrowed eyes, as if peering into his soul. That's when I realized what was really going on. I hissed, "This isn't about helping Jacob at all, is it? This is about you trying to escape the bus debacle."

"That's simply not true!" he lashed back, stung by my words. But based on his reaction and the slight quiver in his voice, I knew I was right.

My father wasn't your run-of-the-mill head of the household. He had a lot of good intentions, but too often they landed him in hot water. What's that expression again? The road to Hell is paved with . . .?

Right.

I was with him when he brought the school bus to Cosmo's Charters. Normally, the school used the bus to shuttle divinity students to and from community projects during the week. But Dad determined that as chairman of the school's budget committee he could rent out the bus on weekends. With enough rental funds, the school library could stay open late into the night. And if they made any extra cash, he planned to replace the broken laminating machine in the teacher's lounge. The one that died when it ate his tie.

Dad began his awkward pitch.

"If I'd been wearing a turtleneck that never would've happened," he said to the thick grunt behind the desk, aka "Cosmo."

"Guess I'm lucky you weren't," Cosmo smirked.

My father buffed a black smudge from the rear of the bus with the hem of his blazer. Meanwhile, Cosmo kicked the tires and banged his wrench against the bus.

"We're trying to raise money for the school. This bus sits around on weekends—so if you can use it, we'd simply request a modest fee."

"Library, laminating machine, I don't care," Cosmo grumbled. He didn't look like the type of man that had gotten far in life by trusting people. "Any catch?"

"Not a one," Dad promised.

I inched toward him, nudging him a little. "Umm . . . the side of the bus, Eli?"

"Oh! Yes, yes, yes. Sorry. It's extremely important that you cover this up." He pointed to the writing on the side of the bus, which read, *Union Theological Seminary—The Bible Bus*. "It's on both sides."

Without a word, Cosmo ambled over to another bus and peeled off a long, thin magnetic sign, which read, *Cosmo's Charters for Hire*. It'd been used to cover up another sign. "No problem." He smiled.

True to his word, after my father dropped off the bus the following weekend, Cosmo affixed the large magnetic sign over the school's legend. A few hours later, a bawdy group of cross-dressers and buxom girls piled on the bus, yelling and singing raucously. They dangled feather boas and silver streamers out the window, which sailed in the night air.

Despite my father's best intentions—yes, there's that word again—and Cosmo's many assurances, the magnetic covering didn't last long. The bus driver swerved too far to the left when passing through a tollbooth, and a metal pylon jarred the sign loose. Of course, no one on board noticed, and if they had, they probably wouldn't have cared. They were on a mission to party. For 137 miles, all the way to Atlantic City, as the passengers drank, danced, and bared their souls (and sometimes skin), the bus proudly displayed *Union Theological Seminary—The Bible Bus* for the whole tristate area to see. Everyone on the highway witnessed the raging party inside. Finally, the bus reached its destination, and the driver parked next to the convention center marquee, which read, "Puffers and Tails: Adult Film Convention."

As luck would have it, an Associated Press reporter was writing a story about how pornography flourishes during tough economic times, and he chanced upon the Bible Bus as the rowdy crew unloaded. He snapped a flurry of pictures and quickly dispatched them to his editors. The next day, every national news outlet ran the story of the Bible Bus, with headlines like "Bible College: Eat, Drink, and Be Mary!" and "Holy Cross-Dressers!"

Needless to say, the university's Board of Trustees was none too pleased with my father.

"Eli, were you fired?" Mom asked, realizing I might be onto something.

"No! No," Dad insisted, gesticulating with exasperation.

"You said the Faculty Committee understood."

"They do. It's just—"

"It's just what, Eli? It's just you thought it would be better to spring this on me sixty minutes before my boss—the *managing partner* of my law firm—gets here for dinner? I honestly don't know what to say to you," Mom chided.

"Look, I'm not saying we have to go. We don't have to make a decision right now. I'm merely asking you both to think about it."

"Okay, I've considered it," I said, standing to my feet. "My decision is: absolutely not."

I stomped upstairs to my room. Mom left in a huff, too, leaving my father alone in his comfortable chair.

# Chapter 3

**T**hree hours later, my parents sat at the dining table, a scattered spread of platters, candles, and two empty wine bottles separating them from their guests—my mom's boss, Byron, and his wife, Kimley. Byron had been over once or twice before. He was an oily-haired beanstalk who dressed in designer suits or, as Mom once called him behind his back, "a well-read lounge lizard."

Nonchalantly, I walked past the dining table to the kitchen, retrieving one of the boxes of Boo Berry cereal I'd hoarded since Halloween—its smiling marshmallow ghost eyeing my "Jesus Hates Your Botox" T-shirt.

"You remember Byron, dear?" Mom intoned. "And his wife, Kimley?"

Kimley's shoulder bones poked through her gold-embroidered jacket. She practically looked embalmed. I imagined her sitting in front of the computer and Googling, "How to lose weight but still enjoy three French martinis a day."

"Why, hello, Jordan," said Byron, flashing me a blinding white-toothed smile. I nodded hello. "Eli, did Rachel tell you about the client she scored today?" he asked.

I watched as Mom traced her finger around the rim of her empty wine glass. "It's no big deal." She laughed nervously.

"What did your client do?" I piped up from the kitchen barstool.

"They promised huge returns that would've grossed millions if it hadn't been a massive Ponzi scheme," she said flatly.

Dad shook his head. "Unfortunate."

"Hey, these investors knew who they were dealing with," Byron argued.

"Wow," I interrupted. "You should run for political office with a moral compass like that."

"Jordan!" Mom scolded.

"No, it's okay." Byron laughed. "I've actually considered it." His eyes darted up at me as a smile spread across his face.

"I agree with Byron about the investors," Kimley chimed in. Her voice was a grating Long Island accent mixed with a thousand smoked cigarettes. "It's like they picked up a baby snake and said, 'Hey, what a cute little baby snake.' And they pet it and loved it. And then one day, BAM! The snake bites them on the ass."

"I'm sorry, I don't understand," my father said. In his defense, he wasn't great with metaphors.

"The point is," Kimley continued, "it's a friggin' baby snake! What did they expect?"

"Eloquently put," I said, pouring milk into my bowl.

"Thank you, Jordan," Kimley clucked.

My mom shot me a disapproving look and pointed to my cereal bowl, looking to change the subject. "Is that your dinner?"

"Boo Berry cereal is much more than *dinner*. It's a metaphysical education in a bowl . . . introducing kids to the concept of life and death." I smiled like a QVC host. "All with the great taste of blueberry-flavored marshmallows."

"Ah, the existentialist of the breakfast cereals." Dad chuckled.

Still fuming about the possibility of a summer in bumpkin land, I tromped up the stairs and yelled, "And there's no way I find Boo Berry in Ashworth."

"Ashworth? Is that the new club next to Soho House?" Kimley asked.

I stayed upstairs reading. Every once in a while, a bit of wine-soaked conversation drifted into my room. I heard Kimley say, "I watched Letty try on a pair of Roger Vivier heels that cost twelve thousand dollars. Twenty-four-carat gold mesh, satin, and taxidermy birds with crystal heads." While I usually didn't read and listen to music at the same time, I made an exception. Kimley's voice trailed off as I took out a book, put on my headphones—listening to a Killers track on repeat.

The next thing I knew someone tapped me on the shoulder.

Ugh. It was Byron. *Do I have To Catch A Predator on speed dial?*

"Uh . . . Uh . . ." he stuttered as I sat up on my bed.

"Yeah, talking's hard."

As if that were an invitation, he sat down next to me.

"What are you reading?" he asked.

"*Stray Shopping Carts of North America,*" I said, pointing to *A Prayer for Owen Meany.* "Shouldn't you be downstairs with the big kids?"

"They won't miss me." Well, I couldn't argue with that. "They think I'm in the bathroom."

Annoyingly, Byron yammered about politics, the strength of the yen, and his forty-two-foot fishing boat. And then he droned on about golf, I think. I wasn't really listening.

Byron said moodily, "Oh, I see I'm boring you."

I didn't look up from my book. "No. No. I always yawn when I'm interested."

*Why won't this creep take a hint?*

He cleared his throat. "You know, making eye contact while speaking to someone shows intelligence, gumption, and demonstrates respect."

"Unless you are walking while talking and giving eye contact and accidentally run into a wall," I said, finally looking up from my book.

What I saw when I met Byron's eyes freaked me out. He didn't respond. He didn't flinch.

Shaking my head, I nervously offered a solution. "Maybe you should check on Kimley. After that shoe story, Eli could be breaking out his exotic bird feather collection."

But I could tell, Byron didn't plan to leave and he definitely didn't think I was funny—not one bit.

"No," he said, slowly leaning toward me. "I think you want me to stay here." Despite his hot breath on my neck, a chill filled the room.

*Uh-oh.*

He spun my shoulders toward him and lunged at me with his lips. Immediately I tried to push him away with all my strength, but his bony hands were too strong for me.

All I could do was scream.

Thankfully, my father heard.

The next afternoon my father loaded our suitcases into the trunk. Mom and I stood in silence, watching him struggle.

"This is the right thing to do," he said. "First the bus, then Jacob, and, to top things off, your boss." He waited for a response. When he didn't get one, he cried, "I punched a man! And I'm a pacifist!"

Mom and I stood in solidarity. Even though her boss was the poster child for "stranger danger," I still didn't want to go to Ashworth.

"Look, this will be an adventure. Who couldn't use three months of fresh air? Plus, we only have a year before Jordan goes off to college. It's great quality time!"

He pretended to be enthusiastic, but my father looked disheveled. It was a lose-lose-lose situation, and only he seemed unaware of it. Ashworth. It sounded like a place where boonie rats in ten-gallon hats spent all day rebuilding engines. Where city girls stared at the sky, cursing their bad fortune.

My mother looked even worse than my father. She hadn't slept and her skin was pale. Even so, she wrapped her arm around me and whispered in my ear, "We'll get this car turned around in a week."

"Here we go!" Dad said with a forced smile.

# Chapter 4

I hadn't said a word since we left New York. In fact, the only noises I made were the occasional squishing of the leather when I shifted around the backseat and the persistent click-click-click of my texting. If my father asked me a question, I put on my headphones and answered him with the muted thump-thump-thumps of bass.

"Saw world's largest Rubik's Cube today," I texted Stryder along with a photo of the multicolored beast. "At top of escalators connecting the Holiday Inn to a mall. In case you ever get to Knoxville."

"LOL," Stryder replied, seconds later. "The longer u play w/ them, the harder they get. I know something else like that! :) ROTFLMAO."

*Okay, I'm going to ignore that one.* Stryder's attempts at innuendo were transparent and annoying—only slightly less annoying than when motion sensor faucets don't work or . . . being dragged to Texas.

From the backseat, I watched my mother yapping on her cell phone. I briefly turned the volume down to hear what she was saying.

"No. Pressure has nothing to do with it. I don't care if Byron said that; it's not true and he of all people knows that. We're going because we need to help my brother-in-law." She shot my father an exasperated look. "A three-month hiatus after twenty years isn't crazy."

I'd been hoping she'd been talking to reporters to tell them about a kidnapping.

As for my father, he was totally uninterested. Actually, I think he was relieved to be away from the city because he started dressing like a color-blind tourist in Key West: Hawaiian shirt, plaid shorts, Ray-Bans, and a pair of sneakers that they'd discontinued in 1989 for being too ridiculous.

We drove for hours and hours, and the hours became two days. We stopped when the car needed gas, when Dad fell asleep at the wheel, for tourist traps such as junk art sculptures museums, or when we were hungry. At a restaurant in Memphis, I put our name on the list as "Donner"—the pioneers that resorted to cannibalism to survive. When the hostess called, "Donner, party of three," I said, "Great, we're really hungry."

Mom gave me her *you-should-know-better-than-that* look. Whatever. But I was surprised my father didn't notice. I remember him debating Uncle Jacob for hours after we watched that movie about the Uruguayan soccer team that crash-landed in the mountains and ate their dead teammates to survive. "Are individual rights more important than the good of the group?" Dad asked.

*Umm . . . Do dead people have individual rights?*

Now, sitting at the diner, he was too busy studying the map and chirping about the historical significance of the cities we drove through to notice anything else.

"We'll be passing through Hope, Arkansas," he explained. "Did you know that's where President Clinton grew up? Maybe we should drive by his old house."

After putting the map aside, he studied the menu. He ordered meatloaf with broccoli, Mom got a salad that was nothing more than iceberg lettuce and a few slices of pellucid tomato, and I requested the "Ernest T. Special." I imagined Ernest T. as the ill-tempered cook behind the counter, a lonely but sincere man with shaggy bristles above his upper lip and a cigarette dangling from his mouth. When the mountain of food arrived, my mother looked at my plate disapprovingly.

"There's nothing green on it, Jordan."

"Don't judge a food by its color," I retorted, stabbing my pork chop sandwich with a fork. "Besides, neither does yours and you got a salad."

She laughed, and to be honest, I was relieved to see her smile.

After lunch in Memphis, we popped over to Graceland. Apparently my father was a big fan. I think Elvis wrote a song about jail, so at least I could relate to that. The highlight was being able to capture my dad tripping on the mansion's front steps with my camera's speed shot function. *Snap-Snap. Snap-Snap.* After the self-guided audio tour, I texted Stryder a picture of my dad midair and another of the King.

"Don't hate! Just saw the Jungle Room. Avocado green shag carpet on the ceiling. Toilet of death was off limits. Bummer."

Stryder didn't respond.

Ten minutes later, I typed, "I signed your name on the wall!"

Still no response.

After four days of steady driving, greasy spoon diners, and roadside oddities, we finally made it to Shreveport, Louisiana, our last stop before crossing into Texas. We stayed at a motel on the outskirts of town and left early the next morning. When we passed "Welcome to the Lone Star State," a sign on the side of the highway, I privately cheered, knowing that the sooner we arrived, the sooner this ridiculous ordeal would be over. My mom had the same thought as she raised her fist in a mock cheer.

The dense trees along the road screened us from what lay beyond. The landscape didn't look at all like the sparse and dusty Texas I'd imagined. To my surprise, it was more green than tan. Dad raced down the narrow two-lane roads, swerving frequently to avoid potholes and the occasional roadkill.

"If you see a gas station or restaurant," he whined, "let me know. I don't think I can make it."

"That was your second bottled water in an hour," Mom said. "What'd you expect?"

"It's hotter than Hell on high!" Dad exclaimed.

We'd been driving since breakfast, and after the last fill-up, my father said it was "make-or-break" time. I think he was losing it.

"That means we're not stopping until Ashworth?" Mom inquired.

"Right-o."

Yep. He was definitely losing it.

A long stretch of road with hardly any traffic opened up in front of us, after a nagging series of twists and turns. It was too tempting—every New Yorker's secret dream, 100 MPH on the open country highway, soaring through the pure, unlimited expanse. He floored it until the speedometer rattled between eighty and eighty-five.

"You'd better slow down," Mom warned.

"There's not a soul out here," Dad responded.

A white truck appeared in the distance, which my father quickly dismissed. As it blinked by Mom threw her arms into the air.

"That was the highway patrol."

"They don't drive trucks, Rachel."

"We're in the country, Eli. Of course they drive trucks. They ride horses. They do whatever they damn please."

I peered through the back window in time to watch the truck whip into a U-turn. It came after us with flashing red and blue lights, brilliant even in the afternoon sun.

I chuckled under my breath as my father pulled over onto the gravel. The cop kept us waiting for five minutes. It seemed cruel, since Dad was about to burst, but it was sort of funny watching him squirm. While we sat there, I breathed steam onto the window and wrote "Help Me" in outward facing letters.

Finally, the officer opened his truck door, and I watched as his ostrich boots hit the asphalt. He donned a tan cowboy hat and moseyed over like a confident gunslinger, a throwback to the wild, wild West. My father rolled down the window and the sweltering Texas heat spilled into the car.

Now this is more like it. Let the calamities ensue.

"Afternoon, folks," the officer said in a husky voice. The name below his bronze badge read, "Officer Eugene Watts." "Is there some kind of emergency?"

*Eugene? Really?*

"No, officer." Dad paused. "Well, sort of. I'm in a hurry to find a restroom."

"Ya have to water the farm, huh?" It was hard to tell if he was being smart or just making a friendly joke.

"Uh, yes—water the farm, I suppose." We'd been dealing with Dad's shrunken bladder for days now, but this made those annoying stops worth it.

The officer glanced at our "Imagine Peace" bumper sticker before stating the obvious. "Y'all ain't from 'round here."

"Correct. We're just passing through . . . to Ashworth."

"Why Ashworth?"

"We're headed to a small church there."

The officer's facial expression changed immediately. "I reckon I'm speaking with the new pastor of East New Hope?"

I glanced sideways at my mother. The knowing tone of his voice gave us pause.

"I wouldn't say new pastor," Dad said. "But I am helping out for a few months."

The officer looked at his driver license.

"Well then, Pastor Klein—"

"Dr. Klein is fine," Dad interrupted.

"How 'bout 'Pastor Klein'?" the officer insisted.

"Yes," Dad agreed nervously. "Pastor Klein."

"Okay. It would be my honor and privilege, Pastor Klein, to escort you to the next establishment for use of their facilities. It's not a restaurant, but it's owned by real nice folk."

My father looked at Mom and me with wide eyes. The cop had behaved strangely. He'd become unusually amiable at the mention of the church. It was so extreme that I wondered if he was being sincere. Maybe he was going to take us to some secret shack where he'd performed grisly redneck rituals to torture us.

*Like forcing us to listen to that "Cotton-Eyed Joe" song for days on end.*

We followed the police truck for half a mile and into the almost empty parking lot of the Bocho Brothers Funeral Home. The marquee read "Hardin Funeral."

"I'll be right back," Dad said.

"Uh, there's a funeral going on right now." I pointed to the sign.

"I don't know that I have a choice," he said, springing from the front seat. Mom followed.

"Since we're here, I might as well go, too," she said.

I didn't have to, but it was too hot and awkward to sit in the car while my parents went facility fishing, so I shuffled toward the door behind them. Officer Watts tipped his hat as I slinked past. *Lunatic lawman or Good Samaritan?* I was still on the fence about him.

Inside, it smelled like stale Fritos. Dusty fake flowers topped a series of tables spread out across the lobby. I recognized "Wind Beneath My Wings" being played on the organ in the next room. A diminutive man resembling Benjamin Franklin greeted us. I deduced from his tan suit, furry ears, and flower on his lapel that he was a Bocho brother.

"Hello!" he said, welcoming us with a smile. "So pleased you folks could make it."

"May we, err . . ." Dad fumbled.

"May we use your restroom before the proceeding?" Mom interjected, her lawyer instincts taking charge.

"Of course. Right down the hallway and to the left."

They dashed away, leaving me alone with Ben Franklin.

"How did you know Mr. Hardin?"

"Oh, Mr. Hardin, he was, uh, my gym teacher," I said.

He looked at me quizzically. "Well, feel free to pay your respects. The visitation started forty-five minutes ago, and you're his first visitors."

I hadn't intended to go in, but now it seemed required. Little by little, I inched toward the casket in the viewing room. The pineapple-shaped lady playing the organ broke into a sluggish version of "Amazing Grace." There were twelve pews, each of them empty. From twenty feet away, I could see the open coffin. It was shiny and black, and a wreath of carnations rested in front, splashing the room with color. I'd never actually seen a dead body, not a real live one.

Finally, I reached the casket. I stared down at the dead man surrounded by gold taffeta. He wore a red plaid shirt and blue jeans with a belt buckle the size of my hand. His ashen white and ancient skin contrasted sharply with a cheap, raven-black toupee. He had a look of triumphant scorn on his face, as if he were poised to reprimand me just for staring down at him.

A cold shiver rain down my spine. *Still, no one cared enough about this old guy to come to his funeral? What was his name?*

I looked at the nameplate sitting on top of the casket. *That's right.* This surly dead man was Mr. Jasper Hardin.

I stood there for a few more minutes, and after paying my

respects to the stranger, I turned back toward the lobby. Stealthily, my parents had been watching my every move from the entranceway. *Good. Maybe they'll think they've driven me into the arms of some weird death fetish. Note to self: Wear all black tomorrow.*

"Would you like to sign the register?" asked the director.

"You get paid by the guest?" I asked.

"We'd be honored to sign," Mom said, quickly picking up the pen and handing it to me. I scribbled "Jordan K." Ours were the only signatures in the book.

As the funeral home door closed behind us, I heard the director whistling along to the organ music. It was that catchy Ray Charles song my father once downloaded as a ringtone. The song that stuck in my head for days after hearing him take an "important call." A song I wouldn't have pegged for funeral, but I dare you to omit from any respectable road trip. Without hesitation, I slammed my car door and gave into temptation:

"Hit the road, Jack."

# Chapter 5

The day simmered. I could feel the sun scorching my arm as I leaned against the backseat window. I glanced out just in time to see a sign shaped like a bigmouth bass: "Welcome to Ashworth. Y'all enjoy!"

"Now remember," Dad instructed, "down here, 'y'all' is singular. 'All y'all' is plural and 'all y'all's' is plural possessive."

I shuddered. I was a long way from the city and now, rather than hanging out in Greenwich Village, I had to concern myself with incorrect, country bumpkin grammar.

As we entered the town, my father hovered just below thirty miles per hour. I guess he didn't want to test the "lightning never strikes twice" theory. Our snail's pace allowed us to tour Ashworth's local economy. We passed a small gym called the "Fit Farm," which featured a picture of a cow holding a dumbbell, and then, there was the Dairy Queen, just as I had predicted. Next came a Piggly Wiggly grocery store and, on the opposite side of the road, a gas station that advertised "Live Wrestling." Apparently their marketing department had hit the financial skids, as the sign was merely a piece of plywood with sloppy, spray-painted lettering.

Further up the road, neighboring a Dollar General was a tanning salon that hadn't quite burnt all the way to the ground. Amid the rubble stood a lone faux palm tree that, surprisingly, had not melted into a puddle of green goo, and a gaudy, tropical-colored sign for "TanYoHide."

I made a mental note to take as many pictures as possible. I could use them when I sued my father for irreparable damages.

*Thunk, thunk, thunk.* Out of nowhere came a paved brick road that led into the town square. The entire car and all its contents rattled and shook about, including us. Mom held onto the door handle and muttered under her breath. At least she was still on my side.

A moment later, a Romanesque-style courthouse came into view. With elaborate stone carvings and a central clock tower, it stood tall overlooking the otherwise modest square. Dad took one quick look at the architectural gem and excitedly explained the town's history he'd discovered on the Internet.

"Ashworth is chicken, beef, and groceries now," he hummed along. "But in the thirties, they found hidden oil reserves nearby. Groups of roughnecks and speculators flooded the area and changed everything. Ranchers received royalties, and Ashworth sprang from nothing. Isn't that courthouse amazing?"

"It gives me the creeps," I declared, taking a picture of the large clock face that read, "Night Cometh." *Snap-Snap.*

Obviously, the oil boom my father spoke of hadn't lasted forever. Now, the square and the sand-swept brick sidewalks on the courthouse grounds served as a reminder of better days.

"I wonder if it's like this all the time," Dad said. He rolled down his window and looked at the crowd gathered on the courthouse lawn. I did the same, lifting up my camera toward the spectacle.

The square seemed to be a hotbed of activity. Women wearing tight clothes that showed every fold of skin chased rambunctious children. *Snap-Snap.* Packs of men grilling steaks at the edges of the crowd. *Snap-Snap.* Old fogies in lawn chairs sipping lemonade. *Snap-Snap.* A roar of laughter boomed from the speakers as a man holding a cigar introduced the "Cajun Cats," and a scruffy band jumped onto the stage behind him. The rotund leader of the band held up his pants while yelling into the microphone, "Yee-haw!" *Snap-Snap.*

Surrounding the stately hall were two antique shops, a diner, a hardware store, three clothing stores, a photography studio, and a coffee shop with a curious sign. A frog, wearing a white-powdered wig and clutching a cup of coffee in one hand and a glass of wine in the other, danced next to the establishment's name.

*"Madame Ribbette,"* Mom said contemplatively. "What a funny little place. Do you think it's a restaurant too? Probably Cajun food, right?"

Normally, I would have replied with something smart like, "Or an amphibious brothel," but the teenage boy in front of the coffee shop had my full attention.

Truth be told, I couldn't stop staring at him.

Tall and dark-haired, he was unloading boxes from a black Chevy Tahoe. When a small box fell to the ground, he paused to sweep a floppy strand of hair from his eyes. I watched the way his T-shirt clung to his slim body: his ribs, strong shoulders, and the round of his chest. Just as he lowered his forearm, he met my stare.

*"Remercier la bonté!"* my father shouted, causing me to jump and quickly turn from the boy, embarrassed that he caught me ogling him. Then, when the Volvo stopped at the last light in town, I did what I knew I shouldn't—I looked back. The boy was smiling, relaxed, staring right at me.

"See!" Dad shook me again from my visual reverie. "I told you Ashworth wasn't completely unrefined. They have a French restaurant!"

Meanwhile, a truck advertising a plumbing company pulled alongside us at the light. On the driver's side door was a graphic of a man, pictured from his chest down, wearing a navy shirt and sitting on a toilet with his pants around his ankles. It so happened that the mulleted plumber in the truck wore the same navy shirt, which completed the picture from the chest up. The plumber, who looked as if he was sitting on the toilet, turned, smiled, and waved, leaving my parents with their mouths wide open as the light turned green.

"Maybe we should paint a lawyer's suit on the side of my door," Mom said. "And Eli, we can paint the body of a donkey on yours."

I, however, wasn't paying attention to my mother's sarcasm or the man in the plumbing truck. I was busy peeking into the rearview mirror, preoccupied with the uncommonly attractive boy I hoped was watching us as we headed away from the crowd.

Half a mile outside of town, a spire peaked over a tree-covered hill. As we continued, the spire grew taller and when we reached the summit, I could clearly see the weathered white church. The clapboard structure looked nothing like our church in New York. It had stained glass windows and a tolling bell, but there were no flagstones from centuries past. And I was pretty sure it hadn't taken years to build.

As we pulled in, I could see that it definitely needed some TLC.

"Doesn't a lightning rod on top of a church show a lack of faith?" I asked, not expecting a response.

Proudly positioned on the front lawn was a handsome brick marquee with permanent raised lettering, "East New Hope," and a changeable sign beneath. I rolled my eyes at the day's pronouncement: "When God winks, miracles happen."

It didn't surprise me. From the backseat of our Volvo, I'd seen a number of these signs as we chewed up the local roads and highways on our trip across the country. Sometimes they announced weddings or church events, but the signs were often funny, providing clever, pun-laden truths to their communities.

Like on a heavily traveled street in Virginia, I saw one that read, "Keep using my name in vain. I'll make rush hour longer. Love, God." In Tennessee, next to a diner with an "Open Sundays" billboard, a church next door responded with its own message: "We're open Sundays, too."

My favorite was a marquee in Shreveport, Louisiana, that advised, "Forgive your enemies—it messes with their heads."

But the main reason the sign in front of East New Hope didn't surprise me was because this was my Uncle Jacob's church. Only Jacob would imagine a God that winks.

*It's gonna take a miracle for me to survive the summer. You can start winking any time now, Big Guy.*

Next to the church, behind an iron fence, an ancient cemetery set an eerie backdrop. I hated cemeteries and any creepy place, really. I kept my distance from haunted houses and horror movies. And I stayed as far away from scary books as possible, because whenever I picked up a book my imagination got the best of me and I was quickly transported to places I could only dream about—nineteenth-century England, a faraway planet, or . . . ugh, a cemetery with brain-eating zombies. So, to have a cemetery next door to where I'd be staying? The next thing I knew, Hannibal Lecter was going to start delivering our mail.

Unfortunately, if the church looked dilapidated, our house was worse. The little parsonage on the other side made the church look like the Sistine Chapel. The house had two dormers and tattered, butter-colored siding, plus a rickety full-length front porch and an odd, cupola-topped carport. I was pretty sure the whole house would fall down if any of us sneezed.

"I thought Jesus was a carpenter," I snickered.

We parked next to Jacob's cream-colored Jeep, and even that had a flat tire.

"Come on, ladies," Dad said with a deep breath. "It's three months."

"Or less," I said. "Or less than three months."

"Of course, or less than three months," he reassured us as he opened his door. My mother didn't budge.

"Three months," she sighed.

As we approached the house, a shaggy dog wriggled out from under the front porch and sprang toward me. He sat down at my feet and raised one massive black paw. "The dysfunctional trio gains another family member," I said, as I shook his paw in an overly formal manner and dismissively patted his head. "You must be Sticky."

Not long ago, Jacob told me that he had adopted Sticky after a group of local lowlifes taped the dog to an abandoned refrigerator at a nearby landfill. A man happened to be collecting cans that morning and freed the puppy from the tape with his pocketknife. He brought him directly to Jacob.

I crouched down to pet Sticky. "I see you're still abused, what with that horrid haircut and all."

Sticky turned toward the road and barked. A man approached on a Harley, his gnarled fists clutching the handlebars. A portly pig—yes, a pot-bellied pig—sat in the sidecar. The man sped by on his motorcycle like a roll of thunder, but he took the time to wave at us as he passed. Time for us to see the snake tattoo crawling up his neck. My father smiled and waved back.

"Are you trying to get us killed?" I snapped.

I smirked when my father stopped unloading to take a second look at the motorcycle man with a beady-eyed pig staring back at us. His face took on a slightly troubled look as he weighed the possibility that I could be right.

"Oh, he's harmless," he decided. "Did you see his little friend?"

"I'd have to agree with your dad, miss," said a voice out of nowhere.

A Hispanic man with a gray ponytail sat on an orange riding lawnmower near the side of the house.

"That's Woulfe and his pig, Notorious P.I.G.," he said, climbing off the grass cutter. "Neither of them would hurt a fly." He towered over us. "Worst thing he ever did was trigger a minor emergency during a town hall meeting when smells wafting from Piggie sparked fears of a gas leak. But it was just flatulence."

"I'm Cesar," he continued, as we stared at him blankly.

"Oh, yes," Dad said. "Hello, Cesar."

"Jacob told me you might be arriving today so I tried to get the lawn in order," the man said, pointing at the small house.

My mother wasn't interested in swapping stories with the yardman. She'd become more sullen since we crossed the Texas border, and now that we'd arrived in Ashworth, reality was setting in. Ninety days of barbeque and cowboys. I checked my phone for reception: two bars. Despondently, we inched along the stone path to the front porch and collapsed on the swing, still within earshot of Cesar and my father.

"Well, I'll let you folks get acquainted with the place," he added. "Let me know if you need anything, night or day. I'm an acre behind you."

"Thank you." Dad smiled. "But I'm fairly competent around the house. We should be fine."

"Of course," Cesar said as he tipped the brim of his hat. He picked up a hedge trimmer from the back of the mower and walked toward the church.

"Since when are you 'competent around the house'?" Mom choked off a laugh.

"Never trust a man who drives an orange lawnmower or a pig with gas," I cautioned an audience who no longer listened.

My father clumsily dropped his bags and picked them up, then dropped them again, before fiddling with the lock.

He pushed open the door and I entered the unlit room behind my parents. Right away, a musty smell assailed us.

"Oh, it's horrible," Mom complained. "It smells like, like . . ."

"Like an old man in a mothball sweater walking a wet sheep-dog," I finished.

"No, it just needs to air out for a while. Give me a second while I turn on the lights and find a fan," Dad muttered. But before he could find the switch, Mom pulled back the drapes and opened the front windows. The sunlight revealed a motley design scheme: art deco lighting, walls papered in a Chinese motif, and scattered Persian rugs on a dry old hardwood floor.

I read a plaque on the front wall: "On January 30, 1951, the church trustees dedicated this parsonage to God and all the ministers and their families that would come to serve East New Hope."

At the end of the room, closest to the front door, was a large sitting area that featured an oddly shaped cuckoo clock, a tangerine-colored French sofa from the fifties, and a modern glass coffee table, all in front of a small fireplace, which housed a tiny television. At the back of the room, the open kitchen featured large windows, some accented with stained glass. It was a scatterbrained way to live, but I couldn't help thinking that the black and white floor tiles, vintage white enamel appliances, and distressed dining table with seven poppy-colored, lacquered chairs were all quite chic. That was, until I stood at the sink.

"The kitchen window looks directly at the cemetery!" I said in horror.

*Note to self: Don't ever do the dishes.*

I took the rest of the tour, starting with the other side of the house. A pair of doors opened up to the bedrooms; one bedroom was much larger than the other. Each had a bath. *Phew.* In between the bedrooms, a thin spiral staircase led to a funky reading loft that Jacob had piled high with purple Moroccan pillows and cashmere throws. I flipped through a few books until Mom walked into the bedroom below.

"No! This can't be the master bedroom!" she called out.

Alas, her last hope was dashed. She wanted the refuge of a decent bedroom, and I could tell her heart was broken. But while I hated this place as much as she did, the house wasn't that much smaller than our brownstone off Third Avenue. I would still be able to hide from them.

"That bedroom is yours, Jordan," Dad called up to me, pointing to the second door.

I scaled down the stairs and turned the old brass knob to my new detention center. The spare room was a shrine to Jacob's teenage years. A poster of eighties rocker David Lee Roth in red leather pants would greet me for the rest of the summer. It hung over a twin bed with a denim duvet cover and, not surprisingly, plaid sheets. A pair of old Hush Puppies slippers—probably from the same decade as the poster—lay under the bed.

My parents peeked into my room.

"Uncle Jacob is seriously disturbed," I said gloomily.

Dad sucked in a deep breath and was about to protest when my mom responded, "No argument there."

"We can unpack later, ladies," he said. "Let's go explore."

My mother and I didn't move an inch.

"Come on," he pleaded. "What else do we have to do?"

"We could go throw rocks at a tree . . . or count clouds . . . or go play on the highway and get hit by a truck," I offered.

"What about going back to New York?" Mom suggested.

Dad gave her a look. "Not helping."

She shrugged. "If God's watching, I hope he rewards us for this suffering."

I got in one more suggestion. "Hey, Eli, we could sit on the front porch with a six-pack and watch the bug zapper."

He paused, and for a second I think he actually considered it. "Wait, you're too young to drink beer," he said, and he motioned us toward the door. "Let's go."

# Chapter 6

My father practically skipped out of the parsonage. Mom and I dragged behind him. We went past a basketball court full of divots and a picnic area, and then weaved between a handful of cars, before reaching the back entrance to the church.

Inside, the stained glass windows let in just enough light for us to see the coffered ceiling. Dad rummaged through the dark and found the light panel. He flicked a switch, and three beautiful large bronze chandeliers illuminated the room. Above us, we could see that the quatrefoils on the ceiling were painted turquoise and red.

On the floor, there were rows of curved pews with a mix of movable chairs lining the edges. Between the pews, a well-worn yellow carpet spilled down the middle aisle like a stripe of old gum. Despite the formal setting, the staging area featured a piano, drum cage, a pair of guitars, and two large amps instead of the expected choir pews.

Dad marched onto the stage and tapped the cymbal a few times with his finger.

"Centuries of tradition, hastily abandoned. I can't believe that Jacob would support—wait, what am I saying? Of course I can believe Jacob would promote such—"

Before my father could finish his rant, we heard the sound of muffled pop music.

"There must be people in the activities room," he said. "I bet they'd like to know we're here." With that, we navigated through a maze of hallways—three blind mice searching for the cheese.

Dad opened the double doors to the activities room. Before us, a group of ladies—and one goateed gentleman wearing spandex shorts—bent, twisted, gyrated, and jumped. It was a blur of animal print, neon, and metallic-colored leotards. The instructor, a peppy, long-legged teenage heart-stopper, bounced around the energized room.

"Come on, ladies! Y'all got to *feel* it!"

As everyone turned their heads toward us, the instructor realized she had company. She paused to roll up her orange legwarmers over her pink tights and yelled to the twin boys in sleeveless shirts manning the stereo system, "Ted! Todd! Turn it off!"

The music screeched to a stop and the entire room gawked at us.

"You must be Pastor Klein and his beautiful family!" the instructor said as she embraced Dad, then Mom, and finally me. I nearly fainted from discomfort. Everyone was watching, and I wanted simply to disappear.

*Note to self: Learn how to teleport.*

"Jacob didn't know if you'd actually make it. But we prayed and prayed, and look—now y'all are here! I'm Bliss LeBaron." She said her name as if we should know who she was.

"Well, of course, Bliss," Dad played along, and gave us a nervous look. "We're here, and happy to be so."

I faked a measured smile. Not over-the-top fake, but enough to let my father know this whole experience was excruciating.

All the aerobics participants lined up to greet us. I tried not to wipe the sweat from the handshakes on my shorts or look at the enormous saggy breasts hanging out of the leotards, but a few times, I couldn't help it.

Out of the corner of my eye, I saw Bliss sidestep my father and with a determined look, she came straight for me.

I'd seen girls like that before, your typical all-American. The kind of shallow girl I loathed—another Sloan or Brianna, for sure—that wore ridiculous clothing, babbled incessantly about movie stars, and always ended up stabbing me in the back. I felt my body tense. If I was going to survive the summer, I'd have to escape from girls like Bliss. I looked for the exit door.

Too late.

"And you must be Jordan!" the bubbly blonde blurted.

I nodded.

"Jacob told me all about you. And he said we were going to get along fabulously because we're like 'peanut butter and jelly!'"

"I'll be sure to thank Jacob for the introduction," I mumbled.

Before Bliss had time to detect the subtle sarcasm in my voice, an out-of-breath, chubby boy—undoubtedly raised on Cheetos and Big Macs—came rushing into the room, dressed in a coach's uniform.

"You're late!" Bliss chided.

"Sorry, Mom couldn't find my whistle," said the boy. He looked prepared for his workout, in polyester shorts, a green numbered T-shirt, and sweatbands.

"And this is my little brother," Bliss announced, pushing him in front of her.

*"Little" brother. Ahhh, irony.*

"My parents, Buck and Becky, have paid homage to the second letter of the alphabet by giving all us kids a name that begins with 'B.' There is Benjamin, Bailee, me, and the little baby of our family, Boyd." Turning to her brother, she said, "This is Pastor Klein and his family, Boyd. Say hello."

But Boyd didn't say hello. Instead, he simply stared at me, tongue-tied, which caused the twins in the corner to snicker. Boyd's head drooped forward and he examined his tennis shoes. Bliss shot the twins a look and they immediately went quiet.

*"Anyway!"* Bliss started up again. "Every Sunday night, the youth group grabs pizza in town. We will absolutely get to know each other then. Oh, the youth group is fab! Last week, we did this one contest to see how many marshmallows we could stuff in our mouths and still say 'chubby bunny' and . . ."

I had a flash image of Bliss standing in a circle of noisy teenagers, nine or ten marshmallows stuffed in her mouth, repeating in slow motion, "chubby . . . bunny . . . chubby . . . bunny . . . chubby . . . bunny." Someone in the circle handed her the marshmallow package, and her eyes widened in horror as she read: "Chubby Bunny Warning: Consuming too many marshmallows at one time may be fatal."

A strange squeaking noise snapped me from my daydream.

"What's that?" I asked, looking around the room.

"Oh, that's Mr. Prickles," Bliss said. "My hedgehog. I take him everywhere, just like the stars in Hollywood."

I thought she was joking, but sure enough, a small orange pet carrier that could double as a purse sat under the table next to the twins. A hedgehog wearing a turquoise rhinestone collar looked bored.

*Geez, get a kennel. What's up with all the peculiar pets?*

"Speaking of stars," Bliss continued, "have you ever seen any in New York? I bet you've seen a ton! One time, in Dallas, I saw Chuck Norris, the guy from *Walker, Texas Ranger.*" Bliss cracked up. "And Doug Walker—a boy in my school—just happened to be with us— we were headed back from Six Flags with the youth group—and we were teasing him because everyone knows he is completely in love with Minna Yeates and won't leave her alone—"

My head swam trying to keep up.

"—So after Mr. Norris *graciously* signed our Titan rollercoaster photos we kept calling Doug 'Walker, Walker, Texas Stalker'!" Bliss laughed so hard she cried real tears. "Oh, we're going to have so much fun this summer!"

I tried to keep things friendly. "Sure. I'd enjoy that."

"Well, we'll let you get back to your workout," Dad said, waving to the group. He knew I wouldn't last much longer.

Bliss hugged us all one last time.

"You sure you don't want to join us?" she asked me. "We've only got ten minutes left."

"Oh no. I don't do pain on purpose."

With that, the group waved and giggled as we left the room. The music started again and I heard Bliss yell, "Repeat after me! No more bat wings!" I looked back and saw the entire room raising their Shaker Weights—furiously shaking their jiggly arms and chanting, "No more bat wings!"

My father closed the door and looked at me with wide eyes.

"Seriously?" I glared at him. "Just kill me now."

We hurried out of the church and had almost made it before I heard a squish, squish, squish behind us.

"Pastor Klein!" huffed a silver-haired lady wearing orthopedic shoes and a denim shirt with black Schnauzer appliqués. She moved slowly, so we stopped before reaching the exit and waited.

*So close*, I thought.

"Pastor Klein! You're here. Wonderful!" She emphasized each word slowly. "My name is Idabell Ray."

She held out a cold hand. I could see her purple veins running under her translucent skin.

"I'm your secretary and church bookkeeper."

"Nice to meet you," Dad said.

Ms. Ray moved closer. "And you must be Rachel and Jordan." She chuckled. "Come on, let me show you around."

My mother followed the vertically challenged octogenarian down the hallway, looking like a Greek goddess in comparison. In New York, Mom positively burst with confidence, but I knew that turning forty-five had really hit her hard. In fact, it was not uncommon for her to walk out of the room if I handed her mail that included those slick brochures pitching gated golf course communities with on-site nursing care.

"Jacob told me you were quite the looker, but he didn't do you justice," Ms. Ray said with a smile as she led my mother out of the kindergarten Sunday school room. "And your suit is beautiful," she added.

"Why, thank you!" Mom said. "According to Eli, couture is my curse."

Dad interjected before the conversation could go any further, eyeing Ms. Ray's orthopedic shoes. "Rachel and I have different styles, that's all."

"Yeah, she has some, and you don't," I jibed.

"Pastor Klein, you must understand," Ms. Ray said to him with a smile. "Women do not spit, belch, or fart, and therefore we must shop . . . or we'll blow up!"

My mother erupted in laughter and gave Ms. Ray a big side-hug as we walked down a tiny hall. "I can tell we'll be great friends."

Ms. Ray's face lit up.

But as I trailed the three of them, I noticed something peculiar about the old lady. Despite her seemingly harmless appearance, Ms. Ray slowly flipped a loose quarter through her fingers like a knuckle roll, never missing a beat.

After hearing a story about every room, piece of furniture, and photograph in the church building, Ms. Ray led us outside and across the parking lot to an industrial-looking building designated "The Lord's Pantry."

"Jacob opened the Lord's Pantry about five years ago," Ms. Ray said proudly.

We didn't react.

"Jacob never told you about it?" Ms. Ray asked.

She moved on quickly when she realized Jacob had not, in fact, said anything about the Lord's Pantry.

"Well, you should be proud of your little brother. He set up this place to help local families with food. But the Lord's Pantry isn't just a food bank—it's so much more."

Dad helped Ms. Ray with the heavy door and we walked into the large warehouse-like room, where no-cook items like Pop-Tarts and canned food lined the metal shelves.

"Our customers receive a shopping bag and then they can take two items from each category," Ms. Ray said, while walking and pointing at the shelves. "Once a family achieves food security, they can move forward with a plan to gain financial independence."

My mother nudged me and picked up a package of Depends, snickering while she pointed to Dad behind Ms. Ray's back.

She whispered, "For the next road trip."

I snorted, and Ms. Ray turned to look at me. Thankfully a loud clang! bang! clang! of pots and pans crashing to the floor in the adjoining room forestalled any reason for me to explain. There was a burst of laughter, and Ms. Ray smiled calmly and walked toward the commotion. She swung the metal doors open into the next room.

Before us lay a spacious, extraordinary, custom-designed, commercial grade kitchen—replete with stainless steel worktables and professional equipment. To my surprise, Bliss was there, peeling carrots at a butcher block. She gave us a cheerleader smile.

*I guess the aerobics class got out early. Maybe everyone got vertigo from all the crazy colored spandex.*

Next to Bliss, wearing white and standing over a hissing grill, was the chef—the same guy we'd pegged earlier as the yardman instead of church-member-extraordinaire. Two men in red aprons mimicked his every move at the grill.

"Two double cheese, hold the onions!" Ms. Ray shouted. Bliss let out a big "Ha!" and the two men in red laughed.

"Our volunteers—who are most of the time, also our customers—use the center's commercial kitchen to create dishes from the perishable donations, and then we serve those dishes. It's a soup kitchen that also provides our customers with the ability to learn a trade." Ms. Ray went on, "We believe the old saying 'waste not, want not' goes for food and talent."

"And Cesar here has the talent," Bliss said playfully. "He's a real live chef, graduated from the Culinary Institute of America."

Cesar shook his head without looking up to see our embarrassed faces.

"Wow," Mom said, impressed as she surveyed the ingredients in front of Cesar. "What are you making? A turkey dish?"

"You got it," Cesar said. "French roast turkey with all the trimmings. It features red wine, Cognac, vegetables, herbs, and a pearl onion and mushroom garnish." He spoke to my mom but gave me a friendly wink.

"In addition to volunteering as our youth group leader, Cesar trains our customers to cook, so that they leave with a food industry certificate," Bliss explained. "Ms. Ray, is it a third of all the restaurants in a forty-mile radius, or a fourth of all the restaurants in a thirty-mile radius, that employ our customers? I can never remember!"

"A third." Ms. Ray beamed. "Roshi's Bakery on the square employs seven."

I knew nothing about cooking. At home, my father always had his nose in the books, and while my mother said she loved to cook, spaghetti was about as creative as she got. In fact, the last time she cooked breakfast, Dad crunched into something hard. Apparently, she'd made Pillsbury cinnamon rolls from the can and forgot to remove one of the metal ends from the bottom of the container. Needless to say, she never taught me anything other than how to order from Shun Lee Palace.

We didn't use a stove to cook—we used a phone.

"Amazing," Mom said, looking around at the impressive facility. "You must have a large donor."

"Oh, well, we've had some large anonymous donations," Bliss said, clearing her throat. "Rumor has it Jacob had a lot to do with that."

My parents looked at each other without a trace of surprise. Uncle Jacob was always giving away his money to those in need, and not in small quantities either. It was something my father lectured him about at least once a year. Jacob would always wait until Dad finished talking, and then he'd say, "All right if I go write my checks now?"

Mom drew close to Cesar. "You know," she said, almost whispering. "I love to cook. Maybe we could take this to a whole new level if we . . ."

As my mother's voice trailed off, I noticed Ms. Ray backing out of the room. Just before the door shut, she glanced back and mistakenly caught my eye. She immediately gave me a quick, brave smile. But it was a smile I knew all too well; it was the same lonely smile I wore.

# Chapter 7

We survived the first day and night relatively unscathed. I even had an opportunity to meet the other tenant at the parsonage—Jacob's old yellow tabby cat named Hal. At six in the morning, Hal introduced himself by jumping on my face and patting my forehead, as if he were auditioning to be an alarm clock.

*Felinus Interruptus. Thanks, Hal.*

"I can't believe Jacob still has her around," Dad said when Hal followed me into the kitchen. "That cat's got to be fourteen years old! She's named after the computer in the movie *2001*."

"Believe me." I pulled one of the hairs from my bangs down to the bridge of my nose and crossed my eyes to look at it. "*He's* not named after the space computer. Hal is short for *halitosis*." Hal twined between my feet and I crouched down to stroke his chin.

"Ladies, I've got an idea." Dad looked at me and then at Mom, who typed away on her laptop at the table. "Why don't we go to that little French café and then look around the town square? It's Saturday morning, after all."

*Uh-oh.*

I froze in my seat while trying to appear relaxed—a hard combo to pull off. The French café was where I saw the boy, the one I couldn't resist watching.

"Eli, I'm working," Mom said. "I want to finish this brief and have it emailed to New York by six."

*Phew.*

"But it's Saturday, and we need to eat. The café isn't far," Dad insisted. "Plus, you're on a three-month hiatus after twenty years, remember?"

I didn't want my parents to know I was bugging out, but I had to say something in protest. "I seriously doubt that place has anything French about it, other than French fries, French toast, French's mustard . . . shall I go on?"

"We need to eat," he repeated, giving me a steely look.

I was going to continue to fight, but my mother sighed and closed her laptop—that's when I knew we were going.

*Whatever.* I told myself I didn't care if he was there. This small hick town was full of nobodies, and he was probably just a redneck like the rest. It didn't matter what he thought of me.

So how come, right before we left, I ran to my room and changed into something more chic? I tossed aside my shorts and flip-flops and threw on my favorite buckled boots, a jean skirt frayed at the hem, an oversized gray T-shirt, and a thin striped scarf that accentuated the nape of my neck—just in case.

On the way, we didn't speak. Even my father stayed quiet, although in the rearview mirror I could see a twinkle in his eye. When we passed the church marquee, which read "Welcome Klein Family," none of us acknowledged it. We didn't discuss the cemetery and its mossy graves, the man cutting his lawn with a four-wheeler tied to a push mower, or the woman who spit out her truck window.

My cell phone rang and broke the silence. It was Stryder.

I shouldn't have answered. As soon as I did, I could hear Stryder's friends laughing, loud music, and most notably, girls giggling in the background.

"Jordan! I wish you were here," Stryder shouted.

"Yeah, me too," I muttered. "But I predict this adventure will be a complete disaster so I'll be home—"

"Dude! If she has a kid, it means she puts out!" Stryder yelled to one of his buddies.

"What?"

"Oh . . . Sorry, I'm trying to be the world's best wingman. Brace is pathetic with the ladies! . . . Brace! This is your mom on the phone. She wants to know if you're done breast-feeding for the day so she can get drunk with her friends."

*I should be in the Hamptons*, I thought. So I could kick Stryder's butt, if for no other reason. I stared at the back of my father's head with the anger of a thousand burning suns.

"Hey, I'll let you go," I interrupted. "You sound busy. We're about to stop anyway."

"You sure?" Stryder asked.

"I'm positive."

"Okay, I'll text you tomorrow, bye!"

The phone went dead and I felt every ounce of confidence I'd built over the last seventeen years collapsing in on itself like an imploding star.

"Seriously, not kidding," I said into my phone, even though no one was there. "There are five thousand people in this town, and only five different last names. It's worse than you can possibly imagine. All right, talk to you later."

As I finished my sentence, I caught my father's eye again in the rearview mirror. I felt satisfaction as I saw his twinkle fading. But at the same time, I abhorred how I'd become a typical melodramatic angst-ridden teenager. Nothing I could say would whisk me back home to the familiar and frenetic sounds of the city, so why was I so bent on taking away his joy?

Because it isn't fair, I rationalized. It's the summer before my senior year and I'm stuck in the sticks. It's his fault.

All I could hope for now was that the people in Ashworth found us so disagreeable that they spit us out like spoiled milk.

"*Alors*, Madame Ribbette," Dad announced as we pulled into the lot.

My mother's lip curled. "Three months without a venti non-fat mochaccino."

The café sat between a small craft store and a barbershop. Just outside the door, a large bronze frog wearing a top hat and western boots held a blackboard with the day's special: French toast.

I bore a look of vindictive triumph, and Mom snickered.

When we entered, a sandy-haired man greeted us, wearing a

nametag that read, "Caleb." I guessed Caleb was around twenty-five but his shoulders slumped over a bit, as if he'd already seen his fair share in life.

"*Bonjour,*" he said with a smile and a slight country twang.

"*Bonjour!*" Dad replied.

Caleb sat us at a table near the front of the café, next to a group of old men sipping coffee and reading the morning paper. Much like the parsonage, the café was comfortable and eclectic, but with a distinctly French theme. Built-in bookshelves holding hundreds, if not thousands, of books covered all four walls of the two-story café. Guests enjoyed their meals to the sound of piped-in Lyle Lovett. Dad hummed as he read his menu.

*It's cute how he thinks I won't remember this when it's time to pick a nursing home.*

"What can I get you folks?" Caleb asked.

My father looked thoughtful, tapping his chin with his forefinger. "Did I see you have a French toast special?"

"Yes. It's a stuffed French toast with fresh summer peaches and ripe strawberries combined with light cream cheese. A wonderful breakfast treat, despite the *light* cream cheese."

I folded my arms, unimpressed.

"Wonderful! Let's get an order to share," Dad said.

I didn't refuse. Not because I wanted French toast. In fact, I wasn't even listening. Instead, my gaze was pinned on the boy I'd seen the day before.

He sat at the back table, reading. A shiver ran through me as he turned and saw me staring. Again. Immediately I stuck my nose into the menu, clutching it tightly with both hands.

"And a non-fat latte, please," Mom said.

"Oh, and a coffee, black," Dad requested, his fingers drumming on the distressed table.

Caleb turned to me, and I could feel the awkward silence as he waited for my order.

"*Peux j'avoir un latte avec deux sucres, s'il vous plait,*" I asked effortlessly.

Dad cleared his throat in disapproval.

Out of the corner of my eye, I saw the boy. He'd overheard me order in French, and he leaned forward, eager for Caleb's response.

*Oh, great. Bon travail, Jordan.*

"One strawberry peach stuffed French toast, one non-fat vanilla latte, one black coffee, and one latte with two sugars. *À votre service, mes amis. Bon appetit.*" Caleb winked.

I flushed with embarrassment, shocked the waiter knew French after all. Glancing toward the back, I saw the kitchen door swinging back and forth.

The boy was gone.

"Excuse me." Dad grabbed Caleb's wrist in that insufferable, cloying way. "We were wondering . . ."

"Yes?"

"What is a French café with a name like Madame Ribbette doing here? There has to be some story, right? Do you serve frog's legs?"

Caleb laughed.

"No, we've never served frog's legs. Although, I guess we should. We've got some mean bullfrogs outside my bedroom window that I'd like to shut up. They commence to croaking about two a.m. every morning." He tossed his dishtowel over his shoulder.

"Justice and Chelsea Colville, the owners of this place, have been in love with French food and Ashworth almost as long as they've loved each other."

"That's sweet!" Mom said. "Are they chefs?"

"No. Justice is a novelist, and he met Chelsea while researching a book about the Cotton Belt Railroad. Not long after they married, one of his books hit the best-seller list. *The Trainmaster's Tracks*?"

We stared back with blank expressions.

"Anyhow, the book's success allowed them to buy their ranch out on County Road 4923."

"How wonderful," Mom gushed. "They must take good care of you. You speak so affectionately of them."

Caleb's face blanched, and his eyes swam away, as if he were remembering a distant time and place, one no longer accessible. Then he shook his head slowly, freeing himself of the thought. "Yes, we're close. Anyway, ten years ago, the only place to get a cup of coffee in Ashworth was the gas station. Chelsea didn't want something like a Starbucks popping up, so she pounced on this place and *voilà*, Madame Ribbette was born."

Mom looked uncomfortable, like the thought of someone

eschewing Starbucks made her physically sick. She was about to protest when Dad piped in again.

"What a great story! How did she come up with the name?"

"Oh, Chelsea's Grandma Juliet was straight off the boat from Marseille."

*Straight off the boat and then, oh, about a fifteen-hundred-mile walk to Texas. Or did they paddle across Kentucky?*

"That makes sense." Dad nodded politely, even though it made *no* sense.

"Nah." Caleb shook his head. A smile curled at the corner of his lips. "I can't fib to the new preacher in town."

Mom rubbed her forehead at the mention of "new preacher." It was a reminder of our purpose in town, one she and I did not support. If she and I had had a contest about who wanted to go back to New York more, I'm not sure who'd have won.

Caleb's voice became much softer as he leaned into the table. "You know that when a frog croaks, the skin beneath its chin gets inflated, right?"

"Sure," Dad said, unsure how to respond.

"Well, Chelsea has a strange but harmless cyst right under her chin. You can't see it but if she presses down on her tongue she can make her skin distend like a frog."

"Really?"

"Yep."

Mom raised an eyebrow toward me and whispered, "Good thing it wasn't on her forehead or they would've called the place 'The Lighthouse.'"

"And what was the inspiration for your literary decorative theme?" Eli pressed on with his interrogation.

"Actually," Caleb explained, "it's not really a theme. Madame Ribbette doubles as the town library. Most people come in for coffee—or in the evening for a glass of wine—and check out a book. You can keep the books as long as you like, but we ask that you only take one book at a time."

"What a great idea."

"Feel free to look around," Caleb addressed me casually.

"Thanks." I smiled, trying to apologize for my earlier rudeness.

After I finished my latte and fought my parents for the last bite of the scrumptious French toast, I got up to inspect the library. Ambling along the sidewall of books, I was amazed at the menagerie of spines lined up in alphabetical order: Jane Austen, the Brontë sisters, Beverly Cleary, Roald Dahl, Ernest Hemingway, C.S. Lewis, J.R.R. Tolkien . . . I was more at ease surrounded by these familiar titles than I had been all week. When I got to the end, *The Shadow of the Wind* by Carlos Ruiz Zafón caught my attention. I'd heard my English teacher mention it, so I took the book from the shelf and skimmed the first few pages.

*"The Shadow of the Wind,"* a voice murmured behind me.

I turned and felt a shiver upon seeing the boy's hazel eyes—a kaleidoscope of shifting colors, green, gold, gray, and brown.

"You'll enjoy that one," he continued.

I turned back to the bookshelf, trying to regain my composure by acting disinterested, and flipping my hair to the side. I had to avoid his eyes. Defensively, I examined the inside jacket of the book. But there was no denying it—my chest felt heavy, and waves of heat tingled the back of my neck.

*Bad time for a heart attack, Jordan. Get it together. He's a hick.*

"It's set in post–World War II Barcelona, and opens with a book-store owner introducing his son to the 'Library of Forgotten Books.'" The boy paused, then came around to the other side, since I refused to turn around.

"Books that are no longer remembered by anyone."

I stood quiet and motionless. I tried to pretend he was a killer bee. *If you don't move, you won't get stung.*

"The boy chooses a book and becomes obsessed with the author."

He paused. I swished my tongue around my mouth, hoping there wasn't anything stuck between my teeth, waiting for his next move. I hesitated. But then, even though I had my back to him, I could feel him inching away. Already he was giving up. Without thinking, I turned to him and, spying the book in his hand, I said, "I never got into *Catch-22.*"

*Smooth move, Jordan.* The boy looked startled, as if he'd heard a talking cat. I continued, "Wasn't there a character that pursued a tedious conversation with a boring Texan? No offense meant, of course," I said with a pitched smile.

"Well, I'm not a boring Texan, so no offense taken."

As he slid toward me, I could hear people's forks clicking against their plates, and the sound of Caleb filling a mug with coffee. I finally knew what "you could hear a pin drop" meant. My heart beat wildly, *ba-bum BA-BUM ba-bum BA-BUM . . .* and I was sure the boy could hear it.

"It's been assigned reading for most high school students for years." He clicked his tongue. "I never understand why school administrators push kids into literature before they're mature enough to digest the subject matter."

"I don't think it has anything to do with digesting the subject matter," I said. "The guy wrote in circles and never got anywhere."

"Much like life itself," he said. Swiftly he walked to the back of the restaurant, and as he exited through the kitchen door, he threw me a half-sad smile and said, "Enjoy the book."

Something happened at that moment, which never had before—I was speechless. Dazed, I tightly held the spine of *Shadow of the Wind* and stumbled toward my parents.

"Who was that?" My mother grinned. "He is gorgeous!"

"No one," I snapped. "Just some kid with a bad case of academic bulimia."

Despite my harsh words, I snuck one last peek at the kitchen door, the one still swinging, marked *"Interdit Au Public ou Willie Nelson."*

Employees only or Willie Nelson.

# Chapter 8

Sunday mornings always stressed me out. Typically, my parents stayed out late the night before, attending some fancy law firm party or an important dinner at the university, and inevitably they'd oversleep. The next morning, to make the eleven o'clock service, they ran around like their hair was on fire.

This Sunday morning, the stress had nothing to do with the previous night. We were all freaking out because Dad was going to deliver the sermon. He'd be the one everybody stared at; the audience would dissect his every word. This was his game day—with my mother on the sidelines and me hiding behind the concession stand.

"Have you seen my lucky blue tie? The one with the sunburst thingies?" he shouted, rifling through the drawers in the antique dresser.

"I thought I put it in the top one," Mom called out from the bathroom.

I heard him slam the drawers shut and stomp down the hall. Whipping into the kitchen, he stood before me in his navy blue blazer, gray trousers, and mismatched dress socks, knotting his "lucky tie." Unfortunately, there was nothing he could do about the silver-tipped mop atop his head.

He always looked as if he was the loser in a hair-pulling match.

Sitting down at the kitchen table, he tore at the pages of his sermon, lip-synching the words, gesticulating wildly into the air.

*If this is the warm-up, we're in serious trouble.*

"What's your first sermon, Eli?" I asked, hurriedly spooning Piggly Wiggly–brand corn flakes into my mouth since there was no Boo Berry anywhere to be found.

"Well, Jacob had the sermon topics pre-arranged, but—"

"But what?"

"But," he said with an assertive look, "I think I'll do something off-menu. Give them something a bit more intellectually provocative. Something they may not get every Sunday here in the country."

"Um, you're giving your creation lecture?"

He put down his papers and curled his lips.

"Yes," he said.

*Awesome. We'll be back in New York City by tomorrow.*

Mom popped into the kitchen, dressed, but with her hair coiled in a towel. In the city, her rich ivory skin was always protected—the tall buildings and the inside of the law firm always blocked out the sun. But our trip to town yesterday left her with a shade more color. She looked flushed and alive in her lilac-colored suit, which I'd never seen her wear back in New York.

Mom gestured at my pajamas. "We don't want to be late!"

She slipped on her expensive nude stilettos and headed back toward the bathroom, but before she left Dad grabbed her elbow.

"You look beautiful," he whispered. Then, after delivering this strategic opening, he asked, "Rachel, do you think it's a bad idea to go with my creation lecture?"

"Jordan and I are here against our will, Eli. However you decide to embarrass yourself in public is your business."

I placed my bowl in the sink and smirked.

*Que les jeux commencent.*

Let the games begin.

Despite the hundred-degree temperature, people packed the church courtyard mingling, with a few yelling at the kids roughhousing by the flower bushes. Muffled pop music emanated from inside the church. A coffee cart with a parasol stood under the back

awning, dispensing good ol' cups of joe—the secular American sacra-
ment—and offering donuts to the mostly heavyset crowd. Fittingly,
the sign out front read, "God Is Not Boring! Some of His Kids Are
Though." I snapped a picture of the sign with my camera.

*Whoever writes these things is hysterical. I should text this pic to Stryder.*

As we walked toward the crowd from the parsonage, Mom's
stilettos sunk into the grass with every step, prompting a steady
stream of obscenities, which Dad tried, unsuccessfully, to hush. We
drew more than a few sidelong glances from the crowd.

*Hello, Ashworth! Please welcome the new preacher, his wildly cussing
wife, and his sulking teenage daughter!*

Dad walked closer to me, edging away from Mom. He wasn't
the kind of guy to lay his raincoat over puddles. Though I'm not sure
what he could've done—carry her to the church? I took out a box of
Tic Tacs and offered him one. It was his game day after all.

Dad looked distracted. "No, thank you."

"It's not a mint, it's a hint."

"Oh," he said, and he took several and gobbled them down.

I recognized a few of the faces as we approached the crowd:
Cesar, a few of the ladies from the aerobics class, Ms. Ray, Bliss, and
her little brother Boyd, who was oddly carrying a bull whip and clad
in a safari shirt, pocket flap khakis, and weathered brown fedora.
Ironically, everyone looked at us and not at chubby Indiana Jones.

The big bald guy wearing steel-toe work boots standing next to
Bliss looked as strong as a weightlifter. He caught sight of us and
moved toward Dad with a gentle gait.

"Greetings, Pastor Klein, I'm Buck LeBaron, your music director. I believe you met my daughter Bliss yesterday." Buck's voice was
deep and soft and there was a kind spark in his eyes. Bliss followed
him, wearing a huge smile.

"Yes, she's quite the drill sergeant," Dad said as a compliment.

Buck slapped my father on the back, almost knocking him over.
"You don't know how right you are! Learned it from her mother. In
our house, there are only three rules: Get up! Shut up! Eat up!"

"Oh, you can't believe a word Dad says." Bliss chuckled. "He's
such a—"

Bliss stopped mid-sentence and frowned at the blue Dually truck
tearing into the parking lot. A ropy young redhead climbed out. His
jeans were so tight—well, let's just say they didn't leave much to the

imagination. The boy pulled off his wife beater and wriggled into a button up, clearly his Sunday best. Meanwhile, a large, matronly woman with the same shock of red hair emerged from the passenger side. She held her Bible close to her purple dress and scowled at her son, who spat onto the blacktop.

*Note to self: Avoid the gingers.*

Buck sighed just before piano music wafted outside.

"There's our cue," he said. Like clockwork, the crowd filed into the auditorium. As I approached the entrance, the redheaded boy appeared at my side to assist with the door. He walked with a swagger—like a cocky, bowlegged giraffe.

"Thank you," I said with a polite smile.

But he didn't say, "You're welcome." Instead, he tilted his head to study me closely and flashed a mischievous grin.

The place was jam-packed, without a square inch of extra space to spare, by the time Dad entered. When he sat down next to Mom and me in the front row, I felt like everyone's eyes were boring into the back of my skull.

*How do you say, "Take a picture, it'll last longer," to two hundred people?*

The pianist (whom I hardly recognized in his tailored suit versus the spandex shorts he wore in aerobics) pounded out a mean intro as Buck rose. He led the congregation in soulful prayer just before introducing us.

"Ladies and gentlemen. As you know, Jacob has asked his brother, Eli, to stand in as pastor while he's, ahem, clearing up a few things. He'll be with us today and for the next few months. We're delighted to have him and his beautiful wife, Rachel . . ." Buck motioned for my mother to stand. "Mrs. Klein, allow us to welcome you."

My mother stood and faced the church members with a smile and an uncharacteristic beauty pageant wave, for which she received a huge round of applause.

"And their precious daughter, Jordan."

*Precious?*

Unlike my mom, I stood up and sat down in a flash while the church members clapped.

The pianist played again, his fingers pirouetting over the keys. The twins from the aerobics class strummed guitars, and Buck climbed behind the drum kit and led the congregation in song. Listening to the off-key, loud, very flat Ms. Ray belt out "Amazing Grace" behind me, I tried to drown her out by singing in my head, "The stars at night are big and bright—*clap! clap! clap! clap!*—deep in the heart of Texas!" but it didn't work.

Then something even worse happened.

My father took the podium.

Halfway through the sermon, which consisted of sixty PowerPoint slides, most of the audience was asleep. The rest feigned interest or they looked riddled with confusion.

"If God *literally* created humans in a hundred forty-four hours, then we have real problems with stars, which are billions of years old, and fossils that date back over one hundred million years."

He flipped through slides of leaf impressions, dinosaur footprints, and petrified wood.

"We'd have no frame of reference for how the history of human-kind fits into the history of the cosmos. Even eternity eludes conception. Isn't it more rational to think: what if God decided to take billions of years to finish Act One?"

He showed a slide of the Earth as a barren lifeless ball. I looked over at Bliss, nodding in agreement, while her neighbor stared into space, his mouth open. I thought about taking a picture but realized they'd kick me out.

*Wait, that's not such a bad idea.*

"What if Genesis 1:3, where God says, 'Let there be light,' and there was light, what if that began the Second Act, the middle of the story? Would everything start to make sense? Yes, I think it would. There would now be room for God to have taken his time, say about thirteen to fifteen billion years, to create world after world full of marvelous and unique creatures. But, for what? Enter stage left: Adam and Eve."

Slides of ancient human skulls flashed across the screen. Mom bounced her knee up and down in nervous anticipation. Around the room, anyone who had fought sleep wore hopeful expressions, now that the Paleozoic era was finally in the rearview mirror.

"We know the rest of Act Two. Adam and Eve sin and are thrown out of the Garden. Then come Abraham and Moses, and God Himself comes down to become one of us, and to die for us, and then Christ ascends into Heaven and the Apostles stand looking at the sky, wondering, 'What's next?'"

The audience squirmed. Dad finally made eye contact with me and flashed a desperate, insecure smile. I think even he knew it wasn't going well.

"When does the curtain come down on Act Two? What are humans going to do with this world?"

A barrage of PowerPoint slides assaulted the audience: smokestacks spewing out pollution, starving children huddled in dark rooms, tanks, images of war.

At that moment I wanted to yell, "Stop the madness!" but I didn't. I simply gritted my teeth and prayed it would end quickly.

"What will we make of Act Three?" he asked gravely.

If I couldn't stop it, at the very least I had to witness the carnage. It was an understatement to call it a worst-case scenario, a torturous train wreck of a sermon. Even if I'd hate myself afterward, I had to look.

I peered out from my pew and discovered most people in the crowd looked genuinely scared, either of the topic or the preacher himself. Even the redhead, who was pretending to read the Bible instead of the *Pro Wrestling Illustrated* magazine he'd tucked inside, swallowed nervously.

Of course, the worst-case scenario got even worse.

I saw, out of the corner of my eye, the dark-haired boy from Madame Ribbette slipping out the door. He'd witnessed the entire flood of failure.

I looked down at my hands clenching the bulletin, and felt more alone than ever.

# Chapter 9

**D**ad blamed the PowerPoint. "Understandably, people here haven't been exposed to the latest technologies," he explained. "So I've decided to drop the multimedia approach."

Unfortunately, this decision didn't make his next sermon any less obtuse or awkward. The only difference was that most people took seats near the back of the church. Just in case they wanted to make an early exit.

After Dad's second grueling Sunday, Buck and Bliss tried to rally around my father. They invited us to accompany the youth group on its Sunday evening outing to Mr. Woulfe's Piggy's Pizza. Mom politely bowed out and went home. She'd been spending more time alone than I could remember.

Honestly, I was a little worried about her.

Piggy's was so small that the youth group took up every table. I had no other choice but to hang with Bliss and her little brother Boyd (who was dressed like an airline pilot). It was either them or Cesar and Dad discussing local politics. The other boys in the youth group, including the twins and the redhead (who I now knew as Moe) jockeyed for control of the Galaga and Street Fighter games in the corner.

*What is it, 1985?*

Moe favored Street Fighter, judging by the ferocity with which he pushed the other boys out of the way. It was as if he wanted to make the video game real, elbowing one of the twins and stealing Boyd's slice of pepperoni.

Moe licked orange grease from his fingers. "You don't need this anyway, Captain Fatty."

Boyd glowered but Moe kept on going.

"Look!" Moe said. "You've got so many double chins you look like you're staring at me over a pile of pancakes!"

Bliss lashed back in her brother's defense. "You're an idiot, Moe! You're the reason I can't go to Walmart and buy blue spray paint. They lock that crap up cuz of huffers like you!"

Boyd gave me an embarrassed smile and his sister a big thumbs-up.

Bliss pressed her hands together and looked up at the ceiling. "Please forgive my foul mouth and, oh, Lord, please let Moe be swallowed by a whale with excessively bad breath or seriously trampled by stampeding pigs—your choice."

As much as I hated to admit it, I was really beginning to like Bliss. Not only was she entertaining, but all I had to do was ask and Bliss would tell me about anyone in town, their family histories going back generations, on what county road they lived, and probably even what color underwear they wore—if I were interested. Unlike the girls back home, Bliss didn't seem to care about boring scandals, cliques, or malicious gossip. She told her stories with a sense of pride in each family's history.

Unfortunately, the one person I wanted to know about most—the boy from Madame Ribbette—Bliss kept close to the vest.

"Oh, Knox Colville. He's named after Fort Knox in Kentucky, and his sister, Skye, was named after a book." Bliss shook her head and continued to pick cheese off her pizza. "Listen, J-Bird, he's absorbingly gorgeous, but a seriously broken soul." Then she looked at me cautiously, as if she were debating what else she should say. "Best to forget about that one."

"Why?" I asked. "Did you date him?"

She blurted out a spastic laugh. "Sure! In the fifth grade!" She shook her head again. "No, we used to be good friends but he's never been the same since his sister died." Accidently throwing her tray in the trashcan, she added, "I'll give you the scoop when you've got a week to be deliciously depressed."

*Note to self: Clear schedule for week of "delicious depression."*

Dad and Cesar were paying the pizza bill, still talking up a storm, when the youth group started to disburse. Most everyone piled into their parents' Chevys and Fords; "Buy American" was the Ashworth motto. The rest of us crossed the parking lot headed for the church van—parked in the last parking space in the lot—to wait for Cesar and "Pastor Klein."

*Why did Cesar park way out there? The van already has so many door dings it looks like a Stegosaurus chewed on it.*

Moe and his redneck sidekick, Travis, yelled over to us from Moe's blue truck. He had a determined look on his face.

"Jordan, I'll take you home," Moe offered, making crude thrusting motions, ". . . in the Big Blue Bullet!"

He and Travis snickered.

Bliss snapped, "You're such a tool."

"You're such a tool," Moe repeated.

"She's riding with us," Bliss yelled.

"She's riding with us," Moe mimicked.

Bliss flipped her blonde hair away from Moe and grabbed my arm.

"Save your breath, Moe," Bliss said, looking at him with narrowed eyes. "You'll need it to blow up your inflatable date!"

"Shut up, whorenado," Moe yelled.

"For the last time and I won't say it again," Bliss shot back, "Jesus loves you, but everyone else thinks you're an idiot."

Moe gave Bliss a dirty look, but he stopped and waved at me mockingly, and a huge sarcastic grin came over his face, sparking a roar of laughter from Travis.

"So what's the story with the cretins?" I asked Bliss, glancing at the boys in their muscle car.

"You mean, why do Moe and Travis not burst into flames when they enter the church?"

"Yeah." I smiled. "That, and why do they hang with the youth group?"

Bliss rolled her eyes dramatically. "Moe's mom is our resident Church Lady," she huffed. "You know, Mrs. Petiot, the one in purple, the shaggy red 'do? Anyway, Moe and Travis spend their days out behind the Wrestling Station getting drunk or high. Dipsticks. Moe just comes with us to keep his mom fooled. As long as she thinks he's an angel, he can get away with anything."

"What about his dad?"

"Ha!" Bliss burst out a laugh. "His dad's in the clink."

"What'd he do?" I asked.

"Told Mrs. Petiot he was going huntin', but they don't have deer in liquor stores, last I checked! He held one up in Shreveport—he was wearing a disguise, like, duct tape all over his head."

"They caught him during the robbery?"

"No." Bliss shook her head. "A five-foot Korean lady chased him with a baseball bat, and the police arrested him the next day."

"How'd they find him?"

"Wasn't hard," Bliss said. "He was the only guy in the casino with no eyebrows."

I watched as Moe and Travis peeled out of the parking lot with an explosion of smoke and screeching tires.

"Seriously, they're hotdogs," Bliss added. "Complete trash."

"Speaking of trash," I said, following Bliss into the van, "the inside of this van smells like limburger cheese and dirty socks."

"I know." Bliss shrugged. "It's so old it's insured for Indian attacks."

I guess they were used to the smell, because Boyd, the twins, and Ally, a tiny girl with a mouth full of silver, piled into the van without a peep.

Cesar was already behind the wheel, and my father sat in the front picking Cesar's brain.

"So I thought this morning went extremely well," Dad said. I cringed, preparing for a terrible blow.

"Yes. 'The Physics of Redemption' was . . ." Cesar reached for the right word, ". . . interesting."

"I bet," Dad mused. "Considering Jacob called his last sermon on Zacchaeus, 'Things I Learned from a Tree-Climbing Little Person.'"

As Cesar chuckled and pulled out of the parking lot, he asked Dad, "So, Pastor Klein, who do I take home first?"

The group—well, everyone except Dad and me—responded in unison, "Ally!"

Ally turned around and flashed me a blindingly silver smile.

"Looks like Ally is the lucky winner," Dad said.

"Ally lives out in the middle of nowhere," Bliss whispered. "It's a fun and spooky drive."

"Spooky, as in local meth producers might ambush us?" I asked. "Pretty much."

"Killer," I said, checking to see if my cell phone had coverage in case I needed to call 9-1-1.

We drove down the highway listening to Paula Abdul sing, "Straight up now tell me" (the only cassette tape Cesar owned), while Bliss and Boyd debated whether the new men's Wranglers with a "lower waist" was a bad idea.

"Um, I am going out on a limb and say *bad idea*," I added.

I couldn't believe how dark and deserted it got way out there. I moved my fingers across the van's window. Only a bright violet light shone in the distance. "What's that?"

"That's the Purple Blossom." Bliss stared, unblinking. "Or as I like to call it, a roofie colada waiting to happen. Super sketchy."

Uncertain whether to believe her or not, I inquired further.

"Really? Why 'sketchy'?"

"Oh, lots of people looking for trouble hang out there."

"How do you know?" I asked accusingly, hoping to get some dirt on the seemingly harmless Bliss LeBaron.

She considered my question. "Well, occasionally"—her southern accent was more pronounced than usual—"you hear about it if a fight breaks out. Like in October, Charlene Carpenter cheated on her fiancé Ricky. Normally, nobody'd care about a nasty break-up, except this was a little different. Ricky lost his arm in the power plant's turbine the year before, and Luke Baker, the guy Charlene was fooling around with, lost his leg in a huntin' accident two years prior to that. When Ricky found Charlene kissin' Luke behind the Marlboro machine . . ." Bliss made a strong and proper fist as she raised her voice, ". . . he threw a mean punch with his one good arm, knockin' Luke off balance, and Luke's leg *flew* out from under him, which knocked a lady off her stool."

"No one in town blamed Charlene, though." Bliss shook her head. "She's got a thing for amputees."

"Okay," I laughed. "You've convinced me. I'll stay away."

"Good," Bliss said, swiping at the air. "Cesar!"

Cesar turned off the radio and the van turned onto a dark and narrow road.

"Yes, Bliss?"

"It's about a hundred degrees in here and it stinks like a rotten horse fart!"

Immediately, Cesar slowed the van to a crawl under a thick canopy of trees and rolled down the windows in the darkness.

"Thank goodness!" Bliss said as she put her nose near the open window.

Without realizing it, the car went quiet as we listened intently to the night outside. Unlike the city, where it's bright even at one in the morning, this Texas night was black. There were no lights, not even stars.

In an ominous tone, Cesar asked, "Have y'all heard the story of the Screaming Bridge?"

"What's going on?" I asked Bliss.

"You've never heard the story?" Cesar answered for her.

I didn't reply, but my instinct for self-protection told me this was trouble.

"Oh," Cesar said forebodingly, "well, then, you must."

The van was silent but for the song of the crickets and the occasional scrape of a tree branch against the side of the van.

"A long time ago, three teenage girls were traveling along the highway when a bunch of bikers started hassling them." Cesar looked back at the group. "To get away from the bikers, the girls turned onto this road and, scared to death, they turned off their headlights—"

Cesar turned off the headlights and the van continued to inch along in the pitch-black night.

"—so that the bikers couldn't see them . . . only to switch them back on—" Cesar turned on the headlights, revealing a long wooden bridge over a lake tributary.

"—just in time to see that the bridge was out. The girls plummeted to the rocks below.

"People say . . ." His voice was a low whisper now, ". . . that on certain nights, at this very bridge, you can hear the screams of those girls falling to their deaths."

There was silence, and then as Cesar rolled the van off the bridge he let out a shrill scream. We all yelled and he started to chuckle, which swelled into a loud belly laugh. The group followed his lead nervously, until everyone laughed hysterically as Cesar rolled the windows up and sped up down the road. Up ahead the warm glow of Ally's house shined through the trees.

*Yes, it's official. This is the insane asylum for the universe.*

The next morning, I walked outside wearing my weathered running shoes. I stretched on the porch, getting ready to relieve some of the stress inspired by my Texas prison. My father, who was on the porch swing with his paper and a mug of coffee, watched me. I retied my shoes and was about to bolt when he piped up.

"The dog down that road, at the blue house, he looks vicious. I'd head east if I were you."

"Thanks," I said.

"Jordan?" he asked.

"Yeah?"

"I had fun last night hanging out with you and the youth group."

*I won't let him do it*, I thought. *He doesn't get to clear his conscience because of one mildly amusing night.*

"Sure, Eli," I said. But before I got ten paces, I stopped dead in my tracks. I saw plain as day that someone had fixed the tire on Jacob's Jeep.

I looked back at my father on the porch. He smiled and dangled a set of keys.

"Let's see how you handle the responsibility for the summer."

I quickly checked my grin and instead gave him a curt nod of thanks before I took off, energized and heading eastward up the sloping hill.

# Chapter 10

I needed to know about Knox so I only waited two days before inviting Bliss over. That was the most I could take.

After dinner, the two of us settled comfortably in the reading loft. Hal curled up on a purple floor pillow, and I turned him toward the wall so we didn't have to smell his bad breath. My parents went to bed early that night, and we only had an hour before Buck expected Bliss back home.

"You see," Bliss started, crossing her legs pretzel style, "Knox doesn't like bells."

"Excuse me?"

She leaned forward. "East New Hope's bell used to toll three times a day, for everyone to raise their hearts to God. For most around here, the bell is just one more thing at the church that doesn't work anymore. But for Knox, that bell is a little more complicated."

"Come on, Bliss. I thought you said this was about his sister."

"It is," she huffed. "Okay, when the bell worked, it always tolled at the end of weddings, special events, and—important for this story—funerals. So, basically, that sound is fixed forever in Knox's ear, along with the vision of his sister lying there in a coffin. Really. Saddest guy in the history of sad."

Bliss paused. "Anyway, the bell is about Knox's mother, too."

"I'm trying to follow, but you make no sense."

"Hang with me, J-Bird," Bliss said, rolling her eyes. "For Knox and his family, the bell is prophetic."

*Uh-oh. If Bliss starts talking about UFOs or crop circles, I might need to cut this evening short.*

"Sometimes his mom hears the East New Hope bell in her dreams. When she does, her dreams come to life. Like, the first time was years ago, when Knox was twelve. His mom dreamt that she was cooking soup for her kids, but the sound of the church bell drew her to the front door. It chimed like crazy in the dark. She crept anxiously through the house toward the door. Knox said she felt scared, not because she was worried about her safety, but because she wanted so badly to protect what was on the other side of the door."

"Knox told you this?"

"Yeah. I told you we dated in fifth grade!" Bliss snorted.

"Okay. So what was on the other side of the door?"

"Two small children," Bliss answered in a low, slow voice, "standing at the front steps in worn and tattered clothes. One of them handed Knox's mom an envelope that was like, two thousand years old. The note inside read: 'These are your children. You must mend their clothes and feed their souls. Love them as you should, but know that your time is done when the bell tolls again.'"

*Hmmmm.* I wasn't ready to abandon my skepticism, but so far, it was just a dream. And dreams were normal (except for that one I had where Sticky played a cowbell). Anyway, if it meant learning what was inside Knox's brain—surely, I could suspend *some* disbelief, right?

"Knox and Skye thought their mother was crackers, but later that afternoon she got a phone call. A hard-luck couple from out of town got into a horrendous car accident out on Highway 110. The parents bit it, but the two kids in the back were strapped in tight and they survived the crash. The parents had no ID and the plates were all burned up, so no one knew who to call."

"Let me guess," I said nervously.

"Yep. Knox's mom took them in, just like her dream predicted. A week went by, then two. The church bell was getting repaired, and when they finally put it back up in the roost, the kids' aunt mysteriously showed up. She'd been scouring the county looking for her sister, and the police brought her to the Colvilles. Then, right before they knocked on the door, the bell chimed for the first time in weeks."

"Weird," I said. *Could be a coincidence,* I maintained.

But it was really odd.

"Years later," Bliss continued, "Knox's mom had another dream with the East New Hope bell. This one was about a flock of birds swarming the church tower, and the bell tolled whenever the birds plunged toward the cross on the top. That was basically it. When Skye heard about her mother's dream, she was like, 'Whatever, Mom.' By that time, she was a med student interning at Mother Frances Hospital and thought the whole dream thing was silly. But then she started treating a new patient, named . . . wait for it . . . Ms. Ray."

"Ms. Ray? Halloween socks in June, Ms. Ray?"

"Yes." Bliss looked somber. "Her part in the story is crazy. Her husband beat her up. That's how she met Skye in the hospital."

"Oh, sorry," I said.

"That's not all."

Hal rose from the pillow and arched his back, yawning and stretching. Bliss picked him up and plopped him in her lap. I guess she needed to hold a furry creature for the rest of the harrowing tale.

"A long time ago, Ms. Ray adopted a beautiful talking bird—a scarlet macaw—from a defunct vaudeville in Shreveport. The macaw was a champion at mimicking and talking, and had a vocabulary of over a hundred words. They became bosom buddies. Often, Joker—that was the bird's name—heard Ms. Ray say things under her breath, things she'd never say in front of her husband. Ms. Ray had no outlet to express her pain and suffering, so I guess Joker became her confessor. One Friday, Ms. Ray's husband, Vernon, came home particularly sloshed and angry. He decided he didn't like the meatloaf she'd prepared for him. He didn't like green peppers. He didn't like the sauce and, in fact, he didn't like Ms. Ray. Violently he smashed his plate to the floor, started hitting her, and eventually had Ms. Ray cowering in the corner when . . ."

Bliss paused to take a drink of water. I'd become so engrossed in the story that I wanted to pull the glass from her mouth so she could finish.

*Don't leave me hanging!*

". . . she was cowering, and Joker had had enough. Out of nowhere, the bird called Mr. Ray a bastard."

"Are you serious?"

"Yep. Vernon whipped around and saw no one there. He was so drunk, he thought Ms. Ray was throwing her voice. But Joker kept repeating, 'Bastard, bastard, bastard . . .' and Vernon lost his mind. Ms. Ray protested. She said the bird didn't know what it was saying, but he moved toward the cage with poisonous fury. He ripped open the cage and grabbed the bird with his meaty hands. Joker kept calling him a bastard and Ms. Ray screamed for him to stop, but it was too late. She heard the bird's neck snap. Vernon stormed out of the house, and she lay crumpled, beaten, on the floor with her dead bird."

I put my face in my hands, spreading my fingers so I could see Bliss through them.

"After that," Bliss sighed, "Skye attended to Ms. Ray's physical wounds and Jacob attended to her spiritual ones—made even more complicated after Vernon died in jail from a heart infection caused by an abscessed tooth. Yes, Skye and Jacob became Ms. Ray's biggest supporters; they became her whole world."

"That was," she paused dramatically, "before last winter."

"Last winter?"

"Yes, that's when Skye died."

"She died last winter?"

"Uh-huh. Early January, in a car accident. Right down the road from here." Bliss tossed Hal back onto the floor pillow. Nonchalantly, she added, "Jacob was in New York visiting you when it happened. He didn't tell you?"

My heart stopped.

"That was the call he took at the restaurant," I said aloud, in amazement.

Bliss looked at me, her eyes two large moons. "But that's not it," she whispered, leaning toward me. "I wasn't going to tell you this, because it's too weird. But on the day of Skye's funeral—"

"Yes?"

"—that was the last day the bell ever worked. It's been broken ever since. Just like Knox."

# Chapter 11

**B**efore she left, Bliss shook her head at the night sky and whistled. "Somebody's gonna lose a trailer."

Within an hour, she proved to be a prophetic meteorologist. A heavy storm came pounding through the night. Thunder cracked and lightning flashed outside, illuminating the world in quick sketches of light.

Each hour, the rain fell even harder.

Sticky pushed his wet snout under my blanket in search of a place to hide. I struggled to find a position that would allow him to escape the roar of the storm and keep me from falling off the bed. In New York, the rain was always an inconvenience, but here it felt like a drop-from-the-sky wind monster was going to pluck an unlucky cow from its pasture and slam it into the house at any moment.

I couldn't sleep. Part of it was the storm, of course. But the other part was Bliss's story. I kept turning Ms. Ray, Skye, and the boy from Madame Ribbette round and round in my head. No matter how I lay, no matter how many times I fluffed my pillow, I couldn't sleep. Nothing worked.

I couldn't stop thinking of Knox.

At four in the morning, I gave up. I left Sticky on my bed,

burrowed under the covers, and with nothing else to do, I grabbed *Shadow of the Wind* and moseyed up to Jacob's reading loft.

*Shadow of the Wind—there's an appropriate title for tonight.*

Hal was still on the pillow, seeking refuge in his dreams. I curled up next to him and, two chapters later, the sound of his gentle purring lulled me to sleep.

When I woke, it was dawn. I yawned, stretched, and stumbled downstairs, making my way out to the front porch. Looking at the sunrise over the stretch of trees, there was a foreign stillness that seeped into me. I didn't hear any raucous street vendors, honking horns, screeching brakes, or wailing babies—I mean, investment bankers. The only noise came from a crew of clucking hens and the water trickling off the gutter.

*Finally. Something good about Texas.*

Sitting on the porch swing, I lazed and finished the last chapter of my book. It was still early, and my parents were sleeping in. I had half a notion to run and jump on their bed like I did when I was six, but since Mom was still hardly talking to my father, my antics would probably only cause more tension.

Instead, I decided to play it straight. I'd take the Jeep and head to Madame Ribbette for another book. If I kept reading all summer, the last book would end with a return trip to New York. Plus, there was always a chance I'd catch a glimpse of Knox.

I cleaned up and put on a black tank, white jeans, and biker boots. My hair went back with my Mom's silk turquoise scarf. Just in case.

Pulling out front of the church, I passed the church marquee, which read: "Each turn in the road reveals a surprise."

*Uh, yeah. Like yesterday when I had to dodge a padded armchair flying out of a truck bed.*

Ten minutes later, I parked in front of the "Good Ole Days" antique store, where my father had freaked out over finding a vintage Lone Ranger lunchbox the week before. I looked inside the window and saw a pair of crazy candlesticks shaped like a couple bandits with handkerchiefs wrapped around their mouths. I was halfway tempted to buy them for Stryder for kicks. Instead, I took out my camera. *Snap-Snap.*

I loitered there another few minutes, taking pictures of the menagerie of odd items, before I realized what I was doing.

*Quit stalling, Jordan. Cowboy up! I mean, cowgirl up!*

I tucked *Shadow of the Wind* under my arm and, taking a deep breath, I entered the café.

My heart pounded.

A few surly old men played dominoes up front. Caleb saw me right away and came over to greet me.

"Bonjour, mademoiselle." He winked. "It's nice to see you back."

"I'm here to return the book," I said flatly. My eyes flickered past the old men to the back of the café where Knox had sat before. *Thank goodness, he's not here,* I said to myself, trying to ignore my disappointment.

That was, until he opened the kitchen door.

Caleb stole a glance back at Knox and then leaned toward me, holding a pot of coffee in one hand. "You'd like another book?"

"Yes." I jumped at the suggestion. "I mean, it's either that or spending time with the 1950s Weepy the Wee-Wee urinating doll next door."

*Shut up, Jordan!*

"Of course," Caleb said with a smile. "And while you look around, I'll get you *un latte avec deux sucres—c'est vrai*?"

"Right, thanks." I smiled. I liked Caleb. He was on the level.

I turned and scanned the walls of books, pretending not to notice Knox. But I could feel his eyes lingering on my skin, or maybe that was just my nerves. I quickly looked back and saw him leaning against the far wall.

He walked over to me.

"So, what did you think?" he asked.

I hesitated. "A little over the top in places. Doomed love and gruesome murders." I turned back to the wall of books. "But overall, you were right. I enjoyed it. Any other recommendations?"

Knox reached across me and slipped a black paperback from the wall. "*Never Let Me Go.* Ishiguro."

The title seemed a little forward, and I smirked. But I didn't say anything. Instead, I concentrated on inhaling and exhaling, because it seemed that at any moment I might forget how to breathe.

*Whatever you do, don't turn around, Jordan.*

I imagined his strong fingers curving to fit the back of my neck and turning me toward him.

*Don't turn around.*

I imagined feeling the broadness of his shoulders.

*Don't turn around.*

But what else could I do? I was powerless.

I turned around.

"Thanks," I said, barely squeezing the word out. I knew he could feel the tension in my voice.

"You're welcome."

We both stood there silently. I studied him with attention, noting every detail of his appearance, my eyes finally coming to rest upon his black lashes. They framed the most jaw-dropping, intense eyes I'd ever seen.

Then I panicked. A total anxiety attack. I had to get out. I saw the front door and fled, leaving Caleb with a hot latte in hand and Knox totally dumbfounded.

*Smooth, Jordan. Real smooth.*

To my unwelcome surprise, my father was right outside, parking the Volvo next to the Jeep.

*Great, just what I need. I'm as lucky as a telepathic schizophrenic.*

Dad popped out from the driver's side and waved hello. He was holding the Lone Ranger lunchbox in his other hand, and seemed way too animated.

"Turns out the thermos is busted. I'm going to see if they have a replacement cap. I saw one for John Wayne in there. Maybe that one will work."

"If I've told you once, I've told you a thousand times, you really shouldn't mix and match thermos caps from different Western gunslingers," I joked.

Dad cracked a smile.

"Not to ask the obvious, but why do you need a lunchbox so bad? Mom sending you back to first grade?"

"No. Buck needs some help cutting up a big tree branch that fell on Ms. Morina's garage, and I wanted to bring a packed lunch."

I leaned against the Jeep, filled with a sudden irresistible desire to laugh.

"*You're* going to help cut up a tree?"

"Yes," he confirmed.

"You?" Somehow, he didn't look like the Paul Bunyan type, with his khaki shorts, white undershirt, black socks, and Birkenstocks. "Really? Will you be using a chainsaw?"

"I assume so."

"And when will you be embarking on this mission to lose a limb?"

"Very funny, Jordan. You know, I've done my fair share of demolition for charity."

"I'm going to resist the urge to make a joke about you dragging us to Texas."

"That's very kind of you. Did you go to Madame Ribbette?" he asked, eyeing my book.

"Uh, yeah," I stammered. "Coffee's good as ever."

"Great. I might head in there myself. All I had was a cup of your mother's swill." He stared at his thermos. "Well, I think it was coffee. She's experimenting with the blend. Hopefully she'll get it right soon, because I've told her if she doesn't, it's *grounds* for divorce."

I left Dad at the town square and began driving back. Crooked front porches lined the houses on each side of the road, and here and there, trees lay strewn across the streets, felled by the storm. The steady blast of cold air from the A/C and the hum of the tires provided the perfect soundtrack for me to replay the scene from Madame Ribbette, over and over again. I seethed inside, wishing I could take the moment back.

*You shouldn't have run, Jordan. That was stupid, now he thinks you're—*
POP!

I felt the steering wheel jerk to the left, and fishtailed across the road. I could hear the rim scraping across the tarred surface and the tire flapping wildly as the Jeep zoomed forward. Pumping the brakes, I tried to regain control, but instead that created more friction and I swerved onto the shoulder, coming to a screeching halt.

After I regained a normal breathing pattern, I turned on the emergency flashers and got out to inspect the damage. The back right tire was completely shredded. The flat Dad fixed hadn't stayed fixed for long.

*What a surprise.*

There was nothing much around me. The only sign of life was a dilapidated barn ready to collapse after too many years of wind and weather. I took out my cell and called my father. No answer. He was probably on his way to the hospital, missing an arm. Then I called Mom. Nothing.

"Fine, I'll do it myself," I said aloud, as if someone could hear me.

After converting Mom's scarf into a wild hair ponytail holder, I wrestled with the spare tire attached to the rear of the Jeep. I found the jack in the rear compartment and examined it the way a bird might inspect a machine gun.

*I'm a New Yorker. What the hell do I know about fixing a tire? It's a long shot—maybe 100 to 1—but maybe Stryder will know.*

He didn't. After five minutes of Stryder reading me instructions retrieved from Google, I heard a car approaching.

I realized how vulnerable I was. *Perfect.* All I needed was some creep to come along, toss me into his unmarked vehicle, and sell me into slavery to lick envelopes for Publisher's Clearinghouse . . . or worse. I shuffled to the passenger side of the car, popped the glove compartment, and snagged the can of pepper spray Mom gave me.

A large black Tahoe pulled up behind me, and out sprang none other than, yep, Knox Colville.

*What was I saying about luck?*

"Hey, Stryder, I'm gonna have to call you back," I barked into my cell.

Whatever I felt for Knox—intrigue, infatuation, even my recent embarrassment—was replaced by a great sense of relief. I had a real fear of being stranded on the side of the road, so I was more than willing to take any assistance he might provide.

"You plan to blind me with that?" he asked, nodding toward my pepper spray.

"It depends." I didn't move an inch as Knox walked toward the Jeep to inspect the tire. He kept looking at the road for passing vehicles, even though we would've heard anyone coming a mile away.

"Would you mind getting off the street?" he asked courteously.

"Sure."

Crouching down, he dragged his finger across the barb of the stripped rubber. "So, I'm guessing you haven't read this month's edition of *Modern Automotive Mechanics*."

"No. And obviously neither has Eli."

"Who's Eli?"

"My dad."

"Hmmm," he said, flipping the jack up into the air like a little stick. "Why don't you call him 'Dad' then?"

"Why do you care?"

"I don't," Knox said.

We stood there: a standoff.

"Come on," he said finally. "I'll take you home."

I still didn't budge. We heard the guttural sound of an engine coming our way.

"Really," Knox said. "The Jeep will be fine here until the morning."

"Thanks. But I was about to call Eli to come get me," I said as I kicked the tire again, "and the doom buggy."

Knox didn't take no for an answer. Instead, he moved between the road and me.

"I'd be surprised if he can hear his phone over all those chain-saws," he said.

I looked at him curiously.

"He came in right after you left and I heard him telling Caleb about his project."

I rolled my eyes. A truck came around the bend and pelted our cars with gravel. I took my hair out of the ponytail, causing it to spring out like a freshly watered Chia Pet.

Knox glared at the retreating truck, then turned to me and said, "Ready?"

"Wait." I stopped, studying the Tahoe suspiciously. I had a sudden wave of paranoia. "How do I know you're not some kind of psycho that's going to hack me into little pieces?"

"Why don't you call your friend and let him know you're about to get into my car? That way I won't be as tempted . . . if I really am a psycho."

"How did you know it was a him?"

"I didn't, but I do now," he laughed.

Knox ushered me to the passenger door and I reluctantly climbed aboard. As he walked to the driver's side, another car approached. Curiously, Knox froze in his tracks. Instead of passing, the approaching vehicle slowed and pulled right behind the Tahoe.

"Um . . . Is this when the banjos start playing?" I asked.

"No," he said, leaning into the driver's side window. Taking a deep breath, he continued, "I know this car. Give me a minute."

Knox walked back to a long white Oldsmobile and stuck his head inside the car. After a few moments, he returned with an obviously manufactured smile.

"Who was that?" I asked.

"Ms. Ray."

I swallowed unexpectedly hard, like I knew something maybe I shouldn't.

"I told her we were fine and both on our way home."

The old woman gave a friendly honk on her way past. I could see her two hands gripping the wheel and her silver hair barely visible through the sun-stroked windows.

"Should she be driving? I swear she told Eli that she can hardly turn her head because of arthritis. And doesn't she have cataracts?"

"She's more resilient than you'd think," Knox said as we watched the Oldsmobile fade in the distance. The entire time, its hazards blinked. "But I wish she wouldn't drive on this road."

"What's wrong with this road?"

Knox looked sharply in my direction, then regained his composure. He pointed at the Jeep. "Exhibit A."

There was not much to see as we drove down the road, other than fields, barns, and an occasional ramshackle trailer with folding chairs and ATVs parked out front. We passed a huge cattle yard with dozens of white-faced Herefords grazing on dry grass. And hawks lazed in the late morning sky, searching the ground for scuttling mice.

Finally, he broke the silence. "You're Jordan, right?"

"So are you a creeper or Rosemary the Sage?"

*Uh! Why so obnoxious, Jordan?*

Unfazed, Knox replied, "No. That's what your parents called you the other day in Madame Ribbette, then I heard you introduced at church, and finally, Ms. Ray just asked about you because she recognized Jacob's Jeep."

"Oh." I felt a bit embarrassed. "Nice to meet you—"

"—Knox," he said with an outstretched hand. "Knox Colville."

We shook hands and I felt a rush so real it almost swallowed me.

"So how long are you and your family here?" he asked.

I hoped the warm buzz wasn't apparent on my face. I looked away, just in case. "Only until Jacob gets back. Another ten weeks, hopefully sooner," I said. "But ten weeks max, *thank God.*"

Then it got quiet. The kind of quiet that loudly fills a space.

"Sorry," I said. "This is a great place and all, but it's . . ." I stopped. ". . . It's not home."

Knox shook his head. "You don't have to apologize to me."

*Yeah, keep insulting him and his town, Jordan. That'll really win him over.*

I looked out the window at a giant farm complex; it smelled like manure even through the windows. I bit my tongue, resisted the urge to make a joke, and instead I asked, "So you always hang out at Madame Ribbette?"

"Caleb's a family friend—was my sister's boyfriend. It's technically my parents' place, but he runs the place now. I just end up there a lot."

Bliss had told me so much already that I felt awkward sitting next to Knox and dancing around the subject of his sister. It was weird, knowing the answer to a question I ought to be asking. So, of course, typical Jordan-style, I just blurted it out.

"I'm really sorry about your sister."

He looked at me pensively before answering, "Wasn't your fault."

A moment later, he straightened up. "Jacob leads quite the life, doesn't he?"

"You know Jacob well?"

"It's a small town, remember?"

"Ah, yes."

"Yeah, there was mixed reaction around here when he left to save the world—seeing that this community has more than its fair share of need for saving."

"Well, Jacob's always loved China, so I'm not shocked he ended up there. In fact, Eli calls him hardboiled."

Knox looked at me questioningly.

"You know, white on the outside and yellow on the inside?" I continued.

Knox chuckled. We were getting close. The Tahoe climbed the sloping hill on the other side of the parsonage, and Knox turned and stared at me for a few seconds. His face looked oddly content, though melancholy lived there, too.

A minute later, he pulled into the parsonage carport. "Safe and sound," he announced.

I was about to jump out, but Knox said, "Hang on," and he went around the truck and opened my door.

"Oh, thanks," I said, and I pretended to look for my cell phone so he couldn't see me blush. "And thanks for not hacking me into little pieces."

"Anytime."

On my way to the front porch steps, I noticed the church marquee: "Behold the Lord Himself Will Give You a Sign. Maybe Even This One."

Knox noticed the sign too. He stood staring at it, not saying a word.

"Yeah," I said, turning back only briefly. "Whoever changes that sign has an incredibly whacked sense of humor."

And with that, the conversation was over. For the second time that day, I left Knox standing there, watching me leave. As soon as I closed the front door, I dashed to the living room and peeked through the front curtains as he backed out of the driveway.

"Where's the Jeep?" Mom asked, making me jump. She was sitting in a chair by the window, reviewing her endless case documents for the Ponzi scheme client, and drinking a light beer. She was still trying to run the show, all the way from Ashworth.

"The tire Eli *fixed*?"

"Yes?"

"Flat," I sat, glancing out again.

"Hmmm," Mom murmured. "Is that the boy from the café?"

"Yep. The local librarian," I called out as I escaped to my room.

The next morning, I woke up and found the Jeep in the driveway, complete with a brand new tire. It was spotless. Out of the corner of my eye, I noticed a green book in the driver's seat. I opened it and saw the title: *Deliverance*, by James Dickey. Unlike my chicken scratch, his handwriting was flawless on the inside cover:

Jordan—
    Do you hear the banjoes yet? Welcome to Ashworth.

                                    —Knox Colville

# Chapter 12

It was our third Sunday at East New Hope and, just as I had so many other mornings, I woke up way too early. This time I even beat the sun.

I poured myself a large cup of coffee, adding cinnamon, fat-free milk, and two tablespoons of sugar. Alas, even with all the *accoutrements*, it still tasted gross.

*A month ago, I spent Saturday at MOMA, drinking a delicious latte with frothed milk and powdered chocolate. What happened to my life?*

Sipping the vile brew, I stared out the kitchen window and looked out toward the cemetery. The gravestones shone faintly in the moonlight. Little flags of red white and blue stood sprinkled throughout the grounds honoring veterans. The tall trees surrounding the cemetery gave it a closed-in appearance, as if the hallowed acre was a world of its own.

A quick flutter in the far shadows of the cemetery drew my attention. I peered out the window but saw nothing. It could have been a stray dog, or a coyote.

Or a ghost.

*Okay, Jordan, the only thing you've got to fear in that graveyard is a collapsing monument or maybe stepping on a beer bottle—not ghosts.*

I rubbed my eyes and concentrated harder. An impulse came to me—the kind people get in horror movies right before the slasher pops out with a machete, while the audience is screaming, "Don't go in there! Don't go in there!"

With my pajama bottoms tucked into Jacob's rain boots, I grabbed a flashlight and slipped out the side door. Halfway across the yard, I thought about turning back, but instead, I lifted the latch on the chain-link gate and stepped into the garden of gravestones, crumbling saints, and baby-faced cherubs.

A great hush fell over the cemetery as I meandered through. The crickets stopped chirping and the wind went still. The only noise I could hear was the squeak of my boots against the wet grass. I found it strangely comforting that, even though I'd only been in Ashworth a short while, I recognized many of the family names etched into the headstones: Magers, LeBaron, Johnson, Norman, Munoz, Gober.

I even chanced across the man from the funeral we crashed—Jasper Hardin. His epitaph read, "From This Vile World I Have Fled."

*Wow, my old gym teacher must have been a real funster. No wonder no one came to his funeral.*

The crickets grew more comfortable and chirped again. I stood there and absorbed the tranquil energy of the graveyard. There was no boogeyman hiding in the shadows. It was a quiet place, a sleepy hamlet of local ancestors.

As I turned to leave, I almost tripped across a small stone. I dropped to my knees and brushed the grass clippings away, and shined the light. The inscription on the cold flat stone read:

ABIGAIL RAY
1947–1949
SLEEP ON SWEET BABE AND TAKE THY REST

A fresh flower lay beside it. I reached to pick it up when I noticed the headstone three down from Abigail Ray's—with one of the same flowers.

A headstone for Skye Colville.

"Have you seen my Bible?" my father shouted, rushing around the house. The tie with "the sunburst thingees" trailed behind him like a foxtail. Somehow, he'd managed to tuck it into the waistband of his pants.

Still in my pajamas, the cuffs still wet from the graveyard, I ate cereal and watched the morning's fiasco unfold. I resisted the urge to fake "sick" to get out of another painful Sunday. Unlike most teenagers, I enjoyed school and never feigned an illness to get out of it. So, if I did fake it, my parents would surely believe me.

*Maybe some exotic disease that would require a specialist back home. Do they have Ebola in Texas?*

"Your Bible or Jacob's Bible?" Mom called out from the bathroom.

After a moment, Dad yelled, "Jacob's."

"I think I saw it next to the couch."

Dad hurried across the room and scanned every crevice of the couch, even lifting up the cushions. Finally, he noticed the Bible on the end table in plain view, next to the ancient fax machine, which was spitting up papers. He examined the documents cursorily and turned back toward his bedroom.

"Rachel, some papers came in for you."

"Oh, great, I was expecting those. Leave them on the table, please!" She sounded excited. "I don't know why they couldn't email it."

He sat down at the table with me, eating his granola cereal and fervently flipping the pages of Jacob's Bible.

"So Eli, what's your sermon about this week?" I asked.

Dad glanced up, excited that I was taking an interest, but he frowned when he saw my grin.

"Look, I get it. I know my first two sermons failed to wow the crowd, but I've got a good feeling about this one. I'm going to talk to the common man about everyday issues."

"Like?"

Sticky's ears shifted forward.

"The fig tree, the temple, and theological injustice. What do you think?"

*Might as well check the train schedule and see what time we'll be getting into Grand Central.*

"You're a little burning bush, Eli."

I almost felt guilty, but my father needed confidence. If the congregation got bored, or angry, or both, and they decided to send us back to New York, well, that was an added bonus.

"Thank you!" Dad continued, with his cereal spoon raised. "Yes, I feel good about today."

About that time, my mother popped out of the bedroom wearing a blush pink dress and black heels, beautiful as always.

"Jordan," she said on her way to the pile of paper, "are you going to do something with your hair? Maybe put it up in that cute clip Kimley got you?"

She grabbed the faxed documents and rifled through them with eager anticipation.

Dad continued. "I think it is important to emphasize—"

"N-n-n-n-n-n . . ." Mom stammered. "They can't . . . n-n-, no, they can't, no . . ."

"Rachel, what is it?" Dad asked with concern.

She looked at Dad balefully. "This is a Notice of Substitution of Counsel."

"A what?"

She glared again at my father. "I've been fired, Eli. The client needs someone more responsive. Someone who is actually in New York."

My mouth dropped, and Dad looked like he got kicked in the stomach.

Mom stormed out of the room. "Why did we ever come to this godforsaken place?" She slammed the bedroom door behind her.

After a moment, I looked away from the closed door, behind which I could hear my mother crying. My father stared down at the end of his lucky tie floating in his cereal bowl.

I told Dad to tell people she wasn't feeling herself.

"That way you won't have to answer the same question a million times."

He nodded unenthusiastically. I'm not sure he even heard me. It might have been because of Mom, or because he was too nervous about his sermon.

Maybe both.

That Sunday, the band instruments were gone and the stage was bare. An audience of approximately eighty people—significantly less than the week before—sat expectantly in the pews: young couples with their children, elderly white-haired ladies, a cluster of beefy ranchers dressed in tight Wranglers and white shirts, and a rowdy group of Sunday school teachers cackling in the back. My father sat on the front row, drumming his fingers on his knee.

*I'm shipwrecked in a sea of Aqua Net*, I thought, scanning the pews from my middle seat. I stopped. I didn't see Knox. The youth group members were absent, too. No one except Moe.

*Looks like I should've played hooky after all.*

Moe caught me scanning the room and sent over a vulgar air kiss. I glowered in response, but laughed when I heard the lady beside Moe say quizzically, "I smell Jim Beam." Honestly, I couldn't tell if it was said in disapproval or jealousy. Either way, Moe gave a confused look to his mom and turned to face the front.

"Where's the youth group?" I whispered to Dad as the service began.

"You'll see."

I didn't have long to speculate. In next to no time, Buck stood in front of the piano with a microphone.

"As most of you know, before the good Pastor Klein delivers his sermon this morning, our own East New Hope Youth Group will present a dramatic performance, titled 'Turn Around.'"

Buck stepped back and puffed out his chest, winking at Mrs. LeBaron in the audience. "And I'm sure proud to say this production was written by my daughter Bliss and won best skit at last summer's Timberline Youth Camp."

There was an impressive applause from the pews. Mrs. LeBaron looked especially energized.

As the lights dimmed, Buck added, "And don't forget, if you'd like to sign up for this year's camp, talk to Cesar after the service."

The light coming through the stained glass windows created purple and red shadows across the pews. Other than a brief whimper from Annie Oliver's newborn and the occasional scrape of a boot against the floor, the church was completely silent.

The sound system clicked on and I recognized Bliss singing the opening salvo of *Total Eclipse of the Heart*. Her raspy, yet beautiful voice reverberated throughout the auditorium.

*You've got to be kidding me. Stryder would die laughing if he saw this.* The spotlight illuminated Bliss, tiptoeing around the stage as if a ferocious animal were lurking nearby. One by one, the other members of the youth group pranced onto the stage and surrounded Bliss. They looked at her with hard faces and demonic eyes while the song kicked into gear. Each of them wore a black T-shirt with a white sign pinned across their chest. One read, "Lust"; another, "Greed." The others: "Pollution," "Envy," "Drugs," "Lying," "Stealing," and "Hate."

Bliss trembled.

Then, a second spotlight flicked on, revealing Boyd. He stood on a platform on the side of the stage. He was dressed like Jesus, with a white robe, fake beard, sandals, and a crown of thorns. My mouth dropped when Boyd began lip-synching to what had to be his father's voice. He gestured to Bliss with painful intensity.

"Turn around . . ."

At the same time, the youth group tightened the circle around Bliss. She tried to avoid each of them, attempting to break away from the "sins," but she was repelled every time. As this dramatic dance unfolded, Boyd/Jesus continued lip-synching.

"Turn around, my child."

Then for the finale, the spotlight illuminated Boyd throwing imaginary lightning bolts at the sins, while Bliss's dramatic refrain boomed throughout the church.

I don't know what to do
I'm always in the dark!
There is no place left to turn
but the Gospel of Mark!

Bliss dropped to her knees to pray, her eyes fixed on Boyd . . . I mean, Jesus. She lip-synched, too. "I need Jesus tonight!" Each of the sins fell to the floor. "Forever's gonna start tonight. Forever's gonna start tonight."

The song faded out and the crowd stared, transfixed, then leaped from the pews, cheering and clapping. Even me. Sure, it was a bit daffy, but it was actually pretty good.

"You know," Dad whispered, "that was better than some of the off-off-Broadway productions I've seen."

I surveyed the crowd and the proud looks on their faces. I was genuinely excited for Bliss.

But then my stomach lurched. Knox sat in the back pew, applauding politely. I turned around quickly.

*Every now and then I feel a little bit terrified . . .*

Buck and a few of the heftier men carried the pulpit back to the stage, and my father took the altar. He cleared his throat and looked down at his notes.

I didn't dare look back again at Knox.

"Vacation Bible School begins Monday, so I thought I'd give you a sense of what our teachers are up against," Dad began.

"A boy named Ryan was in the garden filling in a hole, when his neighbor peered over the fence and asked politely, 'What are you doing there, Ryan?' 'My goldfish died,' said Ryan tearfully, without looking up, 'and I've just buried him.' The neighbor observed, 'That's an awfully big hole for a goldfish, isn't it?' Ryan patted down the last heap of earth, then replied, 'That's because he's inside your stupid cat.'"

There was some scattered laughter, but more than a few audible groans.

"Despite their challenges, God believes in children. So, I'd like to take a moment to recognize a lady who also believes in children."

Dad put his hand over his brow and scanned the crowd until he settled upon a young lady sitting toward the back.

"The lady who is in charge of this year's Vacation Bible School," he announced, "Annie Oliver."

Annie flipped her hand in the air and shook her head vigorously—she was discreetly nursing her newborn.

"Annie, please stand so we can properly thank you."

Annie held the baby tighter and pulled the blue blanket closer to her chest. She continued shaking her head in refusal. By this time, most everyone had figured out the problem. A lot of the women shook their heads at Dad, too, and murmurs trickled through the pews.

"Come on." Dad cluelessly motioned for Annie to stand. "No need for modesty around here."

Reluctantly, Annie stood up quickly, with her receiving blanket covering the newborn's suckling mouth.

"Ooooooh!" squealed an old man with a white mustache, pointing at Annie. His wife hit him in the arm. The crowd chortled. Dad shifted uncomfortably at the podium.

Realizing the awkwardness of the moment, the flamboyant organist saved the day with a rousing rendition of "Hallelujah."

Needless to say, it was not a good day to be a Klein.

And for my father, it only got worse. Whatever excitement had arisen from Bliss's skit and the drama of exposing Annie Oliver vanished two minutes into his sermon. He had a death grip on the podium as he looked down nervously at his notes.

"In 1916, Albert Einstein published his theory of general relativity, which indicated the universe was expanding. But at the time, Mr. Einstein thought he must be wrong. So, he introduced a constant into his equations to absorb the expansion."

Seated nearby, Ms. Ray nodded her head in encouragement as my father continued, spitting out fact after spiritless fact.

"It wasn't until the late 1920s, when Edwin Hubble saw distant galaxies receding from Earth, that we knew the universe was definitely expanding. And, from there, came the Big Bang Theory—which hypothesizes that the universe was formed in a fiery explosion. Many scientists saw this as the death knell for God. But they were wrong."

I took a quick scan of the room. It had taken a mere ten sentences for the audience members to start yawning and checking their watches. Moe's mother inspected the ceiling for water damage. A mousy librarian-type in the back kept pinching her arm to stay awake. A clean-shaven gentleman with a cowboy hat in his lap succumbed to sleep—he snored a few times before his wife elbowed him in the ribs.

The people of East New Hope were lost in the dark thicket of my father's talk. It wasn't that they weren't smart enough; they just weren't interested. And none of it was lost on him.

"A closer look at the Bible," Dad slowed, discouraged by the dazed audience, "shows that science was upstaged by Moses, David, and Isaiah. The Bible clearly states that the universe is undergoing a continual expansion. Isaiah reads, 'This is what the Lord says—He who created the heavens and stretched them out.' The Hebrew verb, translated 'created,' means to 'bring into existence something new, something that did not exist before.'"

And it went on and on and on like that, for another twenty minutes. Even though he saw the lights go out on everybody's faces, he made no effort to improvise or change tactics. He prattled on, until he whimpered a vague conclusion about geophysical discoveries, laws of thermodynamics, gravity, and electromagnetism.

When it ended, a few people sighed in relief. They were finally free from the agony and the ecstasy . . . actually—scratch that.

The sermon was pure agony.

To cap off the service, the congregation held hands across the aisle and sang "Family of God." Eventually, I summoned the courage to steal a glance at Knox, but I found him mixed in with the crowd exiting the sanctuary. I hoped he might turn around, but Buck jumped in front of us, interrupting my line of sight.

"Pastor Klein, may we take you and your family to lunch?" Buck patted Dad on the back. "The Corral has an amazing buffet."

"Thank you," Dad said, in a trying-to-be-mellow-but-failing voice. "However, Sunday lunch is our family lunch."

*Ahh, yes, the Klein family lunch . . . wait—WHAT?*

Usually on Sunday afternoons, my father rushed off to school and Mom ran to the office, leaving me to grab a Reuben from Katz's deli.

"Absolutely," said Buck. "Family first, by all means. Y'all have a marvelous day."

And with that, Buck left us in the empty auditorium.

"I'm sorry, Jordan, if you wanted to go, but I have to get home to your mother," Dad confessed.

I nodded. He looked so glum that I thought of lying again, to tell Dad he'd done a great job with his sermon, but I decided against it. I didn't want to patronize him anymore.

We walked outside and toward the parsonage in silence. The LeBarons pulled out of the parking lot and Buck honked as they passed the marquee. Dad and I read it together.

"Don't Give Up! Even Moses Was a Basket Case!"

Dad's downtrodden expression worked its way into a smile. And then, we positively cracked up. Whether it was from the stress of the morning or the last two years, I don't know, but for whatever reason, Dad and I laughed so hard that we had to wipe the tears from our eyes.

I felt like I couldn't breathe.

After collecting ourselves, I asked, "So what's for *family lunch*?"

"Well, Ms. Morina brought over her famous Taco Tater-Tot Casserole last night, in gratitude for my chainsaw skills."

"Um, do you think Mom's burned down the house?"

"I hope not," Dad said. "It's not even ours."

# Chapter 13

Luckily, Mom hadn't burned down the house. Instead, she sat at the kitchen table, her hands covering her face. She looked up at us with dark circles and puffy eyes. Even worse than two years ago, when the government beat her in a public courtroom battle and she'd finished a bottle of cognac in the bathtub.

This time there was no cognac, but there was a pack of Oreos lay spilled across the table, most of the chocolate rounds emptied of white icing.

"How'd it go?" she mumbled.

Dad and I spoke at the same time. "Good," he said.

"Awful," I said.

Dad looked at me quizzically, then sat down with a gloomy look on his face. "Jordan's right. It was awful."

"Serves you right."

"I'm sorry, Rachel. But look, I didn't want you to lose your client."

"Intentions are irrelevant." She paused, pulling at the cuffs of her sleeves and straightening her hair.

*Uh-oh, Mom's going into lawyer mode.*

She glowered at him before starting in again. "Actions speak much louder than words, so it doesn't really matter what you *wanted*.

Because, at the end of the day, Eli, you sabotaged my relationship with my biggest client and you've positively ruined Jordan's summer. And for what? So you can traipse around town pretending you're a pastor? What's more selfish than that, Eli? You're giving academic PowerPoint presentations to a bunch of people who aren't even interested. They want someone to care about them, not blast them with irrelevant intellectual ideas about whatever. And the worst part is, you don't take ownership of any of this. I can't believe how narcissistic you are."

"Rachel, I'm—"

"This has all been about you. You're probably happy Byron is such a sleaze because there's no other way we would've come and indulged this ridiculous fantasy."

Mom shot me a ferocious look, like, *I'm sorry I said that, but I need to tear this man apart right now.*

"And how are we going to replace that money? If you've forgotten, your job is not going so swimmingly either. You haven't sold a book in years, and your crazy brother has given away half of the family trust. Wait . . . I've got an idea. Why don't you ask the good people of East New Hope if you can take a job as their permanent pastor? Oh yeah, I forgot. They don't want you here either!"

*Okay, she hadn't burned down the house . . . yet . . .*

And just like that, she stormed out the front door, leaving me alone again with my dejected father. His eyes were hollow and his face drained of color. He was like a lone sailboat in the middle of the ocean, stuck there without any wind. With his finger, he dragged one of the chocolate Oreo rounds off the table and it fell onto the floor. Sticky lunged for it. It was gone in two seconds.

"So, um, Eli, you still up for that family lunch?" I asked.

By evening, Mom hadn't returned, so Dad left a note and we joined the youth group at Piggy's Pizza.

I couldn't tell if it was from seeing Knox, the family meltdown, or the Taco Tater-Tot casserole Dad and I unhappily ate for lunch, but my stomach was like plate tectonics, shifting all around and creating seismic tremors. Whatever the cause, I decided not to overdo it with pizza.

Cesar and Dad sat in the back of the restaurant again, this time discussing Cesar's theory that modern-day aliens could actually be angels.

"Think about it. Our UFOs might be similar to the chariots of fire discussed in the Old Testament."

Dad rubbed his chin. "The Bible does say, in the beginning, that God created first the Heavens and then the Earth, so there is definitely the possibility of millions of inhabitable worlds that may contain races of self-aware beings. But to believe that angels or aliens visit Earth is wishful thinking, in my opinion. When we don't understand certain phenomena, we don't need to make up explanations, like the Norse did, blaming Thor's hammer whenever there was thunder."

Cesar already looked like he regretted having the conversation.

"Let me ask you," Dad inquired, "did you grow up with a lot of scary ghost stories at bedtime?"

"Yeah, but ghost stories with flying furniture, screams, and voices saying 'GET OUT' never scared me as a kid." Cesar shrugged and continued eating his pizza. "One of the benefits of having Latino parents."

I got up and joined Bliss at her booth, along with Boyd, Ally, and, ugh, Moe, who was picking a scab on his elbow.

*Ewww. Not near the pepperoni, please.*

Bliss happily clucked about the silly scribbles on the bathroom wall as she pulled the mushrooms from her pizza and fed them to Mr. Prickles.

"Your production was really creative, Bliss," I said before taking a bite of my side salad. "You ought to think about a career in entertainment."

"Really?" Bliss gushed. "Because I do have an idea for a movie. See, this teenage girl from the country teaches her best friend—who's a boy—to play guitar in high school and then he grows up to be this huge egomaniac miserable pop star, but then comes back to the small town because VH1 wants to do a 'Behind the Music' show. Long story short, he reunites with his best friend, and she's really cool and super pretty and they fall in love—with a murder mystery surrounding diamonds thrown in somewhere—but I'm not sure where."

Bliss finally took a breath. "Anyway, I'm going to call it *Pop Rocks.*"

"Lame!" Moe howled as he grabbed Boyd's Dr Pepper and slurped it down.

"Wow, that's a compliment, coming from a guy whose DVD collection consists only of booger-and-gas-passing movies," Bliss responded.

Boyd chuckled and leaned back in his chair, flashing Moe a "West *Siiiide*" hand signal.

It was the fourth or fifth time I'd seen Boyd, and he was always in some kind of costume. First, he was a coach, then Indiana Jones, then an airplane captain, and today it was an old school rapper—complete with gold chain and an Adidas tracksuit. Bliss called the condition "Dipstick-atheria." As far as medicine went, their parents had taken Boyd to an expert in Dallas, who said he was fine and would grow out of it eventually. "Kind of like most kids do with asthma," Bliss explained.

Moe's face reddened and he turned to Boyd. "You shut up, DJ HipHopapotamus!" Then he knocked Boyd's fork off the table, as he and his sidekick Travis strutted out of the restaurant.

"Uh!" Bliss snapped, coming abruptly to her feet. "He is beyond stupid!" Then she looked to the ceiling and threw up her hands. "You can send in the stampeding pigs anytime, God!"

A few minutes later, Boyd and Ally branched off to another table, leaving Bliss and me a few moments to catch up.

"I know you're a big-hearted person, Jordan," Bliss said.

Sad to say, she was the first person ever to use that phrase and my name in the same sentence.

"And yes," she sighed, "getting involved with Knox Colville would be fun for a while. But it's no secret—he's just waiting until he graduates to get away from this place and never come back."

I didn't really see the problem with wanting to escape. In fact, it made Knox a little more attractive. At the same time, Bliss was right. I definitely didn't need any projects. Stryder was enough.

*Speaking of, how come he hasn't called me?*

If half of what Bliss told me about Knox was true, he'd be more challenging than teaching a kid with ADHD how to do taxes.

*No, thanks.*

We all finished up and wandered outside. Just before Cesar climbed into the church van, I overheard my father finally ask the question he'd wanted to ask all evening.

"So, attendance seemed a bit low, don't you think?"

"Nah," Cesar said as he slid across the leather seat. "You hang in there, Pastor Klein. You're doing great."

After everyone piled inside, we were all accosted again with the van's unbearable smell.

I pinched my nose. "Either this van needs a bath or there's a chicken-fried steak hidden under a seat somewhere."

Cesar pulled out of the parking lot and asked loudly, "So, Pastor Klein, who do I take home first?"

"Ally?" Dad suggested.

Right answer. The group—well, everyone except me—shouted in unison, "Ally!"

Once again, we drove down the highway past the acres of tall grass, broken up by patches of pine and pecan trees illuminated only by the headlights. The radio played "Hotel California" as I stared out the window. I watched the dark shapes of the trees passing quickly as the van sped along. We'd been in Texas a month and I still couldn't believe how dark it got.

"See that road?" Bliss pointed ahead to a small county road sign. I nodded.

"It leads to Colville Ranch."

I saw a single lane as we passed, but the trees quickly swallowed it up. I could see a faint yellowish glow in the far distance, presumably from Knox's house.

Boyd leaned forward to whisper something in my ear, distracting me from my thoughts. I laughed as Boyd attempted to give me the large medallion that had been hanging around his neck.

"Oh my gosh!" Bliss yelled at her little brother. "You're cracked! Leave Jordan alone!"

Then Cesar turned down a dirt road and silenced the radio. He slowed the van and rolled down the windows in the darkness. I heard the cicadas hum and the night birds sing in deeper tones.

The night was warm and I watched as a few lightning bugs flew inside the van. Cesar crept by the thick pines that grew close to the roadside. Outside, the lush foliage scratched the sides and a few leaves whisked inside the windows.

It was like a replay of our last trip down this narrow back way.

In an ominous tone, Cesar asked, "Have y'all ever heard the story of the Screaming Bridge?"

"Is he kidding?" I asked Bliss.

"Cesar, you told us about the Screaming Bridge last week," Bliss said.

But Cesar still turned off the headlights and the van continued to inch along in the pitch black.

"Oh," Cesar said in a deep voice. "That's right . . . Y'all already know about the Screaming Bridge!"

Cesar flicked on the headlights, revealing a hulking and faceless figure wielding a massive chainsaw directly in front of us. The grotesquely masked man advanced on the van with his roaring chainsaw wagging wildly.

Everyone screamed, and screamed, and screamed again. Even my father screamed like a little girl. Bliss climbed on my lap and I buried my face in her long blonde hair as if it were somehow a shield of protection.

I could hear Cesar laughing hysterically, and some of the other members of the youth group had mysteriously calmed down. I peeked out from my hideout in time to see the chainsaw maniac yank off his mask.

It was Buck, wearing a huge smile and laughing uncontrollably.

"We got punked!" Boyd yelled.

My heart beat like a bass drum.

*The way things are going, I might need to see a cardiologist this summer.*

Buck opened the van door and scooted in next to me. I whacked him with my open palm and so did Bliss and Ally. Buck covered himself up, laughing all the while.

"Hey, guys!" Buck yelled. "Did you hear the one about the Screaming Bridge?"

"Yo, Dad!" Boyd said with a high-five raised. "Waaay coo'!"

Buck shook his head, but high-fived Boyd nonetheless.

"I wasn't scared at all," Boyd said.

As Cesar rolled the windows up and sped across the bridge toward Ally's, the tires thumped across the wooden timbers. I heard the conversation from the front seat.

"I told you that was coming," Cesar said to Dad.

"I know, I know," my father panted, his voice still aquiver. "But I wasn't expecting it to be so terrifying!"

# Chapter 14

**W**hat I found the next morning was much more frightening than Buck wielding a chainsaw. My mother stood in the kitchen wearing an apron, baking popovers, and whistling a chipper tune.

"Good morning, sweetheart!"

I poured myself a glass of orange juice and watched her nervously, wondering if she'd gotten a lobotomy. It seemed possible, since she'd forgotten how bad a cook she was. At the same time, maybe she was still trying to set the house on fire—this time using the oven.

I could hear Dad's voice outside, and through the window, I caught him slopping a soapy sponge across the Jeep, scrubbing harder than he probably needed to. He was sopping wet. Sticky, who was also soaked, ran circles around Dad, barking all the while.

I was about to crack a joke about how ridiculous Dad looked when Mom dropped a basket of clean, folded laundry at my feet.

"Your breakfast is ready," she said with a nod to the table. A beautiful fruit salad awaited me: little triangles of melons and discs of bananas and grapes. And she'd already placed a tray of steaming popovers, surprisingly not burnt, at the center of the table.

*Great, now they're both crazy.*

Dad came squishing into the kitchen dripping wet, a cluster of suds sliding down his face. His hair was damp and matted.

"Here you go, sweetheart," Mom said as she politely handed him a dishtowel.

For a second, I wondered if Dad had replaced her with a robot, but he seemed as surprised as I was. He looked at the table, then eyed my mother suspiciously, sussing out whether she was trying to poison us. He mopped his forehead with the rag.

I sat down and stabbed a slice of fruit with my fork.

*There are worse ways to go than the sweet taste of kiwi . . .*

After a moment, Dad sat down next to me and broke off the edge of a popover. He slathered butter and jelly on it, dunked it in his mouth, and nodded his approval. Mom looked on, neither happy nor sad.

Her yellow country dress matched the wildflowers on the table. The ones the churchgoers referred to as "weeds." For New Yorkers, anything that resembled a flower *was* a flower. Mom must've gathered them in the early morning.

She had her hair neatly scooped back into a bun, and I could see little dollops of flour on her elbows. She looked like the mother from a sitcom of the nineteen fifties.

After a second bite, Dad stood up and sulkily addressed Mom. "Rachel, I want you to know—"

"Please, Eli, finish your popover. I made them for you."

Her voice was clear and perfect, machine-like. Dad returned to the table, an obedient husband who knew to listen, lest there be consequences.

"I'll be sewing on buttons later this afternoon, so if you have anything you'd like me to mend, please leave it in the sitting room." She paused, remembered to turn the oven off (*there goes that theory*), and glided toward the back door. "Just going to get some mopping done before I plant marigolds outside . . ."

Dad and I exchanged a look, like, *WHO IS THAT STRANGE WOMAN?*

Then an idea came to him. I could tell, because he moved his thumb back and forth, like he was fighting a thumb war with an invisible opponent.

"So, your mother is clearly going through a lot," he started. "And I'm thinking maybe we need to get out of her hair."

"Like take a drive or something?"

"We need to give her a little more time than that. You'd do that, wouldn't you?"

"What do you mean?"

"Hypothetically speaking. If you had a place to go, like with Bliss, for example."

"Are you trying to get rid of me? Put me up for adoption or something? Because you could've done that a few weeks ago before dragging me to Texas."

"Very funny, Jordan."

"What are you trying to say?"

"Okay, okay." He stared at the floor, summoning the courage before dropping the bomb. "How do you feel about church camp?"

The sun started to peek over the pines when my father and I set off toward camp. As he turned in the opposite direction from town, I caught the day's musing from the church marquee: "Vengeance belongs to God alone."

*Geez . . . What up, friendly?*

Even though most people hadn't even brewed their coffee yet, the air was stifling hot and humid. On the radio, a weatherman with a thick Texas accent said, "Folks, it's only going to get worse."

*Tell me about it, dude. I'm on my way to friggin' church camp.*

I rested my head against the window. After twelve miles of trees and trailers, we made our way over a steep hill. Dad took a left onto a dirt road, and soon we were passing under a plank of wood engraved with "Camp Timberline." Right as we passed under, the Volvo hit a country pothole, and I banged my forehead against the windshield.

"Thanks for being such a good sport," Dad said.

"Oh, I'm thrilled. I've always heard camp offers a rare opportunity for reinvention . . ."

My father smiled hesitantly, and I continued, ". . . What with the oppressive heat, a lake I might drown in, the ceaseless symphony of crickets and frogs that'll keep me up all night until I go bonkers— not to mention the co-ed sleeping arrangements . . ." I watched my father's eyes grow wide.

"There are no co-ed sleeping arrangements, Jordan. If you absolutely hate it, you can come home. I promise."

I didn't reply.

I wanted to ignore the nagging inner voice that reminded me I'd always been curious about camp. But the camp I imagined sat on the Connecticut shore, where I could learn to sail and sit around the campfire, holding court on the political issue *du jour* and debating which was the most significant scientific achievement of the decade— not marching around some picnic table singing "Father Abraham."

And yet, I agreed to go. So Mom didn't end up in the nut house. Or so I didn't have to see them haul her away.

Dad parked next to the main camp building. Countless teenagers scurried about the grounds, all of them dressed in khaki shorts and yellow and green T-shirts conspicuously marked "Camp Timberline." My father rolled down the window. The sounds of laughter and shrieking teenagers surrounded us.

I got out of the car and muttered, "The Kurse of Kumbayah."

"Jordan, it's only two nights. Try to have fun."

"Sure," I said. "I'll try to stay away from the homicidal maniac that's always at these camps hacking, burning, and mutilating everyone."

"Thanks, sweetie."

He started to drive away, but stopped to offer one more bit of parental wisdom.

"Oh, and I heard the local librarian kid will be here too."

I stopped. "Here? At church camp?"

"I assume so."

He drove off, leaving me in the dust with a group of overzealous locals.

*Note to self: Never agree to do anything Dad asks. Ever.*

I did a visual sweep across the camp, looking for the boy Bliss called "absorbingly gorgeous, but a seriously broken soul." I didn't see him. By then, I'd walked into the middle of a clearing where teenagers were jumping on giant trampolines. Bliss was there showing off, doing back flips, her yellow shorts and green tank top bright against the black trampoline. She waved her arms at me as she bounced higher than what looked possible.

I had that sixth sense that someone else was staring at me. I wiped the frown off my face, just in case.

*Oh, brother.*

"Hi, Boyd."

He scrambled over to me in his Roman soldier helmet, a red

cape flapping above his yellow T-shirt, and offered me a piece of his wet chocolate bar.

"No, thanks."

He took a bite, and with his mouth full, Boyd yelled, "You've got to watch this!" He pointed to a group of kids outside the pool area. They were standing around a metal tub. One of the kids was on his knees with his hands clasped behind his back and his face in the tub. "You put your face in the Timberline Toilet of Mountain Dew and bob for Baby Ruths!"

Any distant hope I had of discussing that political issue *du jour* simply vanished.

Boyd knelt to tie his shoelace, which gave me another opportunity to scan the crowd.

No sign of Knox.

*No sign of hope.*

After the worship service, the entire camp headed to the shore of Lake Pine. We all looked up at a deer stand, once used to house hunters. It now elevated the wiry camp director above the throngs of teenagers. Everyone had a flashlight, and the bobbing beams illuminated all the green and yellow T-shirts—and my splotchy orange one. Apparently, Mom washed my yellow camp shirt with Dad's red golf shirt.

*Ladies and gentlemen, the latest from Rachel Klein's "Upchuck" clothing line.*

The director yawped through a bullhorn. He sounded more like a drill sergeant than a church camp leader.

"Okay, people! For all you Camp Timberline capture-the-flag newbies, I'm only going to state these directions once, so everyone listen up. You're either wearing a yellow shirt or a green shirt. If you're wearing a yellow shirt, you're on the Yellow Team. If you're wearing a green shirt, you're on the Green Team. *Capice?*"

The two teams immediately ran to different sides and stared each other down. Friends were adversaries. Brothers opposed sisters.

*For civil war, just add different color T-shirts, and stir.*

"The goal is to capture the other team's flag. You can sneak or you can sprint, but remember, if you're tagged, you go to jail, where you remain until another team member gets you out."

All the kids started bickering madly, trying to appoint their captains. Boyd was soon elected the leader of the Yellow Team.

*Another strike against democracy.*

"We start in five minutes!"

"Team Yellow!" Boyd yelled. "We need border guards, reconnaissance, sneakers, and rangers. We'll come by and give you your assignment. Then . . . Game on!"

One of the twins assigned jobs to the Yellow Team members. When he got to me, he looked frustrated and turned to Boyd. From twenty feet away, I watched the boys eyeing me and trying to decide what to do with my amazing athletic ability.

Boyd pointed to the tree line.

"You think you could stand in that area and blow this whistle if anyone tries to get through?"

*Ah-ha, so they've set aside this special time to humiliate me in public.*

"Sure," I said.

The Camp Director raised his starter's gun.

BOOM.

Streaks of yellow blurred past me. I was the eye of the hurricane.

I walked around the edge of the woods for a while, and then sat on a stump to brood. In the distance, Boyd yelled, "I got you!" having caught a "Greenie" on the yellow side.

Soon, the shouts and laughter faded away into the distance. Most of the action was concentrated down by the ridge and in between the cabins, which made for good obstacles. But then I heard the sound of approaching footsteps. Right away, I knew it was trouble.

"Hey, Mama."

*Ugh, Moe. In a green shirt . . . and skinny jean shorts. Nice.*

"You look lonely," he slurred. "You got double-Ds for that big flashlight?"

"Wow, a new low, even for you. Drunk at church camp."

He snatched the flashlight from my hand, but fumbled it, and it slipped into the air like a bar of soap. It landed on the pine needles, and Moe reached for it but his feet kicked it away. Finally, he seized it in his hands. He shined the light on his face like a psychopath, and then he smiled proudly, as if he'd just learned to use the potty.

"So what if I'm drunk?" He paused. "Actually, I'm intoxicated . . . by you."

I groaned. I thought about running, but Moe had me cornered. I had to wait for the right opening.

He flicked the flashlight off and on, strobing the beam across my feet, my legs, and finally my chest. He wiped sweaty palms against his T-shirt and fumbled the flashlight again. I let it rest on the ground, anxious to pick it up.

"You know what, Moe. All this time I thought you were so repulsive, but now that you shined the flashlight on my chest, I can see what a true romantic you really are." As I spoke, I stepped back, laughing. Moe was harmless, but that didn't make him any less annoying. Plus, if I created enough space, I could dart to his left and make it past the branches into the clearing. "Do I need to break out my warning whistle to call in the troops?"

"Nah," Moe slurred. "I thought I'd join you . . . *or*, we can get out of this place. Maybe slip into something more comfortable."

"Leave her alone, Moe."

Knox appeared from the shadows and scooped up the fallen flashlight, shining it straight into Moe's eyes. Moe screwed up his face, annoyed by the brightness.

"Piss off, Knox," Moe hissed, the edge of his lips twitching in amusement. He turned his attention back to me and leaned forward, as if he might tip over on purpose, trying to knock me down like a bowling pin.

"Come on, Moe. No hard feelings," Knox said, approaching slowly. "She obviously isn't impressed by someone who can't count his balls and get the same answer twice."

I had to stifle a giggle.

Moe, still spotlit, cracked his knuckles and looked menacingly at Knox. "That's funny, chief." Moe threw his head back and laughed delightedly. "Because your *sister* didn't have any trouble counting them."

Knox froze. He was just a silhouette behind the barrel of the flashlight, but I could almost see the wave of anger surge through him. He tossed the flashlight to the side and it landed on a root, where it spilled a cone of light onto the three of us.

In a blink, Knox's fist sent Moe staggering and the redhead struggled to keep his feet. He took a wild swing back, but Knox leaned out of the way and connected another right. He sent Moe to the ground, and Knox leapt on him, cocking his arms back and forth, whaling on Moe, his punches accompanied by a deep animal growl, "Don't you ever . . . breathe a word . . . in my presence . . . again!"

Moe spat a mouthful of blood into Knox's face, as if begging for more pain. Knox complied.

I screamed for him to stop but he didn't; he couldn't. He landed a series of punches across Moe's ribs, his face, wherever he could connect. Only the camp director, with the surprising help of Boyd and the twins, could pull Knox off Moe.

"You're both out of here!" the camp director yelled to the boys. "Now, before I decide to call the police!"

Knox didn't argue, but Moe lay there mumbling about suing Camp Timberline, about not being drunk and how his mom was going to hear the real story.

I caught my breath, holding my stomach with one hand and covering my open mouth with the other.

Knox's face shone with sweat as he worked to control his breathing. Once he did, he met my eyes.

"I'm sorry," he said, ashamed.

I quickly looked away.

From the ground, Moe wheezed with wet, bloody laughter, which echoed through the forest and rang in my ears.

# Chapter 15

**B**liss was unable to contain herself. She was blowing up my cell before I even made it into the kitchen the first morning back home.

"Are you all right?" she asked repeatedly. "I mean, that was worse than when those two fat guys fought over the last motorized wheelchair at Walmart. And to think, in this case, *you* were the scooter!"

While Knox beating the snot out of Moe was major drama at camp, it wasn't front-page news. I know, because as I shuffled into the kitchen I found my father reading the *Ashworth Herald*. The main headline was: "Local High School Dropouts Cut in Half."

*He hasn't heard about it yet. Maybe he won't.*

The always-redolent Hal had positioned himself on my mother's stack of cookbooks she'd pillaged from Madame Ribbette. And I waltzed through a few pages of the novel Knox recommended, but I found it hard to concentrate.

Dad laid his paper on the table next to his vanilla diet drink—the kind that tastes like chalk—and looked at me. Apparently, the country casseroles, barbecues, and fried pies were beginning to catch up with his waistline, and it was time for some drastic measures.

After several long minutes, I found it impossible to ignore his staring any longer. I laid down my book and looked at him impatiently, desperate to avoid the subject of camp, a subject that might lead to the fight. No sense getting him all riled up.

"Do I need to be concerned?" I asked him directly.

"What do you mean?"

"I mean, you're looking at me like I'm some kind of circus freak." I grabbed a bowl and the milk from the fridge. "If this is the sex talk, don't bother."

"What?" Dad stuttered. "Um—"

I pursued my advantage. "Because I think you scared me enough with the book you gave me in the fourth grade."

"I don't remember any book."

"Remember the one you checked out from the university library?" I reminded him. "The one that explained sex by saying it tickles like a *sneeze*."

Dad froze in horror.

"Um . . . Um . . ." he stumbled. "Maybe you should talk to your mother about this."

"So I can get the same advice she gave me in the ninth grade?" I poured a magically delicious cereal into a bowl. "You know the one, right?"

Dad answered my question by scrunching his forehead and looking confused. My plan was working perfectly.

"Where she told me that if a boy tried to French kiss me to step back and say—and I quote—'Sorry, fill-in-the-blank, French kissing is upper persuasion for lower invasion.'"

He buried his head in his hands. "Can we change the subject, please?" he begged.

"Sure," I said, crunching on my cereal and waiting for him to recover. I saw him searching for something . . . anything . . . just not camp.

"What's so lucky about 'Lucky Charms'?" he blurted out.

I shrugged. "If you eat Lucky Charms on a regular basis and don't develop diabetes, you must be lucky." I spooned another mouthful. "A chicken/egg thing."

"Oh," Dad said, thrilled we'd moved on. Taking another swig of white lumps, he wiped his arm across his mouth and grimaced. "By the way, your mother—"

*Great, Mom checked herself into the insane asylum while I was away. . . . I wonder if they have extra cots.*

"—She and Ms. Ray are working at the Lord's Pantry, and then she'll be attending Cesar's cooking class. She said they're going to learn to make roasted butternut squash and apple soup."

"Mom's tackling gourd vegetables? During the summer?"

"Yes," he chuckled. "And then Mr. Hannah is going to give her a riding lesson. He swears he can turn a total amateur into a rider in just weeks. So she's got a busy day. Pretty exciting stuff."

I shook my head. "In other words, she's gone completely nutters."

Dad sighed, puckering his brow.

Mom went bananas after she lost her client. She'd tried so hard to work from Ashworth, but when that didn't work, she blew her stack. We figured she'd stay mad for a week, and then calm down enough to get through the summer. But the morning with the popovers, and now butternut squash soup and riding lessons? Plus, with all the plants she'd placed throughout the house, it was beginning to look like Vietnam. She'd definitely gone off the deep end.

Who knew if she'd ever come back?

And while it played to my father's advantage, I could tell even he was a bit worried.

"No, no," he said, brushing the thought away. "She's just, uh, transitioning. I think she's starting to like it here."

"Mmmhmm. In a completely nutters sort of way."

The phone rang, cutting our psychological evaluation short. Hal jumped toward the sound, as if he planned to answer the call.

"Good morning, Parsonage." Dad cradled the receiver on his shoulder. I snatched the *Ashworth Herald* from him and examined a picture of some quadruplets born in Chapel Ridge.

"Let me check. May I ask who's calling?"

*Bliss again?*

Dad covered the phone with his hand and scowled. "Knox Colville?"

He waited, but I didn't say anything. I was in shock.

"I'll tell him—"

Before my father could finish his sentence, I grabbed the phone from his hand and motioned for him to give me some privacy.

"This is my house, too," Dad argued, but then he realized, no, in fact, it was not his house, and he walked onto the front porch and moped. Moped while he started to hang the new wind chimes made of forks we'd received from a church member.

"Hey."

"Hi," Knox said. "I wanted to call and apologize. You must think I'm completely deranged."

I held my breath for a few seconds before responding, "Well, not completely deranged."

"Can I make it up to you?"

"I don't know. You can't go around bludgeoning people who say things you don't like. Even scumbags like Moe. I mean, you're not a caveman."

Suddenly I pictured Knox cloaked in nothing but bear skin running through a prehistoric landscape for absolutely no discernible reason at all. *Snap out of it, Jordan!*

"I know," he said quietly.

To tell the truth, I wasn't sure how to feel: honored because Knox stuck up for me at camp, or terrified of his unpredictable rage. I decided to give him a little more rope, and prayed he wouldn't wrap it around my neck if I misspoke.

"Well, I guess when life hands you lemons, you squeeze the juice back in life's eyes, right?"

"Interesting way to put it." Knox laughed. "Does that mean you'll come out with me?"

"I'm listening."

Knox paused, as if he were considering what to say.

"Have you had the full tour of Ashworth yet?"

"Let's see, I've seen all the shops on the square, the Snow Cone Hut, Movie Time Video, Piggy's Pizza, Camp Timberline—a place neither of us wants to revisit—and the llama that looks like Rihanna at Cesar's place. Oh, and the Screaming Bridge."

"The Screaming Bridge? Where Buck jumps out of the woods with a chainsaw?"

"That's the one."

"Well then, you still have a lot to see." There was a smile in his voice. "Pick you up in thirty minutes?"

I fell silent. I wanted to go, but I couldn't shake the image of his fists ramming into Moe's face.

"Yeah, thirty minutes," I capitulated.

I didn't think a church sign could make me blush, but it did. Of all things, why did it have to say, "Go On! Love and Be Loved!" when Knox picked me up? Instead of ignoring the sign and letting the awkwardness fade, I blurted out the first thought that came to mind as we passed: "You know what they say, 'Never take love advice from a church sign or a dude in a neckerchief.'"

Knox smiled and kept driving.

*Crap! Filter, Jordan. Filter.*

But I didn't filter. Our next conversation was about ice road truckers. Actually, the word "conversation" might be overdoing it. As we drove away from the parsonage, past tottering barns and infinite hayfields, my nervousness manifested in an endless ramble. After ice road trucking, I discussed the merits of Diet Sunkist and how I loved fuzzy hair in the mornings. I moved onto light sabers, poets, allegations of copyright infringement in the karaoke establishments of Tokyo, and our family trip to the Snow Cone Hut.

"It was so embarrassing," I said with a sigh. "Eli asked the girl behind the counter what the manliest snow cone was. She answered 'Spiderman' but after five minutes of indecision he ordered 'Pink Bubble Gum.'"

Finally, I stopped babbling and breathed in the warm summer air. I turned to Knox. He looked so harmless behind the wheel, steering us cheerfully though the sticks. But a few days earlier, I'd watched as he slammed his fist into Moe's chin and pounded the degenerate's chest with reckless abandon. I would never forget the sickening dull thud his punches made.

"That was a mouthful," Knox said.

"Yeah, sorry." I shook my head. "I'm going to shut up now."

"Good. Because I have something to say."

*Uh-oh. Buckle your seatbelt, Jordan.*

"You were right. About Moe," he continued. "And my temper. I never should've lost my cool. When I saw him creeping on you, I got angry, and I lost control when he . . ."

He looked at me helplessly.

"It's okay," I reassured him, grateful for his epiphany.

"No, it's not. And I won't let it happen again." He said. "I'm sorry."

For Moe's sake, I hoped he was right.

He turned the Tahoe east, away from the square. We both kept quiet, but I reached for his hand and held it in mine for the better part of a mile. Soon we passed a convenience store where a bus, covered in "Casino! Casino!" stickers and logos, idled in the parking lot. A long line of senior citizens snaked around the gas pumps. I guess they were anxious to get their slot machines on. A man in a Pokémon yellow baseball hat handed out coupons for the "Golden Bun Buffet."

"Two dollars off the Buffet!" a banner on the side of the bus said.

"Next stop for the Ashworth county elderly," Knox said, finally breaking the silence.

"What?"

"That's the bus to Shreveport. The casinos."

I remembered Bliss's story about Moe's dad, and I scanned the crowd for a man with no eyebrows.

A little fellow in a pink sweater vest and a glazed look in his eye stepped onto the bus. He dropped his ticket and stood there indecisively, unsure of whether to pick it up.

"These old-timers shove nickels into the slot machines all day, run out of money, and go home six hours later. Sometimes they go back the very next day." Knox sighed. "They love it."

"Then they pass on to that great craps table in the sky," I added.

As we started to pull away, I did a double-take. The woman fidgeting behind the man in pink looked so familiar. I couldn't be sure, but . . .

"Was that Ms. Ray?"

"What?" Anxiously Knox looked over his shoulder at the bus and then in the rearview mirror. "No, definitely not. She makes donation pick-ups for the Lord's Pantry on Thursdays." He glanced back again.

Before long, we approached a large circular driveway lined with oaks, a few roughly manicured bushes, and tufts of periwinkles. A large red and white sign at the entrance announced our arrival at Ashworth's high school campus.

"Home of the Fighting Mighty Pinecones?" I looked at Knox and giggled. "You're the Fighting Mighty Pinecones?"

"Go Big P. Fight for Victory," Knox chanted. "I'm surprised Bliss didn't teach you that one."

"Wow, that's intimidating."

"Excuse me." Knox looked at me accusingly. "Aren't NYU's teams called the 'Violets'? Let's be honest. No one is intimidated by a team called the Violets from a school in Greenwich Village either."

"Hey, they're mean fencers. Besides, I don't go to NYU. Our school mascot is the Thunder Owl."

"Which is only intimidating to the rodent teams," Knox said, trying hard not to bust a gut.

"Say what you want," I said with a smirk, "but many an Eskimo child has been abducted by the great northern Thunder Owl . . . so they say."

I accepted victory and moved on—taking a gander at the Mighty Pinecone campus before me.

Red aluminum breezeways connected the school's sprawling buildings. An American flag flapped in the hot wind, and the day was clear and bright. Sunshine baked the yellow-green grass of "Pinecone Stadium," which was situated next to a massive parking lot.

"All this for a town of four thousand?"

Before Knox could answer, my phone started blowing up.

*What now, Eli?*

I fumbled through my bag, pulling out lip balm, a bottle of water, the candy bracelet I was saving for a special occasion, my Velcro wallet, sunflower seeds, hand sanitizer, my camera—basically, everything except my phone. When I finally found it, the phone slipped through my hands and onto Knox's lap.

"It says 'Stryder,'" he read innocently, handing me the phone. "Do you want to take it?"

"Nah, that's no one. Just my friend's cousin's sister's massage therapist. He's always calling me, trying to get me to make an appointment."

*Nice, Jordan. Smooth as silk.*

Knox chuckled. He glanced at all the junk I was stuffing back inside my bag and spotted my digital camera.

"Have any pictures of New York on there?"

"What?"

"On your camera."

I turned bright red. "I don't know," I said awkwardly. "They're not your typical snapshots."

"Something avant-garde? Like photos of other photos?"

"Yeah, that's it." I laughed. "I take photos of all my other photos. Not in the name of art, but just in case I ever lose the originals."

"Okay, you're going to make me do this the hard way," he said with a smile. "Let's see, would your pictures get you arrested if Walmart processed them?"

I looked out the window. A lady planted plastic flowers in her front yard. Everything in this town seemed from outer space. "No. It's a bunch of artsy photos of things I find interesting or ironic."

Knox seemed satisfied with my response.

He slowed down the Tahoe and pulled in front of a gas station. "Well then, this town is your perfect backdrop."

"What are we doing?"

"Giving you some material." Knox pointed to the gas station's sidewall. There, painted in loopy, large orange letters, was a sign advertising "Diesel Fried Chicken." An elderly man sat in a metal chair along the wall smoking a cigarette and tapping his ashes into a plastic ashtray, which he'd placed on stacked milk crates next to a propane tank.

I smiled and rolled down the window, snapping a picture just as the man flashed a gap-toothed grin. *Snap-Snap.*

In that moment, I had my own epiphany.

It was simple, actually. I could either stay a seething ball of anger, or I could allow Knox, Bliss, East New Hope, and this quirky little town of shoulder pads and overalls to become a weird but surprisingly welcome reprieve from my citified comfort zone.

I was determined, from that point on, to be more open. More relaxed. Not just with Knox, but with all of Ashworth. I shook my head and came back to Knox. Knox, the beautiful boy I would have never known had I stayed in New York.

We turned down a back road toward the Lake Pine marina, and he pointed out a small building with picnic tables on the lawn. "You hungry?"

I looked suspiciously at the restaurant and at the line of customers waiting to place their order. "'You Will Eat Here Café'?" I asked. "Seems a little pushy, doesn't it?"

"It's marketing genius. They only play songs that have to do with hunger—*Everybody's got a Hungry Heart, Cherry Pie, Eat It*—"

"—*I Wish I Were An Oscar Meyer Wiener*?"

Knox laughed and opened the passenger door for me. I slipped my hand into his and let him lift me down from the Tahoe, muttering a quick, "Thanks." After we settled at a picnic table, Knox stood. "And what shall I bring you, Miss Klein?"

I deliberated over the menu, finding it hard to concentrate on something other than his closeness. *Honey glazed onion rings? Grilled artichoke? Pulled pork sandwich?* Finally, I made a firm decision. "French fries and chocolate pie."

"Yes, Ma'am," Knox said with a big grin before he strode toward the counter.

I inhaled deeply to catch my breath.

*Yes, this town might actually be fun,* I thought, as I hummed along with Rufus Wainwright singing about cigarettes and chocolate milk.

# Chapter 16

That next Monday, I awoke early, as usual. As I lay in bed, I replayed
the events of the last week—everything from the meltdown at
Camp Timberline to my extended tour of Ashworth. In one month,
Knox had gone from a drive-by crush to a monster crush and now
maybe possibly sorta kinda my almost boyfriend. It thrilled me whenever Knox revealed another local treasure. He'd raise his eyebrows
and curl his lips into a smile, obviously enchanted by his hometown.
Without a doubt, the last few days were like magic—riding horses
at the Colville ranch, trying every snow cone flavor imaginable, and
memorizing Lyle Lovett songs as we picnicked by the lake.

When I finally made it down to breakfast I sank into a chair
at the kitchen table. On cue, Hal plopped onto my lap. He seemed
impatient with me.

*Brush your teeth and next time I'll get up sooner, cat.*

Mom had left us funny-face pancakes, complete with whipped
cream noses, chocolate chip smiles, and maraschino cherry eyes.
I wondered if consuming them would break the vegetarian rule,
"Never eat anything with a face."

"Where's Mom?" I asked Dad, who'd bitten the cheek of his
flapjack and then abandoned it. He was scribbling notes for his

sermon, still clad in his formerly white robe (now pink, thanks to Mom's laundry care) and black dress socks. It was obvious he wasn't going into the office.

"She's taking a sewing class. She says she wants to make our clothes from now on."

"Cool. Then you guys should definitely home school me for college—so I don't have to go out in public."

"Be nice. It's a phase."

His nose twitched and he looked up with misty eyes at Hal, who was curled up in an orange ball on my lap.

"I think I'm allergic to her," Dad snorted, stirring his coffee.

"Him," I corrected. *Pity. Dad obviously suffers from FGC—aka "Feline Gender Confusion."*

Dad looked as if he was on the verge of discussing the dangers of addictions to allergy medication for the umpteenth time, but the doorbell rang and rescued me from his deep cogitations.

Actually, I expected it to ring.

"Don't get up, it's for me," I said.

"What do you mean?"

"It's Knox."

Dad simply frowned.

I pranced toward the front door. "We're going sailing."

"We didn't talk about this, Jordan," Dad said, drumming his fingers against the table.

"Seriously? It's just the lake."

"But it's also Fourth of July. Think of all the drunks that will be on that lake—you said it yourself a week ago. Plus, I'm not too sure about this boy. Wouldn't you rather stay here? We could ride horses or play basketball or watch a movie."

He came over toward me, and the doorbell rang again. I tossed up my hands in exasperation. "Eli, come on."

"Don't you have a boyfriend?" Dad asked. "What would Slider think of you going boating with another boy?" He seemed pleased with this tactic.

"Stryder," I corrected, "won't care at all. We broke up."

"Why?"

"I dunno." I shrugged. "He doesn't think tacos are funny. Who can stay with someone like that?"

Truth was, after I met Knox, I rarely spoke to Stryder other than an occasional text here and there—opting to leave my phone off whenever I was with Knox—which was most of the time. So when Stryder accidently texted me, "I'll show u my tan lines if u show me yours. Come over now," I figured it was a good break point.

Dad sighed. Obviously, he wasn't going to get a straight answer out of me about Stryder. And although he definitely didn't approve of Knox after finally hearing about the fight at Camp Timberline, he had to let me go. Involving himself in my day-to-day activities wasn't his strong suit. Plus, he'd hit a man just over a month ago. He didn't have the moral ground.

I slung my bag over my shoulder and opened the door. Knox was busy winding up the garden hose that lay jumbled on the front steps.

"Hello, Dr. Klein," Knox said with a polite nod, trying not to look at my father's ridiculous bathrobe. "Just thought I'd clear the road hazards," he said, laying the hose on the ground.

Dad furrowed his brow. He tried to sound imposing, but it came out like a whine. "Son, have you had boating lessons?"

"Yes, sir. I've been sailing since I was ten. We'll be safe, I promise."

Knox was tanned all over, which was all the proof I needed.

Still, Dad hesitated. He was at a loss, unsure of which of his many protests to voice. This gave me the perfect opportunity to jet out the door.

"Bye!" I yelled, lowering my sunglasses. "Tell Mom not to worry about dinner."

"She's making a pot roast. It is we who should be worried!" He smiled, then remembering to be authoritative, he cautioned, "Ninety percent of all boat drowning deaths involve victims who weren't wearing personal flotation devices!"

As I climbed into the Tahoe, I caught sight of the church marquee. "Dysfunctional Families Welcome; You'll Fit Right In." I sighed. I actually felt bad for my father, pacing around the house like the ghost of his brother.

The pastor everybody in Ashworth loved.

"Seriously, I'm about to lose my mind with my parents," I huffed. "I'm not saying I agree with the Menendez brothers, but I'm starting to understand their point."

"Why? Your parents don't seem so bad. I mean other than your dad's fashion choices," Knox said.

"You have no idea. In the last week, my mom has transformed into this crazy Stepford wife. She's busting out these matronly flowered dresses and garden-party hats. She's gone nutso over country crafts. And the house smells like cupcakes. It's disturbing. Mark my words, she's gonna take us hostage soon. I can feel it."

"And your dad? Other than the fact I'm not his favorite person in the world."

"Oh, don't get me started on Eli." I rolled my eyes. "He brought us here with some twisted fantasy that a good old-fashioned country sojourn might bring us together as a family. But"—I stopped and I looked back at the parsonage—"I think he's disappointed his zany family adventure ended with me hanging with the cutlery challenged." I turned to Knox. "Not that you are, for sure."

"Thanks for the acknowledgment."

I smiled.

"Even Sticky's gone crazy. He's totally obsessed with squirrels. Can't focus on anything else when he sees one. Just one skittering up a tree trunk and he's off like a missile."

"That's what dogs do."

"Yeah, but the other day, he literally hurled himself against the tree for thirty minutes. The squirrel chattered down at him. And then, when the squirrel got bored and tried to jump to another limb, it—no joke—fell right on top of Sticky's head."

Knox smirked. "Lunch?"

"No! Sticky got so freaked he ran away. The little acorn-muncher ran back up the tree, and Sticky spent another half hour hitting his head against the tree, trying to get the same squirrel. Dumb dog." I paused. "Uncle Jacob has no idea the amount of crazy he unleashed by asking us to come here."

"Speaking of Jacob, has your dad talked to him lately?"

"Don't know." I shrugged. "Last we heard, he was released and is someplace in China, legally working with a mission. He's supposed to be back soon after we leave."

Knox cocked a brow. "That's a little weird, don't you think?"

"Yes. But Jacob's always been way weird."

I glanced out the window as we passed a ranch entrance with a pair of signs: "Hardin Farms" and "Warning: If You Can Read This

Sign, You're Within Rifle Range." Scraggly overgrown bushes crowded the ranch entrance, and the place looked deserted.

"Hardin Farms," I said quickly. "Did the owner die?"

Knox's eyes tightened. "Why do you ask?"

"I don't know," I said. "The name looks familiar, that's all."

Knox knew everything about Ashworth, so it was hard for me to miss the obvious—he didn't want to talk about Hardin Farms. At all.

"Sorry," I continued. "You were asking about crazy Uncle Jacob?"

"Just curious. From what I've heard, it doesn't appear that your dad and Jacob are close."

I sighed. "I guess."

After one particularly stressful Thanksgiving dinner, Mom told me her theory on why my father always seemed on edge with Uncle Jacob.

Practically every Sunday morning when he was growing up in Brooklyn, Grandfather Klein took Dad to the park, while Dad's mother and little brother—my Uncle Jacob—went to the big red church on the corner. Grandfather Klein wasn't a particularly religious man so he insisted that at least his eldest son accompany him to learn the proper rules of chess instead of participating in the same foolishness.

It wasn't until Dad's fourteenth year, and days after his mother passed away, that he realized what he had missed . . . and what his brother hadn't. At the wake, while all the friends and relatives were comforting their grief-stricken father, Dad and Uncle Jacob sneaked into her bedroom to get away from the kissing great-aunts and closer to the mother they always thought would be there. That's when they saw her diary lying open on the dresser.

"Are you going to read it?" Jacob asked, his big young eyes looking expectantly at his older brother. Dad didn't answer. He could feel the paper under his fingers and could read his mother's flawless handwriting easily, except for a few tear-stained words. He read their mother's last entry aloud, words that both boys committed to memory.

*Dear God—Eli will be outside today, while Jacob sits by my side. I'm confident that Jacob, even at such a young age, understands your unspeakable goodness and eternal love. I pray that, one day, Eli will also learn to turn to You for guidance and strength. May they both know You are the strength of the weak and the comforter of the heartbroken. This is my prayer for them, the ones I love the most. Amen.*

It was this prayer that caused Dad to swear that he would learn what his mother and Jacob knew. It was this prayer that seeded a resentment of Jacob in my father—jealous that Jacob knew their mother in a way he never would. And it was this prayer that caused both Dad and Uncle Jacob to turn their back on Grandfather Klein's marble business so that it became nothing more than a quarterly dividend check from the construction conglomerate that purchased the company.

"So, why aren't they close?" Knox wasn't dropping it.

"I don't know," I replied coolly.

The marina's restaurant, aptly named "Chubby's," seemed empty at first, but all the action was on the enormous patio overlooking the lake.

A big-busted blonde waitress greeted us with a massive smile. She popped her hand on her hip and hollered, "Lawd, guess what the cat done dragged in! Why, it's none other than Knox Colville!"

"Hey, Val," Knox said with a grin.

"You know Ms. Ray already came this week for her pick up. But I can check to see if we have anything else."

"Oh, no. I'm not here for the Lord's Pantry." His eyes moved to me. "I was wondering if you might have a table for us."

*Knox worked for the Lord's Pantry?*

Val bit her red lip. "I bet I can find the perfect spot for you two," she said, winking at me. "Right this way."

She led us to the corner of the patio and seated us at one of those triangle-shaped booths where you have to sit close together rather than across from each other. As we strolled across the deck, I felt the probing eyes of almost every person on the patio.

*Am I being paranoid, or did everyone hear about the fight?*

Two tables away, a bearded man with a forkful of fajita took a long stare at us. He wore a tank top under his overalls, and had been reading *Men's Health* magazine.

Knox shifted in his seat, shielding me from the intrusive stares. He lobbied for me to try the famous Flaming Angus. I surrendered easily.

"So, at least your dad is doing well at the church," Knox said earnestly.

"Wow. I don't know who you heard that from," I laughed. "I told Eli, but he didn't listen, if you're going to bore people, don't bore them with God. Bore them with calculus or tax law."

Three heavyset women had spread themselves out around a large table in the middle of the deck, and the sun was cooking them. A scrawny busboy installed an umbrella to protect them, and they cheered, "Hercules! Hercules!"

I continued, "But my cynicism isn't righting the world any faster than my father is, so who am I to judge? Anyway, enough of my family drama," I said, leaning my elbows on the table. "The only one I haven't complained about is Hal—who is wildly under stimulated, if you must know."

Knox smiled.

*Note to self: Stop talking.*

"Tell me your deep-seated issues so I don't feel so crazy," I said.

"Hmmm, I guess you'd want to know that I'm scared of Pinocchio?"

"Not surprising, being afraid of a big nose is a common phobia."

Knox shot me a crooked smile.

"Or Disney," I added. "Did you know 'Kurt Russell' was the last thing he said before he died? Why Kurt Russell? Because he's one of the few people that can pull off the mullet look? It's a brain teaser."

*Note to self: When I say stop talking, stop talking!*

"Okay, sorry, I did it again. Now, tell me about Pinocchio."

"I saw the movie when I was ten and never fully recovered. It's messed up. The boys on Pleasure Island become donkeys and get shipped off to work in the salt mines just because they smoked and played cards? Seems harsh."

Knox snapped off the top of his drink. "But it was when Pinocchio tried to kill Jiminy Cricket with a hammer, that's when I lost it."

I leaned forward, as if sharing something conspiratorial.

"You're right. Pinocchio is disturbing."

"Yes, I know," he whispered back, as if one of the twisted characters might be hiding in the restaurant. "I had nightmares for years about demented little boys, wounded crickets, and—"

Knox's chair lurched toward the table. A blue Dually truck lugging a fishing boat toward the water, not thirty yards from our table, had grabbed his attention. When the tinted windows of the truck rolled down, I saw Moe and Travis.

"Uh, speaking of demented little boys," I hissed under my breath.

Moe scanned the patio, his miscreant eyes looking for trouble. When he saw Knox and me, he contorted his face lewdly and smiled.

I touched Knox's arm. "You okay?" I could almost see the fury in his eyes behind his mirrored sunglasses.

Val came over to the table and placed her hand on Knox's shoulder. She also stared at the blue Dually with narrowed eyes. "That just ain't right," she said, turning to Knox. "I'm sorry, sweetie pie."

"Should we get out of here?" I asked.

"No. It's no big deal," he said, trying to act casual. He ran his hand through his hair. "But if you're ready to hit the lake, I'm ready."

"What about the burgers?" I asked in a soft voice.

Val said, "We can box 'em up, right now."

"Thanks," Knox said to Val, and she rushed to the kitchen.

Knox snapped back to life as we walked toward the cashier. He put his arm around me and gave me a quick squeeze.

"I'm glad I didn't scare you off with my Pinocchio confession," he said.

"Are you kidding? Dolls terrified me when I was little."

"Really?"

"Yeah, my parents gave me a collector's doll when I was six, and the next morning I told them I didn't want it because it scared me. Sure, they blew it off . . . until I told them it scared me because I'd heard it trying to get out of the box it was sealed in."

As Knox paid for lunch, I noticed a familiar-looking can sitting on the bar. In fact, it looked like the piggy bank I'd made in Bible School when I was small. First, Dad cut a slot in the center of the plastic coffee can lid, then I glued construction paper around the can and added sequins and macaroni for decoration. The can on the counter at the marina was the same breed, except that glued to the construction paper was a picture of an old lady sticking out her tongue and a puff paint description below: "Help an Old Bat."

Knox put a dollar in the can. "Val's eighty-year-old mother spent all her money on a young lover who jilted her."

"No way," I said, mesmerized. "A mountain lion fund."

"Well," Knox said, "are you going to do your part?"

I giggled uncomfortably but stuck two dollars and some change in the can. Several of the customers turned their leathery faces at us when the coins clinked against the bottom of the empty can. In the corner by the bar, a chain-smoking lady yawned.

"Their hearts are in the right place," Knox said as we walked out the door.

And then I said it.

I took in a deep breath and spoke in calm voice.

"Knox . . . You don't have to tell me now, but when you're ready, I'd love to hear about your sister."

Knox didn't reply. He simply brushed his lips across my temple.

# Chapter 17

**M**om opened the door to the Lord's Pantry, and a gust of hot air followed us inside.

"I'm terribly sorry I'm late, Ms. Ray, but it couldn't be helped." Mom tucked her hair behind her ears. "You don't mind if Jordan joins us, do you? I thought it would be a great experience for her to help with the fundraiser."

I hesitated, and then raised my hand to wave, offering an embarrassed half-smile.

While Mom had invited me, the truth was I leapt at the opportunity. Not because I wanted to cut angels out of doilies or man the phones. No. I wanted to spy on her. She was getting out of hand, and I thought maybe if I witnessed enough of her behavior, I could figure out how to pull the string that would bring my mother back.

A man with a skinny face and greasy curls sat across from Ms. Ray. He flipped on his feed store hat and rose to leave, scraping the metal chair against the linoleum floor. Tipping his cap to Ms. Ray, he whispered, "Thank you, ma'am," before nodding at us and slipping out the door.

"Well, what a morning!" Mom said. She slid into the abandoned seat and fanned herself with a *Trucks & Ducks* magazine.

*Don't mind me. I'll just stand here next to this coat rack.*

"First, Sticky took off with the laundry. Heaven knows it would cause quite a stir if anyone saw him dragging my bra through the church yard!" Mom threw her designer purse onto the table. "Can you believe that? Anyway, Buck said we only have thirty thousand dollars to go. Is that right?"

"Yes." Despite her smile, Ms. Ray looked exhausted. I knew from experience how draining my mother could be. Ms. Ray continued, "But we'd always planned to raise more so we could add services—I mean, more than just food pantry and culinary training—"

"What other services would you offer?"

Ms. Ray hesitated. "The idea was to start a small clinic where medical students from Mother Francis could get some experience and provide a valuable community service at the same time."

"That should be easy to sell to the community." Mom took a pen from a coffee can on Ms. Ray's desk. "How much would it take to get that program off the ground?"

"We need a minimum of a hundred fifty thousand, but to do it right, Skye . . ." Ms. Ray cleared her throat, opening a large red leather ledger. "Skye figured one million, one hundred fifty thousand."

Ms. Ray sighed.

*Yeah, I think we could all use that kind of money, honey.*

"One million, one hundred and fifty thousand dollars?" Mom shifted uncomfortably in her chair. "Well, that's a bit more than I thought."

"Is it too much?" Ms. Ray asked.

Mom smoothed out her skirt and raised her chin. For the first time in a week, my mother's eyes glistened. She had a sudden spark. I recognized that look. I'd seen it whenever she went to court, ready to do battle with enemy lawyers.

"Why not?" she blurted out. "You know, I did the Lawyers for Lemurs charity dinner, and we raised a million dollars."

"One *million*?" Ms. Ray's eyes opened wide.

"Yes," Mom said matter-of-factly. "A *million* dollars—"

I cleared my throat.

"—before expenses," she continued. "Close to four hundred thousand after expenses."

Ms. Ray's face twitched.

"Now, tell me a little about the kinds of fundraisers that normally take place in Ashworth."

Ms. Ray enthusiastically recounted the town's history of fundraising. She mentioned the Harvest Festival in Ashworth, explaining how each September the local school received a year's supply of food through donations from the community.

"Last year, Bliss was Harvest Festival Queen, and Garnett Chicken Farm donated a thousand hens to her fiefdom. The Randall ranch gave her five prize cattle. Madame Ribbette provided a year's worth of coffee for the teacher's lounge. Just to name a few. That way, the school uses the money they planned to use on food for something else, like new books or keeping good teachers."

Mom pulled a small spiral pad from her purse and jotted down a note. "Interesting."

"Another event that draws at least ten dollars a head is when the high school teachers play Donkey Basketball against the seniors."

"Donkey Basketball?"

"Yes," Ms. Ray said, "They play basketball while riding donkeys."

"Where?" I asked.

"Outside the school gymnasium. On the outdoor court."

*I can see the sneaker line now. "Air Hee-Haw."*

"Those are great ideas," Mom snipped. "But I was thinking we could do a really nice dinner for, say, one hundred dollars a seat, and showcase Cesar's talents. Or better yet, a silent auction."

Ms. Ray looked at my mother in disbelief, but my mom was back in the saddle, thinking big. She asked, "Now, where do people have their wedding receptions or large sit-down gatherings?"

"The first floor of the courthouse," Ms. Ray said. "It holds about three hundred people on a good day."

"Perfect! That's a beautiful building and right on the square, so it's convenient for people to come."

Ms. Ray's eyes shined as she listened to my mother talk about flowers, invitations, menus, and table linens. I could literally see the joy rising in her chest. After a long silence, Mom woke Ms. Ray from her reverie.

"What do you think, Ms. Ray?"

"I think," Ms. Ray said at last, "I think it sounds perfect."

*Beep, beep, beep.*

Knox and I were heading back from the lake and discussing the viability of female sumo wrestling when my alarm went off. Well, not my alarm, exactly. It was Jacob's. I'd found his digital watch on my first night in Ashworth, and I'd programmed it to beep exactly forty-five days into summer.

*The blessed halfway point.*

"Late for a hot date?" Knox snarked.

"Oh yeah," I responded, grinning deviously. "I didn't tell you about him? We're going to go cow flipping. It's like cow tipping, except we follow the tippers around and then flip the cows right-side-up. I'm surprised it hasn't caught on here yet. It's gonna be a *big* night."

"I'm jealous." Knox pretended to sulk. It was the twelfth day in a row we'd spent together. Almost two whole weeks.

*Way to kill the vibe, Jordan.*

I was careful to sound dismissive. "Way back when I set the alarm to mark the halfway point to the summer."

Knox pursed his lips as he measured my words. "Halfway point to your going home, you mean."

We locked eyes and then sat in silence. I flushed and his shoulders shifted back. This was the first time we'd acknowledged life after summer—other than humdrum discussions about college plans. He was looking out west while I planned to stay east.

"Congratulations on getting closer to the finish line."

It was almost twilight, and Knox had discarded the sunglasses that too often hid his spectacular hazel eyes. His black lashes flickered. I could feel goose bumps on my neck. Knox Colville had a thousand reasons to be arrogant, yet he wasn't—a fact that always left me lightheaded.

Slowly, I reached for his hand.

"I'm just wondering," I said, "if I've missed anything."

"In Ashworth?"

"Yeah."

Knox meditated on my question, and my mind drifted to the

previous evening, when I'd run my fingers over his chest and down his rigid abdominal muscles, and he didn't move away.

I know breathing is involuntary, but whenever I was around Knox, I had to remind myself, over and over: *Inhale, exhale. Inhale, exhale.*

"Absolutely," he said at last. "You finished the tour, but you haven't partaken in the local entertainment. We'll start with everybody's favorite game, Hey, Cow!"

"Hey, *what*?"

"Hey, Cow!" Knox chuckled good-naturedly. "It's our version of Punch Buggy, but with a twist of country livin'. Plus, it's much less violent. No fists."

"If that's what you need to tell yourself," I sighed. "But I know the truth—you don't want to get beat up by a girl."

"No, no." Knox shook his head. "A Southern man never shoots first, never hits someone smaller and never—"

"—never says, 'I'll take Shakespeare for a thousand, Alex'?" I interrupted.

Knox frowned.

*Uh-oh, did I cross a line?*

"Sorry." I smacked my hand against my forehead. "That was just my internal dialogue bubbling out. It happens sometimes. It should come with some kind of disclaimer."

"No, I understand you're trying to distract me. But I see a field of cows coming up. Yes, I'll start with this one." He pointed to a large steer way ahead of us. It grazed behind a barbed wire fence next to a farmer on the side of the road.

"So it goes like this: when you're driving and you spot some cows grazing—which is not hard here—you roll down the window and yell as loud as you can, 'Hey, Cow!' For every cow that turns its head, you get a point."

*How sophisticated. I can't wait to play "What Up, Goat?"*

"You've got to be kidding."

"Nope. Watch this."

By now, we were zooming toward the steer, and I could see the farmer was Mr. Randall from church.

"Be careful," I warned Knox with a smile. "Bliss says Mr. Randall is heavily armed and a finicky eater."

Knox considered this but apparently decided Mr. Randall was harmless, busy digging a post hole by the side of the road. When we passed, Knox bellowed out the open window, "HEY, COW!"

Mr. Randall and the steer whipped their heads toward us. The farmer shook his head and muttered, and the cow lowered its head back to the grass.

*Munch. Munch. Munch.*

"Two points for me. Your turn."

"No way." I giggled. "One. You got one. Mr. Randall doesn't count."

"I think someone's afraid of losing."

*Whatever.*

Reluctantly, I rolled down my window. A few cows meandered on an upcoming hill, and I pulled my hair back from my face.

"Hey, Cow," I said, barely a half decibel higher than my usual voice.

Not a single cow looked up.

"Okay, that was pathetic." Knox used a fairly accurate sportscaster voice. "Yes, ladies and gentlemen, she's too chicken to play Hey, Cow!"

I scowled at Knox.

*Okay, if that's how you wanna play . . .*

Already we were advancing on another herd. I took a deep breath and leaned out the window.

"HEY, COW!" I yelled as loud as I could.

The entire herd looked up, curious but vacant. They bobbed their heads and snacked again on the grass.

*Munch. Munch. Munch.*

I turned to Knox triumphantly. "Looks like I got twenty-five. That must be completely demoralizing."

Knox gave me a devilish look, but I held fast. If I returned his gaze, it would only be a matter of seconds before I'd smother him with me. Then we'd swerve off the road into a bunch of bovines and a chicken coop and the Tahoe would need a new fender . . .

*On the other hand, kissing Knox would be worth all that.*

Instead, I kept the window down and high-fived the warm wind, my hand waving wildly in the air.

By the time we returned to the parsonage, darkness had overtaken the last bits of blue. Knox cut the engine and leaned back in his seat. Something heavy weighed on him. A few stars twinkled in the darkening sky, and I noticed the lights were on in the house. I could see Mom and Dad tinkering in the kitchen. Mom was still wearing an apron.

*Ugh.*

I saw Hal, too, dozing on the front porch. He looked like a fuzzy welcome mat, dusty from his meanderings. I remembered Jacob named him after an old space movie, prompting me to look to the sky for signs of life.

Knox reached for my arm, and we sat there quietly. He brought his hand to mine and gripped me firmly.

"Skye died six months ago, in January."

I didn't dare make a sound. Although I couldn't see Knox clearly, I could tell his eyes were closed.

"That night, the wind carried the smell of chicken shit from the farms across town. You probably think we're used to those smells, but you never get used to that kind of stink."

"Anyway," he said as he opened his eyes. "Skye held her nose and came to the soccer game anyway. I didn't know she was coming, but it didn't surprise me either. Once she started her residency, she worked all the time, so if she did have some time off, she'd come find me. Ms. Ray was with her, wearing a thick red plaid coat. The one that always smells like old carpet."

"They hung out a lot, huh?" I asked, trying not to betray what Bliss had already told me.

"They were close." Knox sighed wistfully. "They had big plans for adding a free medical clinic to the Lord's Pantry."

"That's right," I remembered. "Ms. Ray told us. That's why they're working on this fundraiser."

Knox looked into the night sky, as if watching a memory play out in the theater of stars.

On the field, Knox dribbled the ball up the middle and sped past two defenders. Skye sat on the edge of her seat as Knox headed straight toward the goal.

"Go, Knox!" Skye yelled.

Knox charged forward and crushed the ball. The goalie leapt but never had a chance. The ball flew straight and hard through his arms.

"SCORE!" Skye jumped to her feet, almost scaring poor Ms. Ray to death. Ms. Ray held her hand over her heart as Skye celebrated the victory with the other thirty or so Mighty Pinecones fans who were now standing in the frosty bleachers.

The referee blew his whistle: Game Over.

Pinecones 2

Buffaloes 1

Knox looked up at Skye and Ms. Ray, and took a bow. Before he could straighten up, his teammates tackled him in celebration.

Afterwards, Knox couldn't shake the shiver running up and down his spine as he climbed in his sister's black Tahoe. He'd never let her know, though. Everything was a competition with them. And since she just came from her shift, bundled up like an Eskimo over her scrubs, he felt a prime opportunity for spooling her up about her inability to take the weather.

The wind blew, flinging her driver's side door open.

"Ahhh! Turn on the butt warmers!" she cried to Knox as she started the Tahoe. She desperately poked at the heat buttons, including the seat warmers, while Knox threw his gear in the backseat.

"I can't believe they didn't cancel that game. It's freezing outside!" she said as she slid the gearshift into drive and pulled out of the parking lot. "I mean, I actually enjoyed it when Ms. Ray spilled that scalding hot coffee on my lap when you scored."

"What a crybaby," Knox teased. He could see his words coming out in short white puffs against the passenger's side window and watched the lights of the stadium fade away.

"Say that a little louder, please."

"What a—"

Skye gave Knox a playful slap to the back of the head before she turned back to the barely discernible road they traveled. The only sounds in the cab came from the hum of the tires and the wiper blades thumping across the windshield.

"Find a fun radio station, would you?" Skye said, turning on the wipers to mop off the drizzle that had started forming on the windshield a few moments earlier. "Caleb gave me that satellite radio thing for Christmas but I'm not a fan."

"Why not? It has every station you could imagine." Knox scanned through the stations as they drove down the dark highway. "An alternative station, a country station, an eighties station, a seventies station, a sixties–"

"—I know," Skye said, throwing a hand up. "That's just it! There's even a thirties station. I mean, should you really be driving if you enjoy the thirties station?"

"This coming from someone whose best friend can't see over the dashboard of her Oldsmobile."

"Very fun—"

Suddenly the Tahoe hit a patch of ice and Skye furiously pumped the brakes to stop the powerful combination of fishtailing and hydroplaning. The beast of a vehicle jerked violently as they skidded into the mud on the right-hand side of the road. A metal pylon hidden in the tall brush had shredded the tire.

"Holy smoke!" Skye yelled.

"Yeah. That was awesome!" Knox laughed. His heart pounded and his eyes flared wide.

Skye opened her door and jumped out of the Tahoe.

"What are you doing?" Knox asked.

"Somebody has to get us out of this." Skye raised her eyebrows and smiled. "And since you're dressed in your sassy little short shorts, I guess I'm it."

Her sneakers crunched the gravel along the side of the road as she walked back and forth and studied the Tahoe's front tires.

Knox reached over and honked the horn, causing her to jump. In return, she stuck out her tongue directly into the beams of the headlights. He held up his hands up in innocence.

While all the other girls that grew up in Ashworth spent hours straightening their hair every morning, Skye had long ago surrendered to her dark locks falling down in unorganized curls. Tonight, as Knox looked out at his sister eyeing the tire like a mechanic, as if she repaired busted-up trucks all the time, he couldn't help but think how cool his sister was. The way the wind blew her hair, the way she stood tall and strong in her ridiculous oversized down coat, the whimsical cock of the head, and the general air about her that said her world was full of heroes and empty of doubt.

"The rim's all jacked up too," she yelled.

Knox cracked the window. The car was idling, the engine gurgling, the radio stuck in the 1930s.

"What?"

"The rim is all jacked up!"

"What?" Knox held his hand up to his ear and pretended he couldn't hear.

Shaking her head, Skye walked to the driver's side and knocked on the window.

"Have you fixed it yet?" Knox joked as he rolled down the window.

Skye sighed, her pink lips turning into a small smile as she ran a hand through her wild hair.

"No . . ."

Over the treetops of the hill behind them, a sudden blast of wind howled, sounding like rolling thunder.

"Let's call Caleb and—"

"Then I realized it wasn't the wind. It was a car. So I yelled, 'There's a car coming!'"

Knox squinted his eyes, as if controlling a sharp pain.

"But she didn't have time to react. And the old guy in the truck was too smashed . . . I just heard a sickening crack."

Knox paused, scratching his jaw where there wasn't any itch. He was uncomfortable. All I could do was stroke his hair.

"I jumped out and found Skye lying in the ditch. Right when I thought she might be okay, I noticed her hair soaked in blood. And then her right arm shredded down to the bone, and her chest concave, her ribs pushed deep into her lungs."

I flinched just imagining what Knox saw that night.

"It should have been me."

"You can't possibly think that it was your fault," I assured him.

"I let her go onto the road. I should have been the one to repair the tire."

"Knox, that's ridiculous. It was an accident."

He looked out his window. Although he sat right next to me, he was worlds away.

"The next day, the *Ashworth Herald* ran the story. The headline said: 'Hometown Sweetheart Killed by Purple Blossom Patron.'

"The whole town was abuzz about the accident, but there was something else, too. Wherever I went, I could hear people whispering about it. As if losing Skye wasn't bad enough, people had to make it into some craziness."

"What sort of craziness?"

He shook his head. "The paper featured a photograph taken the same night Skye died. Put the picture right next to her article."

Knox reached across me and opened the glove compartment. He retrieved a large newspaper clipping that was so worn it draped over his hand like a delicate cloth. I scanned through the article, which highlighted Skye's accomplishments and quoted multitudes of friends, family, and colleagues at the hospital. Each of them professed profound love and grief. There were also a few pictures of her. No doubt, Skye had been a beautiful girl.

Beautiful features. Beautiful smile.

Then I saw what Knox was talking about. In the right-hand corner, above and to the right of the Tahoe on the dark country road, was another photograph. It was of the East New Hope sign, and it read: "Jesus wept."

I gasped. "The sign was like that at the time of the accident?"

"Yep."

"Who changed the sign that day?"

Knox shrugged. "Cesar said he'd put up 'Jesus Packs the Pews' an hour before the accident to encourage Sunday attendance. No one fessed up to changing it."

"What about the extra letters?"

"Laid neatly on the frozen ground next to the marquee without explanation."

I tried to speak, but no words came.

*It's just a coincidence,* I told myself. But what were the odds? I shuddered.

"I don't understand," I finally managed.

Knox nodded. "Welcome to the club."

I continued to stare at the photograph of the sign, as if concentrating on it might erase the mystery, or explain it. Something Uncle

Jacob once said to my father was itching my brain: "God has spoken through dreams, visions, and once a donkey. God created creativity so who's to say He won't talk through Twitter?"

I shook off crazy Uncle Jacob.

"What happened to the driver of the truck?" I asked.

"Nothing," Knox strained, as if that tiny word required a huge amount of effort. "He walked away without a scratch. Got a reckless driving charge and served a few days in county. That was it."

"Didn't they charge him with drunk driving?" I asked, indignant.

"He was brought up on charges of homicide by vehicle, involuntary manslaughter, and reckless driving. But he had money, hired some hot shot attorney from Dallas, and the judge had to throw out the breathalyzer test due to a technicality. Apparently, the police didn't do a blood test because, by the time they got to the hospital in Tyler, too much time had elapsed, and they thought they had him on the breathalyzer.

"His attorney argued Skye's death was an accident because of the road conditions and the old man couldn't see Skye through the ice on his windshield. Without the breathalyzer results, the jury decided the State couldn't prove he was drunk."

I wanted to cry at the injustice of it all. It was a strange thought, but I wished my mother had been there, arguing against the driver.

"To top it off, Moe bought the truck from the driver. The guy didn't want anything to do with that truck anymore. Sick f—" Knox gritted his teeth and swore under his breath.

"Wait, Moe drives around in the truck that killed your sister?"

Knox pierced the night sky with his stare. His silence was my answer.

*Moe is most definitely a portal for evil.*

Someone inside the parsonage flicked on the outside lights, and Dad and Boyd came bounding down the front porch stairs. Not surprisingly, Boyd was dressed like a pirate in high-tops.

"You *do* have a date," Knox chaffed, cutting some of the tension.

"Yeah, you should see him flip a cow. Pretty amazing."

Boyd ambled toward the Tahoe and I rolled the window down.

"Hey, Jordan. Your dad and I were about to shoot some late-night hoops. Wanna play?" He hesitated, then added, "Knox, you can join us, too."

"Thanks, Boyd," Knox said. "I bet you have a good *hook* shot—"

"Don't encourage him," I groaned.

"Unfortunately, I need to get to the café and help Caleb with a shipment."

Dad shadowed Boyd and looked guardedly at Knox.

I opened the door to wave them away, and walked to the other side of the Tahoe to say good-bye.

I smacked a mosquito on my arm. "Sorry about the audience."

*Too bad I couldn't squash Dad and Boyd like bugs, too.*

Knox waited for the two of them to saunter away toward the court. A faraway train whistled as he kissed me on the cheek and then whispered what I desperately wanted to hear: "See you tomorrow?"

I joined Dad and Boyd after he drove off. My heart was heavy with Knox's pain and the story of Skye.

"So is Knox your boyfriend now?" Boyd asked, passing me the ball.

"You know, Boyd, if you still have two legs and two eyes, then you're just a *rookie* pirate, but I can fix that—if you want to continue with your line of questioning."

Dad snorted. The idea of me finding a boyfriend in Ashworth was ironic, considering my protestations back in New York, and Dad's laugh was his way of letting me know that he hadn't forgotten.

I threw the ball to Dad.

Boyd said, "You throw like a girl."

"That's because I *am* a girl, Captain Peghead."

Meanwhile, Dad spun the ball on his finger, and we watched it rotate around and around, a world spinning fast and furious and almost out of control. The ball teetered on his fingertip, but he managed to keep it up for twenty seconds or so.

"Cool! Where'd you learn to do that?" Boyd asked.

"St. Vincent de Paul High School," Dad said smugly.

"It's not that impressive, Boyd." I sighed. "The priest taught all the boys how to play with balls."

I dropped to the grass and sat alongside Sticky to watch the worst display of athleticism on either side of the Rio Grande. That didn't keep the two knuckleheads from hooting and hollering as each of their bricks clanged off the rim.

I continued to watch, but my thoughts drifted back to Knox, his story, and the photograph of the sign. I couldn't imagine the pain in seeing someone you love mowed down in front of you. It seemed almost unbearable. But having the town whispering about that stupid sign on top of that? That might actually be unbearable. In a universe of random possibilities, anything is possible, people!

*Right?*

*Beep, beep, beep.*

The watch alarm sounded again, snapping me from my thoughts.

"Late for something?" Dad yelled to me as he massacred another jumper.

I was about to answer, but my eyes happened across the well-lit church sign that glowed fifty yards away:

"Often when we lose one blessing, another is given in its place."

"Hey," I called out to Dad. "Who changes the church sign?"

Dad halted in his tracks, and the ball bounced off his shoe and skittered across the drive. He was puffing air, out of breath, and his chest heaved as Boyd ran after the ball like a dog tearing after the tires of a passing car. Dad turned and squinted at the sign.

"You know," he said with a puzzled tone, "I don't actually know."

# Chapter 18

I was already outside on the dark porch when Boyd—dressed in a Batman costume—threw his first pebble at my parents' bedroom window.

"Seriously, Zorro?" Bliss hissed under her breath. "That's not Jordan's room! You're going to get us killed!"

"Yeah, Boyd," I said, having crept up behind them, causing Bliss to jump and swat me with her lip-gloss key chain. "When you're a teenager and somebody throws a pebble at your window, you assume somebody's trying to hook up with you. When you're old like my parents, you assume somebody's trying to kill you. You're lucky Eli didn't come out with his frozen pea gun." I waved them along. "Come on. I think I found the perfect place to hide."

For days I'd obsessed over Knox's story and how the sign had predicted the tragedy. When Dad didn't know who changed the sign, I asked Buck. He said it was Cesar. When I asked Cesar, he said it was Buck. After Bliss confirmed her father was not changing the sign, my suspicion jumped to Ms. Ray, until I reasoned that there was no way she could reach the top line of the sign any more than I could. The church marquee now read, "To Give Is Better Than to Receive," which made me suspect the piano player. But he was on vacation. No, it was evident that I was going to have to uncover the marquee manager myself.

Needless to say, it didn't take much convincing for Bliss and Boyd to agree to a stakeout.

As they followed me across the parking lot, Boyd listed off the contents of his backpack, which rested under his scalloped cape, making him look more like the Hunchback of Notre Dame than the Caped Crusader. He'd packed canteens of sweet tea, peanut butter and jelly sandwiches, flashlights, and most importantly, Cheetos. Bliss carried a blanket so we wouldn't have to sit in the grass.

"Where are we going?" Bliss asked, as her pink bedazzled Converses crunched the ground beneath her.

I pointed at the cemetery. "Over there."

Bliss stopped in her tracks. "No way, José!"

I knew this was coming. I turned around and made my case. "Here's the deal. The bench below the cemetery's oak tree is the best vantage point to see the sign. Plus, there is a fence around the cemetery, so we don't have to worry about stray dogs or passing cars seeing us."

"Heelloo," Bliss said as she rolled her eyes. "I'm not worried about stray dogs or passing cars!"

"Then why are you worried?" I asked.

"Let's see." Bliss put her hands on her hips. "Maybe because there are *dead* people in there? Plus, have you seen the movies? Teenage girls are always getting eaten by zombies, especially if they're blonde."

I turned to Boyd. He practically danced with excitement.

"Don't zombies eat brains?" I asked.

"Uh-huh," Boyd answered gleefully.

I smiled and winked at Bliss. "I think you're safe."

"Very funny," she huffed. "But you're not persuading me with your curses and sarcastic gestures."

I turned to Boyd. "Bruce? You coming with me or leaving with Bliss?"

"I'm with you," he said as he shined his flashlight onto the cemetery's green grass.

"Great." I pinched one of his black plastic ears. "I get Bliss's sandwich," I added, leading Boyd to the narrow entrance.

"Errr!" Bliss fumed behind us. "Okay. You seriously have to stop twisting my arm. I'll go. But, for the record, if I die in there you have to avenge my death . . . or at least make sure it gets turned into a movie!"

Bliss looked down at my legs next to hers on the blanket. "Short people have it so easy."

"Why?"

"For one, less leg area to shave."

After two hours of waiting for someone to change the sign, our conversation had deteriorated. Bliss and I were solving the world's problems—like inventing a motorized ice cream cone for hot and *really* lazy days—while Boyd shined a flashlight into a hole in the ground not far behind us looking for some kind of "critter." At that point, the discussion about the creepy cemetery seemed a lifetime away.

"So, come on, J-Bird," Bliss managed while keeping a blueberry lollipop in her mouth. "Spill the goods on Knox."

"There's nothing to spill."

"Uh-huh, right."

"I'm serious."

Bliss turned to face me. "Is my tongue blue?" she asked, sticking it out.

I shook my head no, even though her tongue was a dark shade of azure.

"He's become a good friend," I stated with a straight face.

"The kind of good friend that you've kissed?"

Bliss was obsessed with "the kiss." She'd watched way too many eighties "Brat Pack" movies from her parents' ancient VCR collection, which produced unrealistic expectations about the perfect kiss. It hadn't happened to her yet but she dreamed about that Molly Ringwald moment, when the gorgeous guy kisses her in the dark. A kiss illuminated by candles on top of the birthday cake he made for her.

I shook my head at Bliss and smiled. "No kiss."

"You're such a liar!" she yelled. "Tell me! Tell me everything!"

When the Corps of Engineers made Lake Pine, they chose not to clear the trees in an attempt to make it a prime fishing lake. As a result, there are stumps all over, many of them just below the surface and hard to see. This kept the big powerboats off the lake, leaving it for fishermen and weekend sailors.

Knox named the small Colville sailboat *The Escargot* because "she moves like a snail." But Knox liked it that way. "You don't buy a sailboat on a lake surrounded by hundred-foot pine trees because you want to race."

It was Fourth of July when I first climbed aboard. My father had tried to make me stay at home, but I wasn't passing up an invitation to spend the day with Knox.

With the sun setting, we cruised into a cove and dropped anchor into some nice East Texas mud. Waves lapped against the hull, while Knox unwrapped the sandwiches he'd packed from Madame Ribbette.

Time seemed to stop as we sat shoulder to shoulder with our legs hanging off the side of the boat. Occasionally, our arms would touch ever so slightly and I'd feel my stomach flip. I told myself that it must be due to the rocking boat—or maybe some bad tuna fish—but that didn't explain the goose bumps. Not when it was ninety-five degrees.

Before I knew it, our perfect day of fishing, lounging, and laughing was drawing to an end. It was dark. Pitch dark.

"Um, Captain?" I asked Knox with a raised eyebrow. "How are we going to get back to the marina?"

"We're sailing."

"And how do you plan to do that without the ability to see two feet in front of you and stumps all over the place?"

"Oh, it won't be dark for long."

"Really? How do you plan to manage that?"

"You know what they say about country folks and fireworks, right?"

"Index fingers are overrated?" I giggled.

"No," Knox said with a laugh. "But you're on the right track. Just wait a little while and this entire lake will be lit up for hours."

It hadn't been five minutes before the first cracks sounded across the water. A rocket squealed across the sky, exploding in a spray of purple and green sparks.

Knox explained that every Fourth of July, the town of Ashworth commissioned a fireworks show at the Fighting Mighty Pinecones' football field, complete with veterans in convertibles and the high school marching band. The real show, though, took place at Lake Pine. A 360-degree view of fireworks commissioned by ego—with each lake house striving to be bigger, better, and louder than its neighbors.

We watched the sky for a long time before my curiosity got the better of me. I wanted to know more about Knox. I wanted to know whether he felt half of what I felt.

"So that first day we met in the café—"

"Yes?" Knox smiled. "I remember that day well."

His quick answer surprised me. Before I could protest, he continued.

"I looked up and you were walking toward us, behind your parents. I even remember what you were wearing."

"No you don't." I blushed.

"Buckled boots the color of your hair, a jean skirt frayed at the hem, an oversized gray T-shirt, and a thin striped scarf that accentuated the nape of your neck."

I eyed him suspiciously. "Are you straight?"

Knox laughed.

"It was a ridiculous outfit for the Texas heat, you have to admit."

I looked down at my tank top, flip-flops, and cut-offs. I'd assimilated, all right. "In my defense, I had no idea it would be so hot. It's like living in the French fry bin at McDonald's."

Knox rolled his eyes and continued.

"Just before your dad opened the door, one old man yelled, 'Are her legs that skinny or is she riding a chicken?'"

I playfully hit him on his shoulder while the cornucopia of flares of firecrackers filled each shore with red light. "No, they didn't!"

"I swear."

"No, seriously! What were you thinking? Because . . . I wasn't too sure about you."

"You really want to know?" Knox sighed. "I was thinking you were weedy, cynical, spoiled, irritating—"

I hit his shoulder again, this time not so playfully. "Okay, that's enough! Never mind."

The sound of crackling and pops drew my attention again to the otherwise black night. The show was building, gradually accelerating the splashes of color in the sky. Colors that exploded with happiness.

"It's beautiful," I said, looking up at the celebration. "Don't you think?"

I turned to Knox and realized he wasn't looking up. His face was serious and he was looking at me.

As the rockets rang, he leaned toward me and softly traced the line of my neck with his lips. Heat flared in every cell of my body and my heart pounded louder than the fireworks.

Then he pulled away, only to look me in the eyes.

"Yes. It is the most beautiful thing I've ever seen."

And then, he kissed me.

"No way! That's the most romantic first kiss *ever*!" Bliss screamed. "Under a canopy of fireworks!"

"I guess it wasn't bad." I shrugged, lying through my teeth.

Bliss didn't buy it.

"Okay," I said with a huge smile. I could still feel the pressure of his hand on the small of my back and the sense of delight when I chuckled against his worn T-shirt afterwards. "It was the most amazing moment of my life!"

That was all Bliss needed to hear to make her spring to her feet and jump up and down clapping her hands and laughing. I joined her. Bliss grabbed my arms, each of us bobbing up and down with excitement. I don't think I'd ever actually jumped for joy until that moment. Within seconds, Boyd expanded the circle to three, though I'm sure he had no idea why we were jumping.

"Wait." Bliss stopped. Her face drew grave and she pointed behind me. "Look at the sign."

I turned slowly, breathlessly. The sign had changed.

Now it read: "All you need is the faith of a mustard seed."

"No!!!" we all yelled in unison.

# Chapter 19

**K**nox led me down the narrow, freshly buffed hallway to the long awaited fundraiser. We passed lockers, trophy cases, and hand-made student posters for last year's prom. The sounds of hard-soled shoes against the gym floor lured us toward a pair of aluminum double doors. Knox pushed down the handle and we entered the Fighting Mighty Pinecone gymnasium.

The whole town seemed to be there. A huge crowd milled through the gym, and around the banquet and card tables covered in crafts and cookies. It looked like the offspring of a union between Jeff Foxworthy and Martha Stewart, what with the flowers, fluorescent lighting, and all that plaid. I scanned all the guests until I saw a familiar face. Bliss. She stood in the corner in front of a microphone, strumming an acoustic guitar for a small crowd, dazzling them with her rhinestone charm. When she saw me, she flashed an energetic smile.

My mother scurried around the room in her mushroom-colored silk pantsuit. She greeted guests enthusiastically and gestured to various objects for the auction. Every now and again, she'd toss her head back and erupt into spasms of laughter.

The gym had not been her first choice. But after the mayor closed the courthouse for fumigation due to a water bug infestation,

Mom reluctantly settled on the Mighty Pinecone gym. It was "not a sophisticated location, but it will do," she said. Unfortunately, an entire Macy's store worth of perfume couldn't stymie the pungent smell of stale high school sweat and floor wax.

"The storm clowns are gathering." I said, my eye on my mom.

"Storm *clouds*, you mean?"

I exhaled. "Yeah, those too."

"Hello!" cried a small voice. "Hello, Knox and Jordan!"

I could hear someone addressing us, but for the life of me, all I could see was a ridiculously large flower arrangement on the small round table in front of us.

But then Ms. Ray craned her neck from behind the bouquets, prompting a large grin from Knox.

"Jordan, I do believe you get prettier every day." She raised her eyebrows and shot a sideways glance at Knox. "This Texas heat must agree with you."

I felt my cheeks burn. "Thank you."

Ms. Ray beamed. "Can you believe all this, Knox?"

"No." His eyes gleamed, observing Ms. Ray's delight. "It's remarkable."

"Yes." She brushed a strand of silver hair as she scanned the gymnasium. "Skye would have been so proud."

Knox didn't answer immediately, so I fumbled for my camera to give them some space. Any mention of his sister disarmed him, and I didn't know how he'd react.

He laughed wearily. "She would have been thrilled. You've done a fabulous job."

Her face softened. "Thank you, doll. But I didn't do a tenth of what Mrs. Klein did."

Knox put his arm around me as Ms. Ray pointed at the labyrinth of tables on the floors and lining the walls.

"Jordan, your mother has done so much. Just look at all those fabulous auction items! I don't know how she did it."

*I do: Martinis and mood stabilizers.*

Truth be told, my mother didn't do anything halfway. Whenever people spoke of her, they called her "hard-working," "sharp," and "frightfully together." It was both her strength and weakness. After the law firm meltdown earlier in the summer, she transformed into

Suzie Homemaker, trying to bake fruit pies and washing dishes Jacob probably didn't know he had. When the charity event sprouted, she put her shoulder to the wheel. She devoted herself completely, and hadn't mentioned the law firm for weeks. Everything was about the Lord's Pantry. I remember the day she learned the mayor and city council members were going to attend. Her eyes twinkled, as if to say, "I'll show them what a big-city girl can do."

If all went well, the "Pack the Pantry" fundraiser would launch a medical clinic and supplement the food bank. I didn't see a downside in the least.

I took a deep breath and smiled. "She's amazing, all right."

*At least I didn't lie.*

Ms. Ray chuckled. "Did you see what I donated?" She sat up straight and pointed to the first table next to the stage. "In the front. Right next to Ms. Cheek's flip-flops—the ones with a bottle opener on the bottom. Ingenious, if you ask me."

Next to the flip-flops were two pies and a sign that read, "One Pie a Month for a Year."

Knox and I exchanged glances and smiled at the enthusiasm in her voice.

"Gave you top billing, huh? Mrs. Klein knows what she's doing." Knox raised his chin. "I know I'm bidding if one of them is your lemon icebox pie."

Ms. Ray glowed in celebration of his compliments. She *adored* Knox—which I understood. And I knew that Ms. Ray and Skye were close, but as I watched, I couldn't help but notice that Knox's eyes lit up with genuine affection for her.

*Looks like I got some competition.*

"Of course," she added, "Cesar and Pastor Klein did all the heavy lifting."

I followed her eyes across the gym, where Cesar and my father lugged chairs from the back parking lot. Dad struggled with two while Cesar easily managed four.

Knox chuckled and ran his hand through his tousled hair. "Maybe I should go help?"

"No!" I protested, as Ms. Ray turned to check in more guests. "Don't you dare leave me."

"Afraid this place might rub off on you?"

"No." I grimaced. Actually, I was more concerned about my parents embarrassing me. These country people cherished how connected the community was, and my parents were anything but "connected"—to anything, reality included. While I wanted Mom to succeed, I needed to maintain a low-pro. "Cesar's got it covered."

I watched as Mom headed to the stage. Cool, poised, and lovely. She waited for a few people to find seats, while others drifted through the gym, examining crafts and tags. When she cleared her throat into the microphone, a hush fell across the space.

"Ladies and gentlemen. Distinguished guests. I would like to take this opportunity to congratulate each and every one of you on launching this outstanding fundraising campaign. With your help, we can keep the Lord's Pantry open for business for a long time."

There was a smattering of applause, and she went on. "Charity is often perceived as a donation or offering to people who are less fortunate. Charity has different names: philanthropy, benevolence, altruism, magnanimity, and so on. But, to me, it is what God wants us to do."

She raised her head toward the crowd. Dad waved, rocking back on his heels and inhaling a basket of Ms. Herrington's fried pickles. He'd lost a few pounds, so no more strict diet. The horseradish dipping sauce slathered on his lips and chin suggested a full-on binge.

"At each table, there is a donated item and, in front of the donated item, a sheet of paper with a starting bid. The highest bid at nine o'clock wins the item. It's that simple. Just drop your bids in the boxes on the tables. As you can see, there is plenty of punch and wonderful homemade foods in the back, so please enjoy yourselves. Charity is also about having fun!"

The crowd hummed with approval and people applauded enthusiastically. Though there weren't any air conditioners, the heat didn't bother anyone—the crowd was lifted by its higher calling.

Knox nodded to the tables. "Shall we?" He placed his hand on the small of my back.

*There he goes again!*

I had to remind myself to breathe. Even though we'd been together almost every day for the past month, every nerve still tingled when he touched me. We walked by two tables before Knox wanted to bid.

"Awesome, I'm signing you up for this one." He grinned and placed my name by the thirty-dollar line for Miss. Hackler's "Moroccan Surprise"—two belly-dancing lessons.

I slapped him on the arm. "That's a veiled threat."

Knox groaned.

Next to the belly-dancing table was a collection of cinnamon-colored squirrels in four three-foot metal cages. I crouched, staring through the wire at the little guys making high-pitched "tseet" sounds while they dangled their front feet—like they were drying their teeny nails.

"Cute overload," I said, placing my finger through one of the spaces, trying to touch their kitten-soft fur. "It's the Von Trapp family choir."

"I wouldn't do that, if I were you," Knox cautioned. "Those big brown eyes can be deceiving. See that fold of skin that extends from the wrist to the ankle?"

"Yeah?"

"That's the gliding membrane."

"So why would anyone auction—"

"Nothin' wrong with flying squirrels," huffed Mr. Wheeler, who rose from his folding chair and shook his cane at us. "Did you know they can stretch out parachute-like and glide through the pines—sometimes a hundred fifty feet? And lots of people raise 'em as pets."

"I didn't," I said apologetically.

I peered again at the frantic little squirrels. They looked happy enough, and maybe finding a home other than cantankerous Mr. Wheeler's backyard sanctuary wouldn't be half bad. So I bid on them.

Mr. Wheeler sat down again and smiled in approval. I wondered if this was how he got people to bid on his squirrels, by bullying them into feeling guilty.

*If I win, I'm gonna set the little nuteaters free.*

We continued past the tables. One listed a Madame Ribbette's gift certificate and a bottle of prized Bordeaux from the Colville cellar. Another—compliments of the Wrestling Station—displayed a Troy Aikman autographed football. Ally's table featured her blinding smile and a puff-paint poster advertising five nights of free babysitting. Mr. Randall contributed an interesting oil painting of the Alamo, where the men inside wore contemporary army camouflage and held machine guns. Fred's Midnight Oil Stop + Shop even got in on the gig by donating a free month of premium unleaded and two bottles of Tito's vodka.

Knox squeezed my hand as we headed to the next table, and the next, and the next, and the next. We saw a "Bored Basket," stuffed with games, puzzles, Sudoku, cards, and the classic game Operation. Cavity Sam's large red lightbulb nose was all I needed to see before I bid.

"This game is my favorite," I said, my eyes wide. "I remember being six and asking Eli why we have rubber bands and miniature horses in our bodies. He told me, 'I guess that's why they say everyone has a little horse in them.'"

"What?"

I'd stumped Knox with that one.

"I know. It makes no sense. Confused me for years."

I glanced over at my father. He looked calm, cool, and collected, shaking hands, and effortlessly socializing with the townsfolk. He caught my eye and waved, but when he saw Knox at my side, he winced slightly.

"My dad is crazy," I whispered to Knox as we smiled and waved hello.

Knox skipped over the compliment. "Oh yeah, if you think he's bad, my dad told us that the bumps in the center of the highway were so that blind people could drive. He'd close his right eye, veer into the center, and ride the bumps until we were convinced."

I put an arm around his waist and shook my head. "Not as bad as my parents telling me that when the ice cream truck played music, it meant they were out of ice cream."

Knox touched his forehead to mine as we edged closer to the far door. "Okay. Okay. You win." When the door opened for a janitor, we both saw it: Moe's truck in the parking lot.

Knox bit his lip and said, as if reading my mind, "Don't worry, they won't come in."

"How do you know?"

"Because Ernie is here."

Knox pointed to a short man eating a stick of corn on the cob near Dad and Cesar.

"Why would that matter?"

Knox and I weaved around the dessert table, which featured Roshi's cupcakes. The three large laughing ladies who'd yelled "Hercules" at the marina surrounded the table with rapt attention.

"Last Christmas Eve, Moe and Travis got plowed and decided to play a prank on Ernie. They called and said the plant had a spill and Ernie needed to get there right away. He's a single dad and didn't have anyone to stay with his boys so he had to leave them alone."

"How old are they?"

"Seven and nine," he explained, pointing at a carwash-themed basket, complete with bucket, sponge, brushes, rags, and various cleaning supplies.

I placed a bid. No doubt the Jeep could stand a bath.

"When Moe and Travis got to Ernie's house, they stood on the lawn outside the boys' bedroom window and fired a shotgun into the sky. As soon as they saw the boys looking out the window, Moe yelled, 'I got him! I got him!'"

I placed the pen down hard on the table. "Shut up!"

"Yep. Convinced the boys he murdered Santa."

"That's horrible!"

Knox nodded in agreement. "Ernie caught on when he got to the plant. After he got home and heard what happened, he threatened to kill Moe—or worse, tell his mom."

"Good. Did he? Try to kill him, I mean?"

"No." Knox sighed. "Moe and Travis ended up cleaning out his chicken houses for a week instead. But Ernie threatens to bring it up anytime he sees Moe."

Knox paused to inspect a golf-themed basket. He flipped through the tees, towels, balls, and an alligator club cover until he reached a box labeled, "Potty Putter," which was designed for the avid golfer to practice putting while sitting on the can.

"Ugh!" I grimaced.

"You sure you don't want this?"

I scanned the room. Knox was right; there was no sign of the misfits. In fact, everything seemed to be going perfectly. Mom spun through the crowd, and Dad joined the ladies at the dessert table. The bid boxes were getting stuffed with sheets of paper. And the whole crowd seemed happy to be enjoying this opportunity to come together to make a difference.

Everything looked perfect. But I could tell it wasn't perfect. It wasn't a sixth sense because I heard it. The muted sound of a dog barking.

Sticky's bark.

*What's Sticky doing here? Why would my parents bring Sticky?*

A shaft of daylight shone through the south-facing double doors, and I motioned toward them. It took me a minute to adjust my eyes, but through the crack I could see Sticky's fur, a few abrupt motions, and . . . a shock of red hair.

*Moe!*

Not a second later, Travis peeled open the door, and Moe crouched on one knee, holding Sticky by the collar.

Sticky looked wet. Actually, he looked soaked. Like that time he jumped into the pond chasing that crazy squirrel.

*Squirrel.*

*Oh, no.*

Moe's eyes met mine and he flashed a devilish smile. He whispered something in Sticky's ears as if the dog knew English. Sticky's ears perked up, his nose wiggled in the air, and his wild eyes darted around the room, coming to rest on Mr. Wheeler's cage. Moe slapped Sticky on the hindquarters and with that, the dog took off like a missile, charging through the crowd. Before Mr. Wheeler knew what hit him, Sticky knocked him off his chair.

People began to shout in alarm, and the crash grabbed everyone's attention. People ran to help Mr. Wheeler off the ground, but no one controlled Sticky. They must have thought the worst was over, that Sticky was simply excited and happened to hit Mr. Wheeler.

But I knew better. I was just too far away to make a difference.

Sticky wriggled away and ran in circles, then collected himself and with one giant surge, he knocked the squirrel cages off the table, and they crashed onto the floor. The next thing I knew, the cinnamon-colored flying squirrels took to the air. They swarmed above us like rats with wings, leaping from table to table. Sticky barked and chased at them, snapping his teeth and careening into items up for auction.

The Mighty Pinecone gymnasium, which had once appeared a honeycomb of fellowship, now became a center of pandemonium, as Sticky led the way with his manic pursuit of the squirrels.

"Get Sticky!" I yelled to Knox.

"Get Sticky!" I yelled to my father.

"Get Sticky!" I yelled to anyone who would listen.

But it was too late. The squirrels crisscrossed through the crowd, seeking refuge on the bleachers, the basketball rim, and the gymnastic equipment. A few hid under tables. One climbed up Mrs. Brackin's polyester pants and then ran through the tower of cupcakes, toppling them over. Guests who ran across the cupcakes smeared blue icing onto the floor and slipped and slid into the nearby tables at center court.

An errant squirrel made for Bliss's guitar case, which frightened Bliss enough that she screamed—unfortunately, into the microphone, providing the perfect soundtrack for the unfolding catastrophe.

All the while, Sticky stayed in hot pursuit, and one of the squirrels fled to the top of the flagpole. As the pole teetered, the squirrel steadied himself and soared onto a pendant light above the stage. When the flagpole teetered and fell to the floor, Darrell Moore, a ten-year Marine, dived to keep the United States treasure from desecration. Regrettably, Buck chased Sticky and crashed into Darrell like a linebacker. They lay pretzeled together beneath the stage.

On the other side of the gym, stumbling blindly because someone had kicked Cesar's homemade salsa into his eye, Dad tripped over an end table and splintered it in half.

Sticky still ran free and bounded after a squirrel that was clearly getting tired. It no longer zipped through the air. Instead, it bounced from table to table. Sticky, not to be outdone, jumped onto the tables and smashed bidding boxes, destroying them and everything else in his wake as he pursued the fatiguing varmint. Knox lunged and tried to tackle him, but failed.

It was pandemonium incarnate.

I looked back at the door. Moe was bent over, pressing his hand against his stomach, laughing without remorse. When he saw my vindictive stare, he took off running. Travis followed right behind.

Behind me, I heard my mother scream, "The bid sheets!" She was down on her hands and knees, unraveling, grasping for the bid sheets, the runaway golf balls, and what was left of Roshi's tasty blue cupcakes, sticking them anywhere she could corral them—including her blouse, the carwash bucket, and Mrs. Mager's knitting basket. Dad threaded through the commotion to help, but she was already one wave short of a shipwreck, off her rocker, stark raving mad, barmy, screwy, batty, cracked, touched, demented, bonkers.

*Here comes nervous breakdown number two.*

She had tried so hard, and now she had egg all over her face.

Literally.

The eggs from Garnett's Chicken Farm had cracked and were oozing limpid egg white onto her cheek.

"Where's Ms. Ray?" Knox asked, scanning the gymnasium.

I pointed to the entrance doors. "Over there."

Ms. Ray watched the bedlam in bewilderment. She looked at us for a fraction of a second, before saying something to Bliss, who'd just stopped screaming into the microphone. Then Ms. Ray turned and left through the doors Knox and I had come through. I could barely keep up with Knox on his way to catch her.

"Bliss, where did Ms. Ray go?" he asked. "Is she okay?"

"I don't know." Tears slid down Bliss's cheeks, one after another.

"What did she say to you?"

Bliss stood still, looking at the toppled tables and Buck dragging a glum Sticky behind him. Her whole figure drooped.

"Ummm, something like, 'The Lord helps those that help themselves.'"

# Chapter 20

I overslept on purpose to let the day pass. In the evening, Mom sat in Jacob's recliner, dipping Cheetos into ice cream and watching a show on animal hoarders. I decided it best to leave her alone. Dad and I trekked over to the church office instead. On the way, we passed the marquee.

The sign read: "Jeremiah 17:5."

"What's the reference?" I asked.

Either he didn't hear me or he didn't care. He fixed toward the church and plodded into his office, his thoughts elsewhere.

The office was its own quiet catastrophe, with Bible-verse butter mints littered across his desk, along with torn bid sheets and crushed crafts from the auction scattered across the furniture and floor.

"What's Jeremiah 17:5?" I repeated.

His cell phone, set to that insufferable robotic human voice alert, announced, "You have nineteen new messages."

"You going to check those?"

He grunted in response. I guess recounting last night's events nineteen times would take an entire workday.

"Well, chief, this has been a fun conversation, but I'm going to read on your couch until it's safe to go home again. Did you order the straitjackets for Mom, or should I?"

With that, I flopped down and disappeared into another book Knox had recommended.

While I read, Dad lit his pipe and reorganized his desk, stacking the bid sheets and eating the butter mints. The ceiling fan whirred above us, and for some time it was the only sound. That was, until we both heard a noise in the hallway.

*Click. Click.*

Holding the pipe in his hand, Dad leaned forward and listened. I put my book down across my waist.

Two months at East New Hope and I still wasn't used to the church at night. The creak of loose floorboards in the old place could be unsettling. In fact, one evening last week, my father asked me to accompany him to shut off a rogue light in the auditorium. The place at night freaked him out too, apparently. As we were unsuccessfully searching for the main light switch, there was a mysterious thump in the auditorium. Creeping in to investigate, we found a heap of hymnals strewn across the floor in front of the pulpit. My heart beat fast and I could tell Dad was not in any better shape. A fact I knew because he told me what he'd preached to Jacob so many times before:

"Don't worry, Jordan. All events occur within the natural order, not outside the natural order. Stories of the unnatural are just that, stories. They're parables, told to make a point."

I think he almost changed his mind, though, when a growling noise emanated from the cross hanging on the back wall. I screamed when a gnarly, sharp-toothed opossum scampered across the stage, but Dad seemed relieved. I guess potentially rabid opossums existed within his world order.

*Click. Click.*

"Don't worry," Dad said now. "That opossum is back."

I sat up and leaned forward, trying hard to make out the sound. "No," I said slowly. "It's high heels. I thought you locked her in."

He frowned at me for a quick second before replying: "Apparently not."

Finally, a firm, light tap on the door confirmed there was no opossum.

"Come in," Dad said cautiously.

There was an odor of sweet smoke in the air when Mom entered the room. She paused as she entered, taking in a deep breath. She'd changed clothes since we left her, having traded her bathrobe for a Dallas Mavericks jersey and pajama shorts, along with her nude Louboutin heels. She clutched a bunch of papers and sat down without saying a word.

*Featuring our "Pajama Drama" collection . . .*

Dark circles shaded her eyes, and strands of honey-colored hair escaped her ponytail and ran across her face. I could still see neon orange dust from the Cheetos at the corners of her mouth.

For a few moments, we sat in silence. There was something about her concentration that made me nervous. She'd been driven to the brink, and anything was possible—divorce, career change, changing my name to something country like Irma-Jean.

Eventually, she began, "I'm still trying to figure it out."

"What's in the spreadsheets?" I asked her, hoping to cut off any impending pep talk from my father.

After a moment's thought, she shook her head. "Maybe your father can answer that. Are there more than two accounts for the Lord's Pantry, Eli?"

Dad looked befuddled. "Two accounts?"

"More than the church's account and the Pantry's account at Ashworth Savings."

"Yes, I think those are the only two accounts, but you can always ask Ms. Ray. She handles the books."

Mom went back to studying the spreadsheets, and Dad caught sight of Jacob's Bible in front of him. Smoothing out the pages, he flipped through the book until he found Jeremiah 17:5, which was underlined in thick red ink.

"Cursed is the one who trusts in man, who depends on flesh for his strength and whose heart turns away from the Lord," he read out loud.

"What?" Mom asked.

"Jeremiah 17:5."

"The thing is"—she sounded frustrated—"I haven't been able to get in touch with Ms. Ray. I've called since eight a.m. No answer all day."

Ms. Ray's unavailability didn't surprise me. We hadn't been able to find her last night and despite Knox's concern, I convinced him she'd probably decided not to answer her phone or come to the door. She'd been so excited for the fundraiser, after all.

"I'm sure she's around," Dad assured my mother. "Have you checked with Buck?"

Mom slid the papers across the desk toward Dad. I could see a small area highlighted in yellow.

Dad inspected the numbers. He wasn't much of a financial wizard—that was my mother's gift—but he could still read a balance sheet.

"Did you withdraw that for the fundraiser?"

Mom exhaled with irritation. "Of course not!"

"What are you guys talking about?" I interjected.

Mom continued to look straight at my father. "Who has access to the account?"

"I'm not a hundred percent sure."

"What are you guys talking about?" I repeated.

Mom looked at me, her eyes two red flares. "Someone stole the Lord's Pantry's money. Sixty thousand dollars."

"When?"

"This morning. At four twenty-eight a.m."

Knox sped down the country road, dust flying in our wake.

"I'm glad you called. We might have a chance," he said breathlessly.

"You really think she's at the casino?" I asked.

"Yep. Playing the devil's game."

"The devil's game?"

Knox had a determined, angry sneer, but my curiosity melted some of the ice. "Roulette. It's nicknamed the devil's game because of the legend. Supposedly the guy who invented roulette sold his soul for the game. If you add all the numbers on the wheel together, it equals six-six-six." He paused. "If I had to bet on it, I'd put my money that Ms. Ray is at the Chicken Ship Casino. Ms. Ray disappeared sometimes when her husband flew off the handle, and she usually disappeared to the Chicken Ship."

"Gambling. I never understood the draw," I added.

After flying through four town squares and past two mattress outlets, seven motels, and three car dealerships, we cruised over the

Louisiana border. A few minutes later Knox swerved into the casino parking lot. Docked and facing downstream, the ship was trimmed like a Christmas tree with banner advertisements: *99% return on all slots, single-deck blackjack, $2.99 steak and eggs, players drink for free.*

"You found this place easily."

"I've been here before." Knox shrugged.

"You?"

"Yeah. It's a rite of passage for every teenager in Ashworth. You have to slip past the surly bouncer and play Texas Hold 'Em with Chimney. As soon as you have a decent run, he takes out a pack of cigarettes, taps one out, lights it, and blows smoke in your face. If you finish the hand without coughing, you earn his respect."

We walked at what I hoped was an unassuming pace. The door-man blocked the entrance ahead of us, and we kept our eyes averted from him. Soon we passed a pair of twenty-something *Dukes of Hazard* lookalikes, and they greeted Knox with a "wazzup?" I overheard the short one, who rocked a sweet mustache, brag how close he'd come on *The Little Green Men* nickel slot.

But we kept our focus straight ahead. We had to bypass the doorman, and neither of us had a fake ID.

Then, out of nowhere, popped Mr. Gober.

Usually you could hear Mr. Gober before you saw him, because he had one of the loudest voices in the county. He'd lost some of his hearing after setting off a package of bottle rockets at his kitchen table one year, and now he tried to compensate by yelling instead of talking.

"Knox Colville! And Jordan Klein!" he thundered. "Kids, what in the world—"

"Mr. Gober!" Knox snagged the corpulent man by the elbow, only yards from the door, and led him away, trying not to sound anxious. "Please lower your voice and trust me."

I glanced at the doorman, a big bald brick of a man with a square face, wearing all black—like a cartoon of evil. The giant placed his palm against his ear, tinkering with the earphone inside, and stared at us with beady eyes. We'd gotten his attention.

*Please don't ask me to distract Tiny.*

We huddled fifteen feet away from the entrance, and Knox explained to Mr. Gober why he, a mere seventeen-year-old and soon-to-be senior in high school, was about to enter a 21+ gambling establishment. Knox had no choice but to divulge the truth, and when Mr. Gober was about to speak, Knox put his finger to his lips, begging the half-deaf old man to lower his volume.

"Ms. Ray? I had no idea," Mr. Gober said. His words came out unsteady, but quieter. "This is horrible. We've got to get in there before she climbs fool's hill."

"Can you help us?" I asked.

"Of course." Mr. Gober shook his head. "Now, let's go get her and the church's money." We looked toward the doorman, who thankfully was distracted by the back end of a tanned woman in a tight-fitting red sequin dress. "Just follow my lead."

With that, the three of us approached the entrance.

"Nowadays, you're lucky if you can keep your farm wet and pay your taxes," complained Mr. Gober, his voice booming. "How's your place doing? Gettin' a good price for your heifers?"

My pulse raced, but Knox sounded cool and confident. "Not too bad, I suppose."

"Well then, you're luckier than me. I'd get locked in a supermarket and starve. Guess I should stick by you in here!"

I knew enough to keep my trap shut. If there's one thing that would've given us away, it was my Yankee accent.

Five feet from the doorman, Mr. Gober brilliantly played an ace. "Did you get a load of those bikini models in the parking lot? I wonder what they're advertising!"

The bouncer's eyes flickered with attention, and before we took another step, he zoomed past us, radioing his boss to say that there was commotion among the cars and he needed to check it out.

With that, we were in. Immediately, the sounds of a hundred slot machines assaulted us, all of them scrolling through their lemons and cherries. Pop music resounded through the main room. We passed a pork barbecue buffet and a large bar where a blonde in a low-cut white top and sparkly earrings mixed martinis. She blew Mr. Gober a kiss.

"You take me to all the best places," I said to Knox.

He winked.

We scanned the room, but there was no sign of Ms. Ray. Instead,

Knox pointed out Chimney, and sure enough, the daunting dealer blew a fan of smoke into a player's face.

"Where's the roulette table?" I asked Mr. Gober.

"The devil's game," he answered, pointing to the far side of the room.

The three of us weaved through a swamp of blackjack tables and waitresses doting on old men with walkers. They placed gin and tonics or whiskey sours into the drink cups affixed to the walkers' handles. Halfway across the room, I saw Ms. Ray in the far distance. She exuded joy, her smile like a light in the middle of a storm. A crowd surrounded her, a few of them clapping nervously.

"At least she's doing well." I pointed her out to the others.

Mr. Gober, an experienced gambler, gasped. "Yeah, but look at those chips. We gotta get there before she loses them all."

Knox and I took off. He ran left and I rounded a table to the right, almost knocking down a row of senior citizens. Knox was sandwiched between a cocktail waitress and a geriatric beauty.

I squeezed through the crowd and found myself at the edge of the audience.

"Ms. Ray!" I shouted, blocked by a white-haired man in a pink sweater vest. He whispered to his wife. "She's betting with thousand dollar chips. She's up to a hundred thousand dollars!"

Knox joined me. We yelled, "Ms. Ray!" but the crowd walled us off. She hunched over and fingered her chips. We stood on the opposite side of the table, so we could see her face, but it was difficult to get her attention. We continued to shout, and our neighbors looked agitated. Some of them even turned down their hearing aids.

"Ms. Ray!" I bellowed, and for a moment, I thought she'd heard me. She looked up and her face brightened. But she was lost in her own reverie. She fiddled with the cross on her necklace and with her other hand she pushed the whole stack of chips toward the dealer.

The dealer counted eighteen chips, and then called out to the pit boss, "Coloring up ninety-eight thousand!"

The crowd exploded in cheers. Ms. Ray calmly restacked her chips on the table and slid them into the red betting area.

"Ms. Ray!" Knox pushed and struggled through the crowd. We needed to intervene.

"Ms. Ray!" I yelled.

"Ninety-eight thousand on red," the dealer barked.

"No! Ms. Ray, no!" we yelled.

But it was too late. The croupier waved his hand and said, "The bets are down." The man's long arm stretched out and he spun the roulette wheel. A hush fell across the onlookers, and Ms. Ray looked up and saw us. Her mouth fell open, but she turned her attention back to the table and watched as the tiny silver ball whirled around the wheel of colors and numbers.

"God," I prayed, "please, let it be red."

As the ball danced around the long circular edge, Ms. Ray took a deep intake of breath and closed her eyes. Suddenly, the whole casino fell still. It seemed to me like everyone—the mumblers, the men with backaches, the pill poppers, the card players, the women in muumuus—everyone strained to hear the soft skipping of the silver ball trying to find its place. *Click-click-click, tick, tick, click. . . .*

The ball rattled from number to number, red to black, black to red, and back to black, only to switch again and again.

"Oh, Baby Jesus." Mr. Gober ran up to us, and pleading to the chandelier above, he said, "Let it be red. Please, let it be red."

The wheel slowed, and the ball plunked into its final slot. No one spoke. The hush deepened as the crowd strained to hear the croupier.

In an austere voice, the croupier announced, "Twenty-two. Black."

The crowd groaned.

Ms. Ray flinched and closed her eyes, refusing to meet her defeat. "Oh God, oh dear God! Oh God in Heaven . . . no," she whimpered.

Then, holding her purse close to her body like a shield, she opened her eyes wide at the croupier taking the stack of chips away.

"Oh, son, I'm sorry, but I wasn't betting all those chips."

"I'm sorry, ma'am." He turned his face from her as he cleared the table for the next players pulling up chairs.

She persisted. "No. You misunderstood me. I wasn't betting those chips."

With a desperate smile, she laid a small hand lightly on his arm. There was no anger in the gesture, just appeal.

"I'm sorry, ma'am. All bets are final."

We watched as her small and fragile hand fell from the dealer's sleeve. The crowd dispersed, eager to leave a scene with so much bad luck and disappointment. Ms. Ray looked confused, like she was stuck in a foreign country without a map.

It didn't take long for Mr. Gober to tear into her. "You should be ashamed of yourself, Ms. Ray," he condemned, nodding toward Knox. "That boy'd fight tigers in the dark with a switch for you. And this is how you repay him? By stealing everything his sister worked so hard to build?"

She shook with guilt. Without a word, Knox stumbled away, past the baccarat and blackjack tables. Past Chimney. Past the gawkers and players straightening their stacks. Past the bartender twisting a lime. Past the surly doorman. Long past where he could hear Ms. Ray abandon herself to a storm of grief that had consumed her since Skye's death.

When I caught up to him, he had his cell phone out.

"It's gonna be okay," I pretended, but I was a bad liar.

He dialed the number without looking up. "Officer Watts, it's Knox Colville. I can tell you where she is."

# Chapter 21

"**B**efore the milk expires," Mom muttered as I walked into the kitchen.

She stood at the refrigerator with the door wide open—not *completely* surprising, since the August sun baked at 100 degrees. Dad sat at the table, scowling at the *Ashworth Herald*. I could see the headline: "Gambling Granny Bets Against God."

We were all in low spirits after all the drama of the last few days. Shuffling toward the table in Jacob's Hush Puppies, I thudded into my usual chair. I plopped pink yogurt into an empty cereal bowl in front of me and took out my phone to play Rocket Weasel.

My father turned down the corner of his paper. "By the way, how did you even get into the casino?"

"I just showed them my ID and told them New York is on the metric system."

He stared at me, annoyed. I chose not to look up from my game.

"I've lost ten times in a row, so I rebooted and showed it who's boss." I took an oversized spoonful of strawberry surprise. "Artificial intelligence, my arse."

Dad frowned.

"Before the milk expires," my mother repeated obliquely. She stood fixed in front of the open refrigerator, staring at the carton of milk.

"Uh-oh, Mom." I put down my spoon. "The *leche* fairies speaking to you again?"

My father lowered his eyes. Apparently, he didn't find my levity humorous.

Mom snapped shut the fridge door and sat down with us. Slowly, she poured herself a large glass of milk. "We leave Ashworth before the milk expires," she finished.

We all stared at my mother's glass of milk.

A few white drops slid down from the rim.

Since I knew the date was approaching, it wasn't a total shock. But the more time I'd spent with Knox, and Bliss, too, the more I'd forgotten about the city. Leaving Ashworth and returning to New York had become a vague, abstract idea. And now, just like that, before the milk expired, we'd be gone?

*Way to harsh my mellow.*

I felt a sudden urge to cry, to scream, to run without stopping. My parents looked as pale as the milk—its small bubbles that popped in plain sight.

"Why don't you invite Knox over for dinner tonight?" Mom said, coming to her senses and breaking the silence. "I'd like to get to know him better."

My jaw dropped open. It was the first time she had spoken directly to me since the fundraiser meltdown, much less shown an interest in Knox.

Dad turned his head sharply. "I don't know, Rachel." His face tightened. "I already invited Cesar to join us. It would be rude to ask someone else."

"Nonsense," she dismissed. "It'll be a dinner party."

Thinking it might be a good excuse to call Knox and raise his spirits, I agreed. He needed a pick-me-up after the Ms. Ray debacle.

Then I gulped.

*Wait, Mom's cooking? Maybe this isn't such a good idea.*

I wrinkled my nose, thinking of the last meal she'd made in Ashworth. It was supposed to be a gourmet lentil loaf, according to *The Joy of Cooking*. But when she emptied it onto the platter in front of us, it oozed into a messy pile that looked like Sticky's canned dinner.

Ironically, it ended up being the dog's dessert.

"Are you sure you want to cook?" I asked. "We could always have Roshi's deliver."

"I want to cook," Mom insisted. "Why not?"

I could think of a million reasons why not—from undercooked chicken to burnt and flaming pineapple beef kabobs—but after all the chaos, I welcomed her enthusiasm. Plus, I desperately wanted an excuse to see Knox.

*What's the worst thing that could happen?*

"Sounds good. I'll call him."

I could tell my father was going through the same thought process as we watched her bob to the counter and flip the pages of her *Southern Gourmet* cookbook—except he was weighing his desire for my mother's mental health against his weird rivalry with Knox.

Ever since Knox took me sailing, my father felt spurned, and he hissed not-so-subtle snarky comments whenever I mentioned Knox's name. He tried to dissuade me from seeing Knox, even suggesting we have "the first annual Klein father-daughter night" when Knox and I had plans to play skee-ball at the dead mall arcade in the next town over. I guess being at home with his crazy wife really was that bad.

"Something more manageable though," Mom continued, still flipping through the pages of the cookbook, humming. My father, on the other hand, folded his paper, rose from his chair, and sighed.

"I'm going to go work on my sermon," he said.

Thankfully, Mom opted for spaghetti instead of a dish from *Southern Gourmet*. It was one of the only dishes she could pull off, and I was glad for it. At least this way, Knox wouldn't witness any cooking disasters, although I couldn't promise much more.

He came over without much of a fight, especially after I told him Cesar would be there to mitigate my dad's cheap attempts at humor.

We all sat down at the table and everyone seemed cheerful. After an initial run of polite conversation, however, our banter died down and we all sat silently, wrapping pasta around our forks and listening to Hal lick his paws. Between bites, my father sat with his steepled fingers beneath his chin, his eyes sneaking glances at Knox.

*Why is he so weird?*

I averted my eyes and Mom swished one last sip of wine in her glass. Cesar was the only one who seemed comfortable. In fact, he cleaned his plate as if the meal were the best he'd ever had. Knox glanced around the table, his eyes smiling when they reached me. Finally, Mom refilled her wine glass and stood.

"I propose a toast," she announced. "To old friends and new, may you always have good wine and never get sued."

"*Gracias*, Mrs. Klein," Cesar answered, standing up with his own glass raised. "I'd like to add a little something to that. To new friends," he said. "May the darkest clouds bring the thickest showers of blessings."

Mom smiled and looked my way. "Jordan?"

"Okay," I said, standing up and raising my ginger ale. "To new friends," I said, smiling at Knox. "May you never get behind Mr. Wheeler writing a check at Piggly Wiggly's self-checkout line."

Knox's eyebrows went up and he responded with a quick raise of his glass. "And here's to the Fighting Pinecones: may they be sharp but never pricks."

I almost spit my drink onto the table. Cesar and Mom snickered, but my father groaned. Not to be outdone, he pushed back his chair, scraping the legs against the tile, and stood with his glass raised high. "May God be with you and bless you. May you see your children's children married in your church. May you be poor in misfortune, yet rich in blessings. May you know nothing but happiness."

I rolled my eyes, but he hadn't finished.

"May God grant you many years to live and may you always have work for your hands to do. May you always eat thy bread with joy, and drink thy wine with a merry heart."

Mom cleared her throat.

"And may God fill your heart with gladness to cheer you," he concluded.

"Well, now," Mom said with a smile. "Who wants seconds?"

While she wasn't the *best* cook, she had skills I'd never seen before. I glowed in admiration of her, happy to see her confident again. No one else but my mom could have defused the bomb that our dinner was quickly becoming.

"I usually add white truffle oil to the noodles, but—surprise, surprise—the grocery store was all out," she explained as she heaped pasta onto our plates.

But something odious was afoot.

Hal waltzed by.

Oblivious to the little orange furball, Mom ladled sauce onto Cesar's dish and accidentally stepped on Hal's tail. The cat let out an ungodly scream and blurred across the room while Mom teetered, dropping the saucepan. She had to brace herself in none other than Cesar's plate of noodles and marinara.

We all held our collective breath.

*Please don't have another breakdown. PLEASE . . .*

Slowly, she tilted her head sideways and peeled her hand off Cesar's plate. She stared at her palm with eerie concentration.

*Oh no.*

Then she grinned. Not maniacally. Normally. She turned her sauce-stained palm toward us. "Look: stigmata!" she giggled, flashing a striking smile.

*Phew!*

We erupted into laughter.

While she cleaned herself off at the sink, Dad questioned Knox. "So, when do your parents come back from France?"

Knox cast a glance in my direction before answering. "In a month," he said. "Right before school starts."

*One more salacious stare and I'll melt.*

"Do they go often?"

"No." Knox shook his head. "We've always traveled, but they bought the flat this year."

"How wonderful!" Mom threw her dishcloth over her shoulder and put her hands on her hips. In her yellow plaid sundress, she looked like a lady from a dish soap commercial. "It's just you at home then?"

I shot Knox a panicked look. Surely someone in the church had mentioned Skye to my parents. Buck, Cesar, Ms. Ray or—*hello!*—me? Apparently not.

Even Cesar froze.

"Yes, ma'am," Knox answered. "Just me."

"Poor thing." Mom shook her head. "You must get lonely."

"My parents love visiting family in France so I'm used to it. Plus, I know getting out of Ashworth every once in a while is necessary."

"I'll say," Dad said, twirling his fork in the air. "Can you imagine the culture shock? One day in Ashworth and the next in Paris."

"Sounds familiar," I muttered.

"Come to think of it, Knox, I haven't seen you at East New Hope," my father stated with a trace of judgment.

"He's been there," I interjected quickly, though I flushed with embarrassment, having spied on Knox so many times in the early days of summer—I'd never told him of my romantic espionage.

I watched Knox shift uncomfortably in his chair. He looked at me and then to my father again. "I used to go every Sunday. But now I just drop in every now and again to listen to Buck hit the skins."

"Church is not entertainment, son," Dad spoke condescendingly.

"Hey," I interrupted. "Speaking of drumers, what do you call a drummer who breaks up with his girlfriend?" I waited a split second before answering my own question. "Homeless!"

Knox smirked. "I don't mind, Jordan." He looked my father in the eye. "I choose, Pastor Klein, not to go anymore."

Dad put down his fork. "Do you mind me asking why?"

"I'm afraid my views are hard earned." Knox crinkled his eyes.

"Explain," Dad commanded.

"Well, did you hear about the alligator attacks in Florida?" Knox asked.

At first I thought he'd come to his senses and was trying to change the subject, but no such luck. Mom answered cheerfully, "Oh, I did. Can you imagine a worse way to go?"

My father stared blankly. If it wasn't mentioned in *The New York Times*, he didn't hear about it.

"A woman was found inside the mouth of an alligator after a snorkeling trip," Knox reported. "Another was jogging when an alligator dragged her into a canal and killed her."

Dad kept munching away. "That's unfortunate."

"Unfortunate?"

"Yes, unfortunate. Accidents happen, Knox. It's unfortunate, but those women chose to go snorkeling and jogging. Death is a part of life."

"Are you implying it was their fault?" Knox asked, incredulous.

"I'm saying it was unfortunate that they were in the wrong place at the wrong time," Dad said.

Knox, his voice cracking with impatience, replied, "Well, I have a hard time worshiping a God who allows such *unfortunate* things to happen."

My father set his knife and fork on the edge of his plate, lifted his paper towel, and dabbed the corners of his mouth.

I slopped spaghetti onto their plates. "You guys need to eat more. Brain cells come and go, but fat cells live forever."

They both ignored the Italian mountains I poured onto their plates. Worse, Knox looked like he'd been waiting for this challenge, like he welcomed the conflict. I could see fire in his eyes.

"Well, son," my father began. "God created us with free will. The consequences are not God's fault."

Knox glowered at my father.

"So it was the women's free will that caused them to be eaten by alligators?" Knox asked. "I'm sorry, but that's absurd."

My father placed his elbows on the table in a pensive pose.

"What I should have articulated was: suffering is the result of free will. Yes, God has the power to prevent all suffering, but only by removing our ability to make choices, only by depriving us of free will. So he can't."

Cesar interjected, "Pastor Klein, free will is one thing but you're not saying that God started the boat then completely abandoned ship, are you?"

Dad gladly welcomed another participant. He turned toward Cesar and tried to cross his legs, knocking his knee against the small table.

"I'd put it another way. The gift of free will demands that God not get involved in the affairs of humans, the way many believe. He's not a cosmic waiter at our beck and call."

I watched Knox avert his gaze out the kitchen window into the darkness of the night. The same kitchen window I'd stared out our first day in Ashworth. He was looking toward the cemetery, where he helped bury Skye.

"Curious." Cesar studied the clump of noodles on his fork. "I didn't think someone that studied religion as a job would think as rigidly as that." He shrugged. "Seems like a waste of time to do all that studying if God only watches."

I could tell Cesar's response surprised my father.

"I do this because we've been given the gift of free will and it is our duty to respect what God gave us and teach others to do the same."

"And that's why we recycle. Ba-dum-bump!" I joked.

No one laughed.

The dinner was quickly becoming painful, like surgery without anesthesia.

"Let me guess. Jacob has been telling the church that God programs events?"

"Oh, no, sir." Cesar shook his head. "Pastor Jacob said that we can never truly understand questions like these. But we can understand God's character of being a loving God."

I pressed my fingers to my forehead and closed my eyes.

"Yes, a loving God but—"

"It's all bullshit!" Knox interrupted, forcing his chair back. The silverware clattered against the dishes and his glass threatened to topple as he stood up from the table. He looked to my mother.

"Thank you for the dinner, Mrs. Klein. I hope you'll excuse me."

Knox turned angrily and stomped out the front door without a word.

I dropped my own silverware in frustration and pushed back from the table. "Thanks for nothing, Eli," I hissed.

I ran after Knox, who opened the door to his Tahoe.

"Knox!"

He turned back. "Your dad's a real piece of work, you know?"

"I think I mentioned that once or twice, yes?" I grabbed his hand.

"He acts like he's smarter than everyone else . . . and he's not. Not by a long shot."

"Wweeelll," I said with an exaggerated smile, trying to take things down a notch. "Once he did find a typo in a Mensa quiz."

"This isn't a joke, Jordan."

"I know," I assured him. I tugged at his shirt collar, pulling myself closer to his distant eyes. "Just don't take him so seriously."

"Don't worry, I won't," Knox spat, stepping away from my hold.

The color drained from my face. "You don't have to be rude."

"Rude? Okay, let's talk about rude. You and your family have walked around here for three months acting like y'all can't *wait* to get away from this place—like it's beneath you."

*Oh no, you didn't.*

My chest tightened, indignant.

"Thanks for gracing us with your presence," he finished.

"Yeah, I'm sorry we're not impressed with gun racks and taxidermy!"

Knox burst out with a booming laugh. "Get over yourself, Jordan!" he roared, squaring his shoulders. "Snobbery is a character defect—in case they didn't teach you that at your fancy school in New York."

I gave Knox the worst stink eye I'd ever given.

He whipped around and jumped into the Tahoe. But he stopped cold, his keys dangling in his hand. Just ahead of us, the church sign glowed in the dark: "Earth has no sorrow that Heaven cannot heal."

"Stupid ass sign!" Knox yelled. He slammed his door shut, revved the engine, and dug the tires into the gravel, leaving me there, livid and alone.

The screen door popped open and my father appeared on the porch. "Is everything all right?"

My stomach lurched.

"No, Eli. Everything is not all right. Thanks to *you*."

My father crept back inside, and Knox sped away. His taillights blurred as my eyes welled up.

Tears rolled down my cheeks, like the milk that had dripped down my mother's glass that morning.

# Chapter 22

Two days had passed since the dinner disaster and I had ignored all of Knox's calls. I was too stung by the truthfulness of his words to speak to him.

Of course, Bliss tried to cheer me up. The night before, she'd taken me to Tyler's Rose Festival because I had to meet some Tyler boys who she explained were better than Ashworth boys because "they bring you mind-blowing first date bouquets." But when she grabbed the first boy's phone and texted HHOGS to 90999—which donated $5 to the Hedgehog Welfare Society—instead of adding her number, I got the sneaking suspicion she only took me to the festival to get my mind off Knox.

It didn't work. So rather than join her for movie night, I sat on the porch swing watching the moon duck behind patches of clouds, surrendering to my melancholy and hoping Knox would drop by.

If I closed my eyes tightly, he appeared. But then light passed through my closed eyelids, vanishing his image. Opening my eyes revealed headlights, but not from a Tahoe coming up the graveled driveway. From a police truck.

"Eli!" I yelled. "The cops are here."

My father plodded to the door like he carried the worries of the world on his shoulders. For the last two days, whenever we'd passed in the halls of the house or been at the same table, I'd looked at my flip-flops, at my hands, at my fork, or at the floor, but never once met his eyes. He's the one who caused this mess.

"Guess you shouldn't have tried to milk Mr. Randall's bull," I said before rising from the swing.

Officer Watts slid out of his truck, his large hat reflecting the moon above. He tipped it our way, just before he opened his back cab door.

I stopped halfway to the door in disbelief.

"Ms. Ray?" Dad said in amazement.

Within seconds, Mom appeared in the doorway. "Oh my."

Sure enough, there was Ms. Ray, walking toward us, while Officer Watts slid back into the driver's side. His door slammed shut. We watched as she slowly crept to the base of the stairs.

"How wonderful," Ms. Ray said with a sad smile. "The entire Klein family."

Officer Watts backed out of the graveled driveway.

"Where is he going?" my father asked.

"Some crazy stole the undies off Mrs. Brackin's clothes line again," Ms. Ray answered. She looked down at her compression support stockings. "I guess Officer Watts doesn't take me for much of a flight risk."

We all stood silent and still.

"I was wondering, Pastor Klein . . ." Ms. Ray turned to face a potted plant near the stairs and tapped her shoe lightly against it. ". . . If I might have a moment of your time. A confession from an old lady."

Mom touched my shoulders to direct me inside the house. "We'll leave you two alone," she offered.

Ms. Ray nodded, mildly. "Thank you, Rachel."

My father looked uncomfortable, but he sat down on the swing and patted the seat beside him anyway. "Why don't you join me here? It's such a nice night."

Standing in the doorframe, my mother and I glanced back. Through the wire mesh of the screen door we saw Ms. Ray start to talk but collapse into my father's chest, sobbing.

Instead of pulling back, my father gently draped his arm around her shoulder and kissed the crown of her hair. When he raised his eyes and gazed upon the church sign, he could no longer hold back his own tears.

"Their sins and lawless acts I will remember no more. Hebrews 10:17."

Moments later, my father looked at us—his wife, his daughter, both watching in astonishment as we saw him cry for the first time. My heart stopped, feeling guilty for trespassing on this moment. But then my mother squeezed my hand, and my father looked at us before he silently whispered over Ms. Ray's bowed head, "I'm sorry too. For everything."

That next Sunday, as I entered the auditorium, I didn't look at any faces in the pews. I already knew what they'd show—shock, heartbreak, anger, disbelief. Instead, my eyes followed the yellow carpet to my usual seat next to my mother.

As usual, she'd pulled her hair back into a ponytail, accenting the angles of her cheekbones. But she wore a dress I'd never seen before. It was wheat-colored, sleeveless, with a tiny gold belt, and cut above her knees. She looked nice and I told her so.

"Thank you," she whispered. "I got it at one of the little shops on the square."

Before I could respond, she found her page in the hymnal and we stood. Softly she sang, so softly that I could barely hear, but it had a lovely tone. I watched as her gaze drifted between the old music book and my father, who stared down at his hymnal. Lost in thought, he made no attempt to join in the song.

The congregation grew loud with the last chord and then, at Buck's direction, we all took our seats in one fluid motion. Every eye was on my father.

*Oh boy.*

Dad shifted uncomfortably. A ray of light from the stained glass window shone across his face, causing him to look up at the expectant audience and, from there, to my mother. With an expression of calm alertness, Mom nodded—prodding my father to stand.

I swiveled my head to the back of the room on the chance that Knox was in the last pew. He'd want to hear this. But I couldn't see past the crowd. Every row was packed to the hilt with searching church members and townspeople.

At the podium, Dad unfolded his notes and smoothed the papers out. "Ahem."

No one stirred.

Then he looked at the congregation and smiled. "Today I am reminded of the Canaanite, Joseph."

Mom let out a quiet sigh of relief.

"At the age of seventeen, Joseph was a tattletale and, some might say, a spoiled brat. But he was also his father's favorite, and for that, his brothers hated him. So what did they do about their 'pest' problem? One day, they sold him into slavery and lied to their father, telling him that bandits killed his beloved son. That's how Joseph landed in a prison in Egypt—a prison where God gave him a mysterious gift.

"You see, Pharaoh had troubling dreams, and when nothing else worked, he summoned Joseph, who rumor had it could interpret dreams. Joseph goes on to predict seven years of abundance followed by seven years of famine. Impressed with Joseph's gift, Pharaoh made Joseph Prime Minister, to govern over the people of Egypt weathering this famine."

My father's voice rose and he spoke with an attitude of wholehearted dedication.

"People came from all over to buy grain from Joseph, including—one day—his very own brothers. Joseph recognized them, but they did not recognize Joseph. After all, years had passed since they had sold him, and I'm sure they didn't expect to see him in such a position of power."

Dad paused and his eyes widened. "It makes for a marvelous sense of drama, doesn't it?"

The congregation responded with eager calls of "Amen!" My mouth dropped as I watched my dad ride this wave of energy.

"Joseph met with his brothers several times without telling them who he was. Finally, he couldn't keep it to himself any longer. He told his brothers, 'I am Joseph!' His brothers were speechless. They were afraid. Then Joseph said, 'Come closer. I am your brother, the one you sold!

"Joseph did something amazing next. He said, 'Don't worry, and don't be angry at yourselves for selling me into slavery. You see, it wasn't you who sent me here. God has put me here to save people from starving.'"

There was no cold philosophical detachment now. He was not

just an advocate but a witness as well—speaking of himself, our family, his brother Jacob, and Ms. Ray.

"What does this teach us?" he asked. He slowed his voice and looked earnestly at the crowd. "It shows us that redemption is a powerful thing. We've all gone astray. We've all been disobedient. But Grace is good; Grace must be embraced; and Grace must be shared. Just as a kidnapped Canaanite looked into the eyes of his betraying brothers, and with love and reconciliation said, 'I am Joseph.'"

# Chapter 23

**M**s. Ray's court date was the hottest ticket in town. Of course, the only competition was the snow cone stand on Crenshaw and the two-for-one sale on Dr Pepper at Piggly Wiggly.

But still, it was a hot ticket.

I watched as members of East New Hope church showed up in droves, bedecked in their Sunday best—except for nicotine-stained Mrs. Logan, who wore jeans and a T-shirt with "World's Best Mom" emblazoned in rhinestones.

I'd borrowed a couture military-inspired pantsuit from Mom's closet. Knox was bound to attend—it was Ms. Ray, after all—and if he saw me, he'd either love me or laugh.

*Hopefully both.*

It had been hard without Knox. Before the fight, I felt floaty, like invisible balloons beyond the clouds suspended me in the air. But now I'd gone five days without seeing him, and those invisible balloons had turned into cinder blocks. No amount of pushing him away would change the truth. I knew that now. And I was ready to let him know.

Dad promised to save my seat, which gave me time to loiter downstairs and ambush Knox when he showed at the ornate courthouse. It wasn't even a blip by New York standards, but all of Ashworth considered the five-story building the finest, most imposing structure west of Shreveport. Workman laid the interior tile at a time when people had pride and patience. The spiral staircase coiled up and up and up, leading the eye to a sky-painted mural on the ceiling where painted swallows circled the tips of spring trees.

I strolled up to the glass cases along the walls which proudly displayed the county's history. Normally I skip stodgy historical text like that, but I needed a distraction.

The first explained how Ashworth became the county seat in the face of a dwindling oil boom and the Great Depression. In 1939, the *Ashworth Herald* listed Ashworth's natural advantages. It boasted, "public buildings erected in Ashworth are not liable to destruction from cloud bursts," and that "Ashworth is free from the annual mosquito infestation that afflicts other parts of the county." Also, "Ashworth has a feed mill, two saloons, two hotels, and one doctor."

*Sign me up!*

I perused another exhibit, titled "Badges, Bandits, and Bars: Ashworth Law and Justice." Stern men dressed in gray uniforms, cradling rifles like babies and proudly wearing oversized brass stars on their chests, stared back at me from an ancient wooden frame. I stopped short in front of a sepia-toned photograph of a grim-looking woman, her gray hair in a tight bun. She held what looked like a warped human head. I leaned in closer and read the courier typed sheet next to the picture. It explained that the woman held a papier-mâché death mask of the first Ashworth County resident executed in the Texas electric chair—the chair nicknamed "Old Sparky."

I took out my camera and clicked a picture of the old woman, and a felt a pang of sadness when I remembered how Knox had joked with me, asking if I took photographs of photographs.

*Apparently, I do . . .*

"You missed the one over there," said a familiar voice behind me. *Caleb! Knox is sure to be with him.*

I turned, my cheeks flushed with anticipation. But no Knox.

"The one about the guy who threw himself from the clock tower during the depression, but landed on a passing poultry truck. Only thing he killed were five fat chickens."

"Hey, Caleb." I spun back around so he wouldn't see my disappointment. "I'm surprised Knox didn't show me this little piece of Treasure Island."

"Yeah, speaking of Knox," Caleb drawled. "He's not coming."

"Why not?" I straightened up, still looking into the glass. I could see Caleb's lean face darken in the reflection.

Caleb looked down at his shoes. "He left this morning."

I turned to him quickly. "Left?"

"He's meeting his parents in France."

It was like getting kicked in the stomach with size sixteen steel-toed boots. I couldn't breathe. I knew the answer to my next question, but I spit it out anyway.

"For how long?" I asked.

"For the rest of the summer," Caleb said. After an awkward silence, he added, "He's probably halfway across the Atlantic."

"But . . . but we're leaving in a week," I protested. "He wouldn't leave without—"

Caleb ran his hand through his hair. He was acting like a surrogate. Knox was breaking up with me from abroad. He reached into his pants pocket. "Sorry, Jordan. He wanted me to give you this."

I stood stiff, and Caleb tucked the note into my hands, pressing my fingers together so the letter wouldn't drop. I stood there as he slipped away, and the sounds in the courtroom became echoes of sounds and the building receded into four distant walls.

It was just me and the note. My heart pounded as I slit the envelope, unfolded the card, and read.

Jordan,

You were right about everything. Your arrival sparked a crazy and selfish thought that if I convinced you this place was something special, you might stay. The truth is, though, it isn't — and you won't.

Bells, signs, whatever. They all urge the same warning: "Leave this land of shadows and ghosts before you become one of them." I'm listening this time.

Congratulations on your own impending escape.

Your friend,
Knox

I stood waiting for the punch line. But every fiber of my soul knew it wouldn't come. Because it wasn't a joke. A windmill kept turning around and around in my head: *"Knox is gone. I'll never see him again."*

Dust danced in the lemon sunlight that spilled through the tall, thin windows. Dust that soon became blurs through the tears welling up in my eyes.

"Are you okay, miss?" It was the mayor. "You're Eli's daughter, right?"

Quickly, I tried to pull myself together.

"Yes," I said, wiping my tears on my mother's suit sleeve. "I am. Sorry, I'm feeling *verklempt* reading that story over there." I pointed, hoping he'd turn his head and give me another chance to wipe my cheeks. "The story about the five dead chickens." I sniffed.

He didn't buy it for a moment.

"Well," the mayor said with a kind smile and nod of his head. "It is a sad story. A dark day in Ashworth's history for sure."

I smiled back at the mayor.

"See you upstairs?" he asked gently.

"Yes." I nodded. "Thanks."

Then the mayor walked away, leaving me alone . . . again.

After a moment, a sigh escaped my lips. I took a step forward. Then I took another. And another.

Slowly, I pieced together a distance of fifteen feet, and then I twined up the spiral staircase, one step at a time.

I wanted to throw up.

Mom's heels clopped against the hardwood floor of the hallway as I reached the fourth floor. I took several deep breaths, still trying to power down the windmill. Mom paced, and my father sat on a wooden bench, watching her.

"Is Ms. Ray here yet?" he asked.

Mom shook her head and stuffed loose papers into her briefcase.

Dad furrowed his brow and fiddled with his tie. I plopped down beside him. I don't know who looked worse—me, Dad, or the papier-mâché death mask in the photograph downstairs. He must have sensed it too.

"Is everything okay?"

I cleared my throat, yet again, attempting to pull myself together. "Let's see," I sighed. "I'd dole out my inheritance, assuming there still is one, to the person who stole my look-alike voodoo doll in exchange for its safe return."

"What?"

"Nothing." I grinned slightly and shook my head. "Everything is great," I assured him.

"Good," he said, twisting his wedding ring, "because I'm a nervous wreck." He leaned forward, looking at the knots in his mismatched shoestrings. "Is Knox here yet?"

"No," I said, taking a deep breath. "He's gone to Paris." This last part came out as a weird primitive noise: part squeal, part whimper, part croak.

I frowned, my bottom lip trembling.

For a moment, there wasn't a word from either of us. But there didn't need to be. My father took my hand and squeezed it. A deeply comforting feeling swept through me as we sat watching my mother search the pockets of her briefcase to take out an empty manila folder. Then it hit me. Whatever crushing disappointment I felt didn't need to distract my parents from the job they had to do.

*Buck up, Jordan.*

"So are you going to have to testify?" I asked my father, nodding toward the courtroom doors.

He fidgeted in his seat. "I'm not sure. Your mother should know." His voice carried a little further than I think he intended. Blame it on the nerves.

"I told you I don't know," Mom huffed.

"How do *you* not know, Rachel?" he persisted.

We waited for an answer while she underlined text in a thick book called *Texas Criminal Procedure*.

"Because," she said, still consulting her book, "it depends on what Judge Cagle wants to hear. He might agree right away or he could want to hear testimony for the record."

"Good!" my father cheered. "That's what we wanted, right?"

Mom paced again. "*Or*, he could shut me down immediately and tell me to get the hell out of his courtroom. Victims of economic crimes are not always permitted to offer testimony concerning a defendant's conduct."

There was something in her voice that made me nervous. My father tapping his foot and continuously smoothing the crease in his slacks probably didn't help, either.

"Do you know what you're doing?" I finally blurted out, afraid that another disappointment today might send me over the edge.

Mom turned her head quickly and met my eye. She looked harried, and I wished I hadn't asked the question.

*What if she flounders?*

But she took a deep breath, and a look of tranquility passed through her like a summer breeze. She placed the book back into her case.

"Yes," she told us smoothly, her eyes newly determined. "In case you haven't noticed—I may be a little out of my element here—but you're looking at Rachel Klein. I've argued in front of the Supreme Court of the United States of America. I've predicted the fate of clients in front of the national media. I was lead counsel on a multibillion-dollar case before we came to Texas." She smiled at Dad. "I can certainly handle this matter for East New Hope."

My mother was the bravest, fiercest lioness, the most expensive jewel, and a delicate, fragile flower—all at the same time. The traits I had once resented were now beautiful to me. Traits I aspired to have.

As my father sighed in relief, a young man, who couldn't have been two years out of law school, bounded up the last step onto the floor. His American-flag necktie lay perfectly folded under his navy suit, and he skipped toward my mother with vigor and an outstretched hand.

"Mrs. Klein?" he asked, not at all winded.

"Yes," she said as she shook his hand. "Mr. Hughes, I presume?"

"In the flesh," the young man sang. "But call me Hamilton."

Mom had always said young lawyers were the most dangerous. For one, people always underestimated them, and two, they prepared twice as much as their opponents.

"Pleasure to meet you, Hamilton."

"Is that Ms. Ray's public defender?" I whispered to my father.

"No. That's the prosecutor."

Hamilton Hughes swayed back and forth on his heels, full of pep. "Unfortunately, criminals come in all packages—even sweet little old ladies," he said. "Burning trash in the summer or chopping down a neighbor's hedge without permission—sure, no problem. But embezzlement? It's a real shame."

"Yes," Mom added with a careful eye on my father. "A real shame."

With a thud, the courtroom's frosted-glass doors thudded open and a bailiff in blue shouted to the almost empty hallway: "State versus Idabell Ray."

"That's us," Hamilton chirped.

"Yes, it's showtime." She winked, stopping the young prosecutor in his tracks.

"You know, actually," he quickly added, falling behind my mother, "this kind of reminds me of this one time I had to charge an eighty-year-old lady with assault. She hit her husband over the head with a toilet seat. Did a lot of damage, actually."

Hamilton dropped his laser pointer pen but didn't bother to pick it up.

*Finders keepers. At least for the time being.*

I turned back to my father. He swabbed his sweaty forehead with his forearm and stared blankly at the courtroom, which was only briefly visible through the closing door.

"Dad." I put my hand on his shoulder. "Stop."

"What?" His eyes widened. It'd been years since I called him "Dad," and it fell out of my mouth so naturally.

I straightened the knot between his worn collar. "You'll need to look sharp if you have to testify."

The wood-paneled courtroom was divided into two parts—the larger area for the judge's bench, witness stand, jury box, and counsel tables, and the smaller section for the crowded rows of Ashworth residents fidgeting in their seats. Late morning sunlight burst through the room through stained glass windows, and goddess-of-justice tapestries lined the back wall. The air smelled of old wood varnish and August sweat.

Up front, my mother—who rocked her Valentino black suit—found her seat at the table closest to the jury box. Hamilton Hughes sat beside her.

Ms. Ray's public defender, an intense-looking man with a blond crew cut, was too engrossed in a crossword puzzle at the other table to notice the flurry of activity around him. He finally tipped his pencil when Mr. Hughes grew exasperated and went to say hello.

I searched the eyes of the congregation members—the same ones that excitedly followed our every move on the day of my father's first sermon. Now, people looked at us with apprehension and grief as Dad and I settled onto the bench behind my mother.

Looking back, I noticed Bliss, Boyd, and the rest of the LeBaron family had filled the entire row behind us. Caleb leaned over Buck's shoulder, whispering something. Boyd, wearing a silver wolf-head bolo tie, gave me a thumbs-up. Bliss waved timidly.

*Even Bliss has lost her pep. We're doomed.*

The rest of the crowd murmured unintelligibly. Occasionally, I heard things like "could be thirty years" and "if he wants to set an example," but everyone's conversations stacked on top of each other, and soon the courtroom sounded like Grand Central Station.

Unfortunately, the one thing I didn't want to hear, I did: Bliss whispering to Caleb, "Where's Knox?"

I focused on the judge's seat, waiting for the judge to shut everyone up.

Caleb cleared his throat, and said, "He's in France."

"Oh," Bliss mumbled. "Of course he is. I'm sure Mrs. Colville is thrilled to have him there." Then she squeezed my shoulder from behind, giving me a final squeeze before she released me.

*Thank God for Bliss.*

At last, a round and red-faced court bailiff entered from a door I hadn't seen. It blended in with the wood paneling behind the judge's bench. He scanned the crowd of familiar faces before proudly announcing, "All rise. Ashworth County Court is now in session, the honorable L.C. Cagle presiding."

Shushes filled the crowd. Even Mr. Gober was quiet.

A spectacled, elderly man with a bushy white mustache entered without looking up. The gallery quickly quieted. We all watched as Judge Cagle shuffled onto his perch, where he would decide Ms. Ray's fate.

Mom had done her due diligence on Judge Cagle. He rebuked teenagers for their reckless underage drinking, doling out the maximum sentence every time. He was tough on business leaders and equally shrewd in divorce hearings, never awarding anyone a penny for "emotional damage." When sentencing thieves, he set a provision—of dubious legality—for victims to take something of equal value from the thief's home. But he had a heart, too. Most of the children in town knew him as the man who handed out pinwheel peppermints.

Apparently, the "Don't take candy from a stranger" campaign hadn't made it to Ashworth yet.

All eyes were on Judge Cagle. That is, until the guards ferried Ms. Ray into the courtroom, wearing handcuffs.

Gasps came from the gallery, and Bliss snapped, loud enough for most everyone to hear: "Oh, come on. Is that really necessary?"

The judge regarded my mother and young Mr. Hughes, and then watched as Ms. Ray took her seat next to the public defender, still absorbed in his crossword.

"I'll hear your announcements," Judge Cagle said.

The prosecutor stood and in a proud voice proclaimed, "Hamilton Hughes, Your Honor. For the State."

"Thank you, Mr. Hughes."

"Jeffrey VanHensel for the Defendant," said Ms. Ray's lawyer, finally stepping away from his puzzle.

Judge Cagle nodded.

My mother followed suit. "Your Honor, Rachel Klein appearing *pro hac vice* for East New Hope Church."

"Mrs. Klein, welcome to our little courthouse. It's a shame you're not here under happier circumstances."

Ms. Ray looked toward my mother, her eyes swollen from crying. Judge Cagle squared her in his sights, and Ms. Ray ducked back into her shackled hands. "Will the defendant please rise?

"Idabell Ray," Judge Cagle declared, "you have pled guilty to one count of embezzlement by misuse of a fiduciary relationship, is that correct?"

Ms. Ray nodded, barely lifting her chin.

"Ma'am, you need to answer with audible words so the court reporter can take down what you say."

"I'm sorry," Ms. Ray croaked. "Yes. That's correct."

"And you understand that we are here today to determine your sentence based on the arguments of the prosecution, your counsel, and your victims?"

"I do."

"Good." Judge Cagle turned back to counsel.

"Is the State ready to proceed?"

Mr. Hughes confirmed, "It is, Your Honor."

Hamilton Hughes had a style that made people sit up and take notice—charming, but heavy on the bombast.

"Your Honor, in the last three years, the church at East New Hope had raised one hundred fifteen thousand dollars for the Lord's Pantry. That's a lot of money."

He continued in an ominous tone. "And it wasn't supposed to be the end."

After a dramatic pause, he continued.

"That money was supposed to go toward a bigger goal of raising one million one hundred fifty thousand dollars for a new facility. A facility that would provide more than a food pantry and culinary training for local down-and-outs. There were plans to build a community center and offer free medical services. But now that money will never come. That dream has died. Why? Because a heinous crime was committed in Ashworth the night after the Pack the Pantry fundraiser."

Hamilton pirouetted across the floor, gesticulating dramatically to the judge and creating great theater for the citizens of Ashworth.

"After the fundraiser, and while the rest of Ashworth slept, preparing to do God's work the next day, Idabell Ray—a trusted church member, volunteer, and employee—stole sixty thousand dollars from East New Hope. More than fifty percent of what the church had raised."

He shook his head.

"She did this, Your Honor, by going to the bank, using her trusted position as church secretary, and taking the Pantry's cash. Cash that was supposed to buy milk, eggs, and staples used to feed the disadvantaged here in Ashworth. Thereafter, Idabell Ray smuggled the stolen funds to Shreveport. To do what? Provide for the sick? No! Feed the poor? No! Ms. Ray *gambled it away*. Gambled it away at the Chicken Ship Casino!"

Then he launched into Ms. Ray with a fever pitch.

"Now, the defendant has already pled guilty to one count of embezzlement by misuse of a fiduciary relationship after admitting to stealing the money. For the record, the State could have also brought charges for—"

"Objection!" The public defender jumped to his feet, surprising everyone—especially Ms. Ray, who looked frightened by his abrupt movements. "She pled guilty. The State cannot ambush this defendant by insinuating there are additional charges without bringing those charges or proving its case at trial!"

"Sustained," Judge Cagle agreed. "Mr. Hughes, please move on."

"Yes, Your Honor," Hamilton responded, unfazed. "For the sentence, the State humbly requests that you make an example of Ms. Ray. That you send a strong message that Ashworth will not tolerate those who betray the disadvantaged, the disabled, the homeless, and the underserved. Law is blind and sees no age, and Ashworth should not look the other way just because of this woman's years. It was an unpardonable sin, regardless of who committed it."

The sharp young prosecutor sat down in his chair confidently, and there wasn't a noise in the courtroom. The only sounds I heard came from the pigeons outside tottering on the rain gutters.

Judge Cagle turned to Ms. Ray. "Idabell Ray, would you like to say anything?"

Before Ms. Ray could open her mouth, my mother interrupted.

Her chair scraped across the floor as she stood. "Your Honor, if I may?"

Judge Cagle raised an eyebrow in admonishment. "Ms. Klein, I don't know how they do things in New York City, but the rest of America allows the accused an opportunity to make a statement. As the representative of East New Hope, you will have the opportunity to comment as to the appropriate sentence."

A nervous shiver ran through the crowd. We all held our collective breath.

"Yes, but I'm not here to communicate a recommendation as to Ms. Ray's sentence," she said. Her shoulders pinched back and she stood tall.

Hamilton Hughes shot her a confused look, and the judge reluctantly allowed her to proceed.

"I'm here because East New Hope has decided not to press charges against Ms. Ray for the full amount."

The young prosecutor looked blindsided. He waved his hands at Mom, as if struggling in the water and forgetting how to speak.

"Instead, East New Hope asks this court to charge Ms. Ray with petty theft only. In regards to *that* charge, we recommend a sentence of time served plus two thousand hours of community service at the Lord's Pantry."

The crowd buzzed, encouraged by this new possibility.

"You can't do that!" Hamilton accused, wagging his finger.

"Actually, we can, Your Honor," my mother said, opening her

rulebook. "Pursuant to the Texas Code of Criminal Procedure Rule 56 you should take the request of the victim into account—"

"This is preposterous, Your Honor!" Hamilton interrupted.

"Further, if necessary," my mother said, with warning in her voice, "I have in my hand a motion to dismiss—"

"A motion to dismiss?" Hamilton screeched. "There are no grounds—"

Judge Cagle cut his eyes to the young prosecutor. "Mrs. Klein gave you the floor for more than your fair share. I believe it is only fair she have an opportunity to respond. Whether you like that response or not."

The old judge turned back to my mother and nodded his head.

"Thank you, Your Honor." My mother continued, "In *Jackson v. Virginia*, the Supreme Court held that federal due process requires that the State prove, beyond a reasonable doubt, every element of the crime charged. So I've done some reading and learned that Texas requires the State to allege the name of the owner of the stolen property in a theft indictment."

The judge leaned back in his leather chair. "Go on."

"As Mr. Hughes so aptly demonstrated, the defendant misappropriated funds. But she did not steal money from East New Hope, as the indictment states."

Mother took three sets of papers from her manila folder. "May I approach?" she asked Judge Cagle.

"You may."

Mom handed a paper-clipped set of documents to the judge, Mr. Hughes, and Ms. Ray's public defender before turning to address the court again.

"As you can see from the materials I've provided, two years ago, the Lord's Pantry applied for and was granted by the United States Internal Revenue Service its 501(c)(3) status. The Lord's Pantry, while a charity supported by East New Hope, is its own entity. An entity with its own bank accounts, its own property, its own money. I don't have to tell you, Your Honor, of the numerous Texas decisions holding that showing that a defendant stole money from one victim cannot sustain a conviction under an indictment alleging a different victim. Ms. Ray did not steal money from East New Hope, she stole money from the Lord's Pantry."

"This is preposterous, Your Honor!" Hamilton interrupted.

My mother wasn't deterred. She held up her folder again.

"And while I'm not as familiar with Texas case law as Mr. Hughes is, I suspect there's enough in this file to tie this case up in the Texas courts for a good two years, wasting valuable county resources, including Mr. Hughes's time. Further, I'm willing to personally represent the defendant in her—"

With the reflexes of a man half his age, Judge Cagle struck his gavel on the wooden stand with three thunderous thumps. "Excuse me!"

My mother paused, and Hamilton looked to the ceiling, as if his appeal to the heavens had been heard. No one in the courtroom stirred.

Judge Cagle took off his glasses and polished them on the sleeve of his robe, letting the silence fester. Finally, he asked, "What about the sixty thousand dollars? That's a lot of money for the church—and this community—to lose. If this is a choice between Ms. Ray and the Lord's Pantry, well, I'm not sure how sympathetic I feel to your request."

"Your Honor, because it might aid your decision." My mother's eyes cut quickly to my father, before taking a deep breath. "An anonymous donor recently gave the church sixty thousand dollars to cover the loss so that the Pantry will stay in business."

Bliss shouted, "Thank you, Jesus," and her voice led the gallery as it erupted in cheers.

I thought back to our last Klein family meeting. Even though my parents always pooh-poohed Jacob's liberal use of Grandfather Klein's money for "worthy causes," right after Ms. Ray's visit, Dad called a meeting to discuss the donation. It was the only Klein family meeting I can remember where no one left the family summit swearing.

Judge Cagle pounded his gavel repeatedly. The crowd simmered down respectfully.

"Yes," Judge Cagle began, "it's a tad unorthodox, but if that's the wish of the church, then I will absolutely allow it." He leaned forward, looking straight into my mother's eyes. "That way there will be no need to invoke any dismissal on a technicality growing out of an immaterial error. Am I correct, Mrs. Klein?"

"Very correct, Your Honor."

"Good," the judge said. He turned to Ms. Ray. "Will the defendant rise?"

Ms. Ray stood, holding onto the wooden banister for support. She was still trying to make sense of it all when Judge Cagle made his pronouncement.

"Idabell Ray, you are hereby sentenced to time served plus two thousand hours of community service to be served at the Lord's Pantry. Forgiveness is a gift. I'm sure I do not need to impress upon you that you should appreciate the magnitude of this gift."

Ms. Ray nodded as Judge Cagle struck his gavel for the final time.

Hamilton Hughes smacked his palms against the table and then lowered his head, bowing in frustration. The whole crowd was on their feet, surging with ecstatic joy. Ms. Ray, on the other hand, collapsed on the defendant's bench, tears leaking from her tired eyes.

"Mrs. Klein," Judge Cagle said, "it was a pleasure having you in this courtroom. You're welcome back any time."

"Thank you, Your Honor," Mom said, just before the gallery erupted again. I heard Boyd, Buck, Caleb, Mr. Wheeler, Mrs. Brackin, Mr. Randall, the twins, Ally, Cesar, Mr. Gober—everyone hooting and hollering with joy.

In the commotion, a gray-haired man wearing a seersucker suit approached Mom and handed her a card.

"My name is Dylan Deskins, Attorney at Law," he said, offering his hand. "Good job today, Mrs. Klein."

Mom took the card and shook the man's hand, before the rest of the crowd besieged her. She smiled at Mr. Deskins and waved as all of East New Hope swarmed around her, shouting her name, laughing wildly, and punching their fists into the air.

# Chapter 24

**W**e planned to leave at noon, right after Dad's last sermon. Dad stuffed the car to the gills. He planned to drop Mom and me at the Dallas-Ft. Worth airport for our flight and then make the drive back. I think he was excited to get rid of us so he could stop at the Billy Carter Gas Station museum a second time.

While some locals argued that Ms. Ray should've "gone to the can," almost everyone in town supported East New Hope's decision. Many stopped by and dropped off desserts with notes that said, "Thank you" or "You're the best" or "You Put the Hope in East New Hope." Mom even made the *Ashworth Herald* in a piece titled "Yankee Doodle Dandiest."

Of course, now that we were the toast of the town, it was time to say sayonara. Everywhere I looked reminded me of Knox, and I wanted to get the heck out of Dodge, but the town was like peanut butter in Sticky's mouth. I couldn't get rid of it. And the thought of leaving without saying good-bye to Knox . . . the thought knotted up my stomach.

*Street art, leather pants, Coney Island . . .*

I tried to think of all the things I loved about New York City, but the list wasn't coming as quickly as it once had.

A noon departure wasn't in the cards because, right before

the service's benediction, Buck announced a surprise lunch in the Fellowship Hall in honor of "the Kleins and all they've done for our community, from the Big Bang Theory lectures to the saving of Idabell's hide."

*Uh, thanks, Buck. No props for falling in love with the town dreamboat and chasing him off to France?*

It felt like half the town had gathered in the Fellowship Hall. Tater-tot casseroles and Frito pies flooded the paper-lined long tables, and everyone chowed down, hungry after a ceremony *sans* Lord's Supper.

*Chinese take-out boxes, red brick walls, steaming streets . . .*

Some of the church members even gave us gifts. Mrs. Brackin framed the church bulletin from our first Sunday in Ashworth. Cesar gave my father a book on UFOs, "to educate him," he said. Bliss burned a CD of all the country music she'd introduced me to—I wasn't crazy about the music, but I loved Bliss . . . and Lyle Lovett.

While I sipped a Coke from my plastic Solo cup, I overheard Moe's mother blathering about how gentle and loving her son was, and that he'd built her a greenhouse for her birthday, in which he grew vegetables and herbs.

*Yeah, right. I wonder what kind of herbs.*

I tried again to visualize all the fun things I had to look forward to in New York. *Walk the High Line. Eat hot dogs and drink Sunkist on the Staten Island ferry.*

Y'all 'member that big storm back in June?" Buck's voice reverberated across the room. A happy crowd formed a half-circle around him and my father, nodding their heads. "I had Pastor Klein with me in my truck going to Ms. Morina's. And y'all know how tall my truck is, right? Well on the way the trees on Pink Ribbon Lane—the ones left standing, that is—were scraping the roof, so I stopped the truck, jumped out of the cab, and yelled to the pastor, 'Gotta git the tree cutter.'"

Dad's face was red and he was laughing, covering his mouth with his hand.

"The pastor is sitting in the cab, and I reached into the truck bed, grabbed my shotgun, and BOOM! I blew the tree branches away!"

Buck roared in front of a laughing crowd. "I told him, that's how we trim trees in the country! Y'all should have seen the look on his face!"

*Awesome water pressure, fire escapes, hot-dog carts . . .*

It was no use. I still thought constantly about Knox. I hadn't heard a peep from him since the letter, except for a slightly blurry black-and-white scenic postcard of Paris.

An hour after the lunch, Dad shut the trunk with a thud. He'd loaded the last of our belongings into the Volvo. "We'll need one stop for gas, ladies, and then we're on our way."

Neither Mom nor I said a word. I wondered how she felt about going back. She'd become the local hero in Ashworth, and now she was going to have to hunt for a job in the Big Apple. Well, at least she'd stopped baking apricot fried pies—unfortunately.

I slapped the backseat and Sticky jumped into the Volvo. Hal was already inside, stuffed inside a carrier so we didn't have to smell his pungent breath.

*When we get back to New York, I'm taking that cat to a dentist.*

Jacob delayed his return—he was busy building houses for refugees. And Buck was looking for a new pastor—but that position could take months to fill. So we couldn't leave Sticky and Hal. What if a tornado blew through? Sticky would barrel through the air like a Frisbee, probably landing in the next county. Hal would probably end up in the catfish pond or as someone's toupee. I couldn't let that happen. Surprisingly, my parents didn't put up a stink.

*I guess Hal did plenty of that already.*

We stopped at the end of the driveway, Woulfe and Notorious P.I.G. sped by like a roll of thunder on their motorcycle, just like they'd done on the day we arrived. Woulfe waved and the pig, sitting smugly in the sidecar, raised his snout.

This time, we all waved back.

As Dad pulled onto the road, I took one last glance back at the church. I had to see the sign one last time.

"There are far, far better things ahead than any we leave behind."

*Nice try, sign. But I'm not so sure.*

I needed to stock up on Pop Rocks and Gummy Bears for the flight so Dad pulled over at a convenience store right outside of town.

The dingy place advertised cheap gas, cold beer, and something called "Bird Brain."

A clerk hunched over the counter with a pack of Marlboros hanging out of his front pocket. He raised his head when I opened the door and polished an apple with a Shamwow.

Then something caught my eye. At the back of the store, behind the shelves of laundry detergent and behind the Fun Yuns, was a large coin-operated arcade unit, bigger than the typical crane machine full of stuffed animals—no, this was the obliquely advertised "Bird Brain." Inside was nothing more than a tic-tac-toe board in front of a barnyard background scene that looked like it had been painted by a second grader.

I pressed my face against the glass, and I jumped back when a handsome rooster entered the box through a small plastic barn door. He stared at me, as if throwing down the glove. According to the sign on the front of the machine, this mighty rooster—named "Er Er Er Er Earl"—would play tic-tac-toe for fifty cents.

Earl clucked and strutted while I considered challenging him to a duel. I felt an odd bond with this flightless bird relegated to the cage. Standing back, I took my camera out of my messenger bag. *Snap-Snap.*

"Got fiddy cents?" asked the clerk in a raspy voice. "You can play him. He gets a treat every time someone plays. Don't matter if he wins or loses—still gets his treat."

Earl seemed annoyed that I was taking so long. In order to appease the impatient bird, I reached in my bag for fifty cents and inserted the money.

Dad entered the store in time to hear the clerk say, "If I had a quarter for every time that rooster beat someone, I'd have more quarters than . . . well, more quarters than that rooster."

Oblivious to the fact, "I beg your pardon? You could beat a rooster?" Dad queried.

"I think he's talking to me," I said. The clerk laughed dryly and watched as Earl and I squared off.

The bird made the first move. Actually, I wanted to go first, but it's hard to argue with a rooster. Earl pecked at the top left corner of the tic-tac-toe board and an "X" lit up. I played my "O" in the center square. He responded with the square below his first "X."

"Some people don't even stand a chance," declared the clerk.

When I blocked Earl's win by placing my "O" in the bottom corner, the clerk snorted.

Earl placed his "X" in the top corner, and soon we reached an impasse. Nonetheless, grain poured into the cage as a reward for his efforts, and the feathered gladiator feasted on the yellow meal.

"That's one smart chick," said the clerk. It was unclear to whom he was referring.

I pressed my hand to the glass and said good-bye to my avian adversary. "You're an eagle among chickens, my friend," I whispered.

His eyes met mine for a split second and, if my deep-seated sense of logic hadn't intervened, I could have sworn the haughty gaming Earl dropped his beak and nodded in acknowledgment before departing through the plastic door. It was a fitting exit.

*Good-bye, Ashworth.*

# Chapter 25

The torrents of summer rain were over and New York City had begun to morph back into its unruly self. Men with black briefcases warred for cabs. Women pitched battles on cell phones and nannies rushed babies in strollers. Delivery trucks rattled down the avenues. An early September breeze tamed the last of the summer heat.

Sticky and I sat in Central Park, watching it all.

We'd been back in New York a week, and life had returned to "normal." Dad was back at the university pushing fruitlessly on the door marked "pull." Mom fielded call after call from every large New York law firm, all of them trying to convince her to come work for them. And I surrounded myself with the joyful chaos of the streets, eating falafel sandwiches and sipping on Yoo-hoos.

But life *had* changed for us.

My parents were tenderer. The previous night, for instance, when I returned home from a walk with Sticky, I found them standing at the kitchen sink. Dad's hands were around Mom's waist as she did the dishes, and he gently kissed the back of her neck and whispered something into her ear. Mom smiled demurely.

"Other teenagers are in years of therapy for seeing less," I quipped.

They didn't even seem embarrassed. And worse, their tenderness made me miss mine.

And today, as I sat clutching a book, attempting to digest the words on the page, my thoughts were someplace else. No matter how I tried to concentrate on my book, he was underneath and in everything around me: the vendor selling oranges with dark hair falling over his eyes. *I almost fainted the first time I watched Knox sweep his hair from his chameleon eyes.* The retired ballerina entranced by the troupe of nimble street dancers just yards away. *She stands tall and quiet—like Knox.* The old man who nursed his Irish brews while reading *Catch-22. That's the first thing Knox and I talked about at Madame Ribbette.* The mother talking on her cell phone, her little boy beside her drawing aimless patterns in the dirt. *He looks alone—like Knox when we first met.*

It was a bizarre feeling, watching life go by but not feeling like a part of it.

"Well, look who's back!" interrupted a familiar snarky voice. "And look, she finally has a friend like her—a mangy-looking dog."

Sloan and Brianna.

I should have smelled them coming—their cigarettes and their overdone perfume and the swirling cesspool of their unmet needs. Both wore tight long ponytails and chic round sunglasses that covered most of their faces.

*Probably so people can't see their red eyes and black souls.*

Sloan locked arms with Brianna as they approached.

"Brianna, did I tell you what an amazing time I had with Stryder last weekend?" Sloan fanned herself with the latest edition of *US Weekly* while Brianna gave her a phony surprised face.

"Wasn't that your *third* date?" Brianna exclaimed. "I want to hear all the juicy details!"

Sloan swatted her friend with the mag and they laughed hysterically.

"Enjoy your sloppy seconds," I muttered, and Sticky gave them both an uncharacteristic growl. Brianna jerked her head my way and flashed a wolfish grin, as if to confirm my fears of a dreadful senior year to come.

*Yep, life officially stinks.*

To think that I once thought Bliss was like Sloan and Brianna. I prayed for her to call right then, to ask me some kind of silly question like she had the day before: "Have you seen Matthew McConaughey yet? TMZ says he and the fam have a new place on Central Park

West. That's all right, I guess. Hey, do you think he would still be as delicious if he went bald? He's not so young anymore, you know. His doctor probably has him on that Propecia stuff, right?"

The phone rang. My prayers were answered! I scrambled to answer it. "No Matthew sightings, yet," I laughed.

"Umm . . . Sorry. I must have the wrong number."

It was my father.

"Sorry, Dad. I thought you were Bliss."

"Jordan?"

"Yep, it's me." He still wasn't used to my use of the word "Dad."

"Your mother called. She needs us home right away. We're having a Klein family meeting."

"You want to bid on Hillary Clinton's black silk knickers for charity, right?"

"No," he continued, unfazed by my remark. "The attorney from Ashworth has something to discuss."

"Oh no, did Ms. Ray's probation fall through?"

"That was my first thought, too, but your mother said Deskins claimed it is something else entirely."

"What then?"

"I don't know. He asked if the three of us could manage a video conference at six tonight."

My mind raced, struggling to keep up with the conversation.

"Even me?" I asked, bewildered.

*Did we leave the oven on at Jacob's? Was someone suing Dad for boring them to death at church? Why me?*

"He specifically said for all three of us to be there. Can you be home in half an hour?"

I looked down at my watch: 5:30.

"Yeah. I'll be home in thirty minutes," I promised, tossing the book into my messenger bag and leashing up Sticky.

"Come on, stick-meister. Let's book."

I threaded through the crowded streets, ignoring the music and happy-hour voices blaring from the pubs, the black-haired beauty breaking up with her boyfriend via cell phone, the spicy aromas seeping from Saffron House, and the teems of brokers grumbling about sour deals. In fact, I hardly heard the yellow cab come screeching to a halt as we ran across an intersection with just six blocks to go.

*Maybe I should've waited for the light to change.*

I had to get back—to the little piece of Ashworth that was calling my name. Sticky wagged his tail and panted. He seemed just as excited.

*But for what?*

When we entered the house, I strolled casually toward my mother's office, pretending like I wasn't gasping for air, like Ashworth didn't matter to me at all.

"Yes," Mom explained as she repositioned the computer monitor. "And he'll be able to hear and see you. Just look at the screen."

"That's amazing. I didn't know we could do that from here," Dad said.

I hovered in the doorway while Sticky jumped onto the black leather couch in the corner. Instead of scolding him, Mom scratched behind his ears and gave me a distracted, "Hey, sweetie."

Dad fumbled in his briefcase until he reached some crumpled pink stationery I recognized as his assistant's. The embossed letters read, "What if the Hokey-Pokey really is what it's all about?"

Smoothing out the note, Mom turned back to the computer while Dad and I watched her type in the Internet address.

Mom turned to my father. "This should be interesting. Eli, why don't you and I sit right here in front so Mr. Deskins has a better view?" It was more a command than a question, and we complied.

In my mind I had a picture of what Deskins' firm would look like: deep-green shag carpeting, padded navy armchairs, paintings of old white guys in custom tweeds bearing down their guns on a field of unsuspecting pheasants, a few silver trophies and shelves upon shelves of books—but not the books I loved, like at Madame Ribbette's.

When the picture appeared, though, there were no boring law books in the background. In fact, I couldn't tell what we were looking at. A pale peach color, out of focus, but definitely moving.

Then there was a quick jolt and the image fell sharply into focus.

*Oh, my.*

We were staring at a giant pair of boobs.

We recoiled but couldn't look away. Mom giggled as we watched the owner of said boobs leaning over a desk, trying to make the connection. She wore a bright blue sundress—and was blessed with an enormous bosom.

"There you go," the receptionist said, standing back to reveal a bewildered Deskins staring right at them.

"Thank you, Gracie," Deskins said as he sat down in front of his computer.

I was glad Gracie left the room. She really was distracting.

"Hello, Klein family! Good to see you again!" Deskins greeted us, grinning wildly.

"You have a beautiful space," Mom said respectfully.

Soft gray and cream walls lit the office and a tweed-covered couch and matching chairs outfitted the room. It was contemporary, unpretentious, and slightly offbeat. I didn't see any paintings of old white guys toting rifles.

*Wrong as usual, Jordan.*

Deskins laughed. "Thank you. Before this boutique hotel look, I had the ships in bottles, nautical charts, and dark wood paneling for years. Sometimes change is good, though, right?"

"Yes, I guess it is." Mom laughed knowingly. Then she began. "Mr. Deskins. We're curious as to why you've called this meeting. If you could—"

Deskins held up a finger. "Excuse me. Hold on two seconds." He pressed a button on his desk phone.

"Send in Officer Watts, Gracie."

"He's here already," Gracie said.

"Perfect! Send him in, please. And why don't you bring—"

"Oh, I'm sorry, is this about a speeding ticket?" my mother inquired coolly. "Because it was our understanding Officer Watts never issued one."

"No, no," Deskins assured us, smiling in response. "Just one more moment."

Officer Watts strode into the office with his slow, casual gait. He glanced at the computer and looked flummoxed. "Well, I'll be," he said. "It's Pastor Klein on the computer." He waved furiously to gain our attention.

"I needed Officer Watts here as a witness," Deskins continued, raising his eyebrows as if in apology.

"A witness for what?" Mom asked.

"Jasper Hardin's will," Deskins repeated.

My parents and I exchanged confused glances as Gracie entered the frame again, this time carrying three glasses of iced tea. She handed one to her boss and the other to Officer Watts, then lingered there, waiting to take part in whatever was about to happen, sipping from her glass.

I felt even more apprehensive as Deskins took off his reading glasses and cleaned them with a white silk handkerchief from his front pocket. The lengthening silence became excruciating.

*Get to the point, old man!*

"I hope you're ready for this." He smiled, putting on his glasses again. He then read from a document: "In the name of God, Amen. I, the undersigned, Jasper William Hardin, residing in Ashworth, Texas, though I am sick and bedridden but of sound mind, memory, and faculties, do hereby offer my last will and testament.

"I have earned my status of 'Most Despised Man' in Ashworth the old-fashioned way: I earned it. I made my fortune by working hard, causing the entire lazy town to despise my success. So I despised them in return."

"He was one nasty son of a bitch," grumbled Officer Watts.

Deskins shot him a *stop talking* kind of look, and Officer Watts tipped his hat before apologizing. "Sorry, Pastor Klein."

"Since no one ever pinched any money from me while I was alive," Deskins read on, "and after what I did—killing that Colville girl and all—"

My heart stopped.

"—anyone that comes to my funeral is obviously someone who had some compassion for an old bastard like me. Consequently, I hereby bequeath my entire estate with all my holdings to be divided equally among those who attended my funeral."

Deskins pushed his glasses up further on the bridge of his nose. He pulled out a small fabric-padded book and opened it to the first page.

We leaned forward, trying to focus on the book. It was embroidered with the words "Bocho Brothers Funeral Home."

He read from the book. "Eli Klein, Rachel Klein, and last but not least, Jordan K." He looked over his glasses. "I'm assuming that stands for Jordan Klein. Yours were the only signatures that appeared in the funeral home's register book for Mr. Hardin's service."

It all came together. Hardin was the dead man I saw my first day in Ashworth. He was the dead man with the angry tombstone. He was the owner of Hardin Farms. He was the old guy that sold Moe the blue truck. He was the man who killed Skye Colville.

"But, but . . ." Dad stuttered. "We just stopped by to use the restroom. We didn't attend the service. We pulled over to use the facilities and—"

"Legally, that doesn't matter. You were there, Pastor Klein. You all signed the book. And Mr. Bocho tells me that Jordan even paid her respects. The Hardin estate now belongs to the three of you."

A few seconds of stunned silence passed before Officer Watts hit his leg with his cowboy hat. "Well, I'll be a bobcat caught in a piss fire!"

"What kind of estate are we talking about?" my mother asked, having regained her composure.

"Well *this* is a full statement of Mr. Hardin's cash and securities at his Ashworth Credit Union account."

Deskins held a piece of paper in front of his camera, and we read the numbers, our jaws on the floor. He confirmed what we already saw, "A nice round number of one million, one hundred fifty thousand dollars."

"Uh, did you say one million, one hundred fifty thousand?" I gulped.

"That's right, one million, one hundred fifty thousand."

My mother asked the question again. "One million, one hundred and fifty thousand dollars?"

"Yes," said Deskins. "It's a lot of money and I can imagine your—"

"Wait." Dad stopped. "One million, one hundred fifty thousand dollars *exactly*?"

I felt a shiver run down my spine.

"We haven't appraised the farm, which is yours as well. But yes, the cash amount is exactly one million, one hundred fifty thousand dollars."

"Farm?" my mother asked.

Deskins's eyes sparkled. "Yessiree. As God is my witness, the house, barns, equipment, livestock, and the pear orchard are all yours. That's four hundred acres of prime Ashworth real estate."

"Wait, Hardin Farms is a *pear* orchard?" my father asked, almost choking on his words.

All summer, we had reminisced about Jacob biting into the

ornamental pear so many months ago, the night he was called back to Ashworth.

*Called back because of Skye's death.*

"One of the biggest orchards in the state," Deskins said proudly. "He used to sell those pears all over the United States. I bet they even made their way up to your neck of the woods."

I took a deep, steady breath just before Deskins made his last pronouncement.

"Congratulations, Kleins. We look forward to seeing you soon."

# Chapter 26

**M**y phone rang and I opened my eyes to a familiar face. David Lee Roth, in a white tank top and red leather pants, feasted on me with his eyes. Early September in Texas is still way too hot to have anything on, and by the sexy smirk on Dave's face, he didn't mind.

"Dave, you're a freak," I mumbled, reaching for my ringing phone. It was Bliss.

"Hellloo." My voice was groggy and a bit grumpy. But after the summer, I was well accustomed to Bliss's early morning, mid-afternoon, and late night shout-outs.

"Hey, hooker! Tell me you're back in town!"

"Bliss, I told you not to call me 'hooker.' I've got enough business without the advertisement," I teased back.

"Yeah, yeah," Bliss laughed. "How was your flight?"

"Good." I sighed, making my way to the closet in search of Jacob's old Hush Puppy slippers. *Nice. Right where I left them.* "On the way to New York, I watched the second half of *The Blind Side*. And on the way back, I saw the first half. It's a movie about a football star that winds up as a down-and-out teenager, right?"

Bliss didn't miss a beat. "I'm sooo glad you're back!"

I looked down at the grungy slippers, which were obscenely large for my feet. "Yeah, me too," I said, slipping into an old T-shirt and cut-offs.

"Okay, now for the real reason I called." Bliss took an exaggerated breath. "Have you talked to Knox yet?"

I glanced at the photo of Knox and me on the deck of the *Escargot*, which sat on top of the dresser. His arm was around my shoulder and he smiled, like I was his prize catch—despite the fact that you couldn't even see my eyes over the clump of wet and matted hair.

"No." I snapped back to reality. "Caleb said he'll be home sometime around three this afternoon."

"I'm sure he's already heard. But what are you going to say about it?"

I fell back onto my bed, staring at the ceiling. My body warmed all over. Of course, I'd rehearsed what to say since we found out. I even wrote out ten pages during the flight. But now that the day was upon me, all my well-rehearsed words seemed *wrong*.

"I don't know."

"*Dirty Dancing* has some great lines you could steal to let him know how much you *looove* him," Bliss advised with a giggle.

"Thanks, but I'll think of something."

Bliss moaned, "Man, would I love to hear that convo. I'm predicting his face will lose all color—complete shock—and then, like in the movies, he'll whisk you off your feet and you'll end up having birthday cake on your kitchen table in the dark."

I sighed and fell upon my bed, kicking the Hush Puppies into the air.

"Or he could freak out and start a blog called 'Hilarious Things I Found in Jordan's Trash,' or worse, never speak to me again," I said.

That seemed more likely, and how could I blame him? We'd inherited the estate of the man who killed his sister, after all. The only difference between my family and Moe was intention.

"True," Bliss agreed. "But somehow I suspect he'll come around."

I hoped she was right.

Upon hearing a lawn mower gurgle outside, I pulled away the curtains to let in the daylight. There was Cesar, saddled atop his old, beat-up Murray riding lawnmower, gliding around the marquee. Today's message was clear as mud: "Love Explosion!"

*Isn't that a Weezer song?*

"Hey, how 'bout we head to town and get you all dolled up. I have a coupon for ten dollars off the works at Pedis, Paws, and Claws. What do you have to lose?"

Normally, I would've given Bliss a list of everything I had to lose: a foot free from gangrene, a life without hepatitis, my dignity. This was a nail salon that also "cleaned" Hal's teeth and shaved Sticky's butt. But last night I'd laid out three different outfits in anticipation of seeing Knox, and I really needed some help, so . . . I cringed as I said it: "Meet me in an hour?"

"See you then, J-Bird!"

Forty-five minutes later, I pulled into the Wrestling Station. I needed to fill up the tank, and I prayed I wouldn't get body-slammed in the process. After topping off, I pulled the Jeep to the adjacent parking lot so other people could get their guzzle on. Plus, I wanted some breath mints for later that afternoon—Hal taught me how critical it was to keep the mouth smelling fresh.

Walking back to the Jeep, I heard a nasal, whiny voice that could only belong to one person: Moe.

"Told you she'd come crawling back."

*Ugh.*

He and Travis leaned against the blue Dually, filling up loose red canisters with gasoline. "Couldn't stay away, could you?"

"I'd rather give birth to a flaming porcupine than have to spend another second with you," I huffed.

Moe lit a cigarette and started to walk my way. I could see the smoke twine into the air. And he was drunk . . . again.

*What's that prayer Bliss always recites around Moe? That's right. "Dear God, please let Moe be swallowed by a whale with excessively bad breath or trampled by stampeding pigs—your choice."*

"Seriously . . ." Moe ambled menacingly toward me. "I could come over tonight—"

"Moe, I'm going to tell you for the last time," I interrupted, using Mom's strong, confident attorney voice.

"Leave. Me. Alone."

His smirk disappeared. "And if I don't?"

"And if you don't . . ." I searched for something . . . anything . . . and then it came to me.

I heaved an exaggerated sigh and turned back to Moe. "I will tell everyone how when you were fourteen, you and Travis went camping. You got up in the middle of the night to go pee and tripped over a burned-out stump. Remember? You had to go to the hospital?" I punctuated the threat with several clicks of my tongue. "With a bull nettle bush in your bum? Or at least that's *your* story."

By the look on Moe's face, it was true. Knox had mentioned it in jest as Moe drove by one day—chalking all of Moe's issues up to that one traumatic event—but I obviously didn't give that story the full weight or attention it deserved. Maybe that was why Moe hated Knox so badly—because it was Skye who fixed him up.

Moe stared at me in horror, without saying a word. His eyes shot fire.

"Moe!" Travis yelled. "Look who we have here!"

A pair of overweight men piled out of a Ford Escort. They wore bike shorts, capes, and masks of pink and purple.

*Ahhh, finally: the men who put the "wrestling" in the Wrestling Station.*

"It's Captain Pudge Muffin!" Travis called out. He pointed at the portly purple-masked man and doubled over in laughter.

Seeing an opportunity to escape, Moe rushed to Travis's side. "No, it's Professor Plumpton!"

The wrestlers waddled up to the two derelicts, rolling up their sleeves. Travis flung the flowing nozzle away and it dripped gasoline all over the truck. Right next to Moe, puffing on his cigarette. I couldn't help thinking that I was watching one of those after school commercials about how underage drinking makes you do incredibly stupid things—like making fun of hillbilly wrestlers, each of them twice your size.

"We're gonna dance all over your ladyboy faces!" one of the wrestlers barked.

Incredibly, Moe and Travis put up their dukes—they planned to fight the overweight brawlers, even though they were outnumbered in pounds, six hundred to two.

Moe and Travis stood against the Dually, looking back and forth between their scrawny fists and the circling wrestlers. Moe's cigarette dangled out of his mouth as he swayed and taunted the masked men with ugly comments about their mother.

Then Moe did the most asinine thing in the world. He let the lit cigarette fall from his lips onto the ground, right into the puddle of gasoline.

Orange flames instantly leapt up the sides of the blue truck. The wrestlers reacted in horror. They quickly abandoned the mission, yelling "Run!" as they fled into the concrete blocked Wrestling Station.

I followed their lead inside.

The only people that stayed behind were Moe and Travis. Seems they thought that they'd actually scared off the wrestlers—that is, until they turned around and found the Dually engulfed in flames.

The store manager rushed by us, carrying a silver canister.

"Get away from there, you morons!" he screamed to Moe and Travis, who finally came to their senses and jumped away from the burning truck.

The manager pointed the canister toward the pumps, but nothing came out. The extinguisher was a dud.

"Run!" I screamed.

The manager, Moe, and Travis all sprinted inside. Just as they made it to safety, a huge explosion rocked the truck. The thunderous boom lifted the truck off the ground and spun it away from the pumps.

Moe and Travis watched it all, jaws hanging.

Within minutes, the fire department arrived. By the grace of God, the explosion spared the gas pumps. Only the Dually had been destroyed. And when I say destroyed, I mean burnt, charred, blackened, unrecognizable, Mom's-old-pot-roast kind of destroyed.

"Mosley Renee Petiot!" a voice rang from across the parking lot.

It was Mrs. Petiot and she was approaching the Wrestling Station with lightning speed, her eggplant-colored skirt swishing like a freight train. Apparently, Mrs. Petiot had stopped at Piggly Wiggly across the street and had watched the entire show. "You are in deep trouble now, mister!"

With reflexes like a puma, Mrs. Petiot grabbed Moe by the ear and marched him toward her car. Travis, on the other hand, didn't wait to learn Moe's fate. Instead, he ran as fast as his boots would take him down the dirt road behind the Wrestling Station—leaving the wrestlers with the last laugh.

"That boy is scareder of his momma than that burning truck," the pink-masked wrestler yelled to Moe, who Mrs. Petiot forced into her car. "That's what happens when you mess with the Hogg Brothers!"

The proud brothers laughed and began their war chant, beating their chests in rhythm followed by a big "Sou-wee!"

*Did he say the Hogg Brothers?*

Caleb called at four with news that Knox just left for the lake. If I went straightaway, I'd beat him there.

I jumped back into the Jeep and pressed down hard on the accelerator. "Thanks, Caleb!" *Put the pedal to the metal.*

On the way, I admired my girly pink nails. Bliss had discouraged me from my usual dark plum. "That's for goth kids. You want pink. Or better yet, Knox will want you to be wearing Barely Bare pink. Trust me."

I hoped she was right.

I sprinted to the *Escargot*, quickly climbing over the stern rail and ducking into the galley. I'd only been there a few minutes when I heard his voice. He sounded irritated.

"Who's below?" he called.

I felt stupid. It had seemed like such a good idea, but now I felt like an unwanted intruder. I couldn't move or speak. Images of Knox flashed in my head. The good times: when he leaned against the Tahoe, waiting for me to come running from the parsonage, or when he arched his eyebrows, revealing another Ashworth treasure, or when he kissed me, the fullness of his lips. And then I remembered the last time I saw him: his face angry, chiding me. And his note.

I struggled to breathe. Which Knox was up there now?

"I said"—the volume of his voice rose—"who's below?"

Finally, I bleated, "It's me, Jordan."

He didn't come down, and his silence was unnerving. I thought maybe he'd left. But when I popped my head out, I saw him against a cloudless sky. He stood on the deck with his feet wide apart and his piercing eyes studying me from between his heavy dark lashes. I wondered if he could see me shake.

"I'm sorry," I blurted out.

After a long miserable hush, he spoke. "What do *you* have to be sorry for, Jordan? I'm the one that left the cowardly note."

"Yes," I agreed. "But—"

I looked to the sky, trying to remember one word of my obscenely prepared speech, but nothing came to mind. I couldn't articulate my feelings. I was speechless, yet again. The water lapped upon the boat, rocking it back and forth. I grabbed hold of the wire cable along the side before I took a deep breath and dived into an apology.

"I'm sorry for getting frustrated with the people buying scratch-offs and holding up the line at the Wrestling Station when I just want to pay for my beef jerky and go. I'm sorry for being the kind of daughter who dismissed my parents without realizing they've been just as unsure of life as I am. Yet they have some wacked kind of love for me I can't even pretend to understand. I'm sorry for telling Bliss hedgehogs are silly pets. I'm sorry for calling Moe a summer teeth slimebucket and for helping to blow up his truck. Wait, no I'm not. Oh, remind me to tell you what happened earlier today."

Knox stood staring, his mouth partly open in a kind of loose grin. I didn't blink; I powered through the rest of my satisfying, emotional purge.

"I'm sorry for telling Stryder that Ashworth is worse than Flint, Michigan. I've never even been to Flint, Michigan. What do I know? Flint's probably great, too. I'm sorry for wishing that Hal used Listerine. He wouldn't be Hal if he did. I'm sorry for my intense self-ishness, my inability to step outside my tiny borders, and my conceit that led me to believe I was better than this place—than these people.

"But most of all," I said, meeting his intense golden hazel eyes. "I'm scared of 'never feeling the rest of my whole life the way I feel when I'm with you.'"

*Dang it, Bliss! I will not win his heart with lines from Dirty Dancing!*

I bowed my head, to gaze down at my Barely Bare toes, as if I could hide the embarrassment of my incoherent confession in the chemistry of perfectly set nail polish.

Then somewhere in the distance, I heard something remarkable, something I hadn't heard my entire time in Ashworth.

I heard it clearly, as if it lay right across the bay, even though looking toward the sound I only saw the soaring pines and the majestic blue afternoon sky.

It was East New Hope's bell.

The bell tolled over and over, ringing with powerful jubilation.

It surprised Knox, too, because he looked in the same direction with a fearless concentration.

"Can you believe it?" he asked, staring toward the trees.

"Yes," I whispered. "I can."

When he finally turned back to me, he didn't speak of my apology, ask any explanation as to why I was back, or comment on the bell. He smiled, and it seared my soul as he wrapped his hands around me.

"Welcome home, Jordan Klein."

# Chapter 27
*Two Years Later*

I drew open the curtains over the sink and opened the kitchen window for a shot of the familiar aromas—honeysuckle, pine trees, and cow manure.

Our new house didn't have a cemetery right outside, but still, the view was growing on me. Llamas, cattle, and goats roamed the fields in the distance.

*Not a bad view at all.*

I smiled. Shielding my eyes from the sun, I turned to watch as cars drove up our long, pear tree–lined driveway and parked in the large lot beside the new Lord's Pantry—a state-of-the-art food pantry, culinary center, and medical clinic. In just two years, Buck and a small army of handymen converted Jasper Hardin's 10,000-square-foot barn into an emblem of charity and goodwill.

After two years of planning, today was the grand opening.

"Morning, sweetheart," Dad said cheerfully as I turned and shuffled toward the coffee pot. Before I could respond, Hal shot through my legs like a bolt of furry lightning, and I tripped, almost crashing into the large Chinese vase Jacob sent us for Christmas. I don't know why I was surprised. Hal had been circling my feet sounding like an idling diesel engine ever since I got out of bed. Still, I glared at him.

*Keep it up, furball.*

"Did you sleep well?" Dad asked with a smile. Not only did he look calm and rested, he was fully dressed. His light blue suit complemented his hair nicely. At the same time, his royal blue-checkered bow tie matched my Star Trek bathrobe, which was also a gift from Jacob.

*Don't beam me up in this, Scotty.*

"Yes, anything beats my dorm bed." I sniffed at the coffee pot.

Knox and I didn't surprise anyone when we announced our senior year that we would both attend Southern Methodist University. Knox was following in Skye's footsteps by going pre-med, while I chose a less practical path—a double major in photojournalism and philosophy. I was quick to point out that the philosophy had nothing to do with my father, but most people didn't believe me.

"It's like sleeping on a chicken coop," I continued.

Actually, it was like sleeping on a magical marshmallow but Dad didn't want to know that. Even if parents won't admit it, they all want their college student to miss home. A few complaints about college life are simply welcomed affirmations of that belief.

"Well, you can come home and sleep in your old room any time you want."

*See?*

In his left hand, Dad held a greasy paper bag.

"Fried Twinkies?" I hoped. It was vacation, after all.

"No." He dangled the bag in front of me. "Fresh bagels."

My eyebrows raised. "Even better. Roshi's makes bagels now?"

"Nope. Cesar added bagels to the baking menu at the Lord's Pantry," he said, taking two out of the bag and handing one my way. "They're really good."

"Wow, a lot has changed." I took a sip of my coffee. But then I spit it out. "Actually, I take that back."

As I reached for a paper towel, the house telephone rang. I picked it up. "Hello."

"Hi, Rachel," the voice on the other end said.

"Hey, Uncle Jacob. It's me, Jordan."

"You're kidding? You sound so grown up."

"That's what two packs a day will do," I joked.

"Careful," Jacob said in a teasing voice. "That's what got Michael Jackson kicked out of Boy Scouts."

I groaned. "Still too soon, dude."

"Oh, sorry," Jacob said with a chuckle. "Is your Dad around?"

"Maybe, but first I need you to tell me the truth." I smiled at my father, his hand outreached for the phone. "Did you really have Dad wear a T-shirt that said 'Stupid American Tourist' in Chinese"?

"You heard about that?" Jacob asked with a chuckle. "Did you also hear how he wore it three different days before one of the other aid workers told him?"

"He left that part out," I said, shaking my head. "Nice talking to you, Uncle Jacob." With an exaggerated grin, I handed the phone to my expectant father.

Right after we got back to Ashworth, Jacob took a position operating an orphanage in the Yunnan Province. Dad went for a month last Christmas to visit and help with the semi-annual medical exams. He must have had an amazing trip, because now he and Jacob spoke at least once a week. They traded sermons, swapped funny stories, and shared prayer requests.

Luckily, Dad wrapped up his call with Jacob explaining all the day's planned activities right before Mom yelled from the next room. "Jordan! People are arriving. Don't you think you ought to get dressed?"

*Can she see through walls?*

"I laid out my olive military suit for you," she continued. "The one you love! And you told Knox to wear something nice, right? The *Herald* is in the parking lot and Channel 4 is supposed to be here at any minute!"

Dad shrugged. I tried not to laugh at the cream cheese all over his chin. It was a valiant attempt.

"I already showered," I charged back. "It will take me two minutes to change, I promise."

Mom's heels clicked against the parquet floor. She looked dazzling in her navy pinstriped suit and cream silk blouse. She insisted on wearing a suit every day, despite the fact that at Deskins & Klein, P.C., the clientele didn't always dress so, uh, formally.

She dipped pearl earrings into her ears and asked my father, "Did Boyd set up the stands last night or this morning?"

"Last night. Right before it got dark," he answered.

Bliss had told me that Boyd was working with the Pantry and had traded his costumes for a permanent collection of Dickies—Dickies that fit him now that he was four inches taller without putting on a pound of weight. But still, it was hard thinking of him as anything other than the tubby little kid in an Indiana Jones ensemble.

"How's Boyd doing, by the way?"

"He's done an amazing job," my mother interjected. He's really handy and Ms. Ray loves him. As Bliss would say, 'They're peanut butter and jelly.'"

I had to laugh. Sure enough, as I squinted out the window, I saw Ms. Ray directing Boyd on where to place folding chairs on the small portable stage. She threw back her head and giggled when he said something to her with a smile.

"Speaking of Bliss, she texted last night," I told my parents. "She got in yesterday. She'll be here by ten."

"Actually, she's already here." Mom pointed out the window.

Indeed, Bliss sauntered across the parking lot with Ally behind her carrying Mr. Prickles.

Bliss always said she'd be a star, and it hadn't taken long for it to happen. Only a few months after she graduated, she auditioned for one of those sing-yourself-into-national-humiliation kind of TV shows. Not surprisingly, she impressed the celebrity judges before she even belted out a note. And while she didn't win the competition, her fourth-place ranking secured a small record deal before she boarded the plane back to Dallas.

"Is she cutting the ribbon?" I asked.

"No," Mom said. "Knox didn't tell you?"

I hesitated. "Tell me what?"

"That we asked his mom and dad to do the honor. This was Skye's dream, after all, and the church voted to name the medical clinic after her."

*I guess that's what he meant when he said he wouldn't miss this for the world.*

How fitting, I thought. Now that the Lord's Pantry had come to Hardin Farms, it was only appropriate for Skye's family to cut ties with their grief and move on, claiming the Hardin ground and transforming it into something powerful and healing.

"Come on, Eli." Mom grabbed Dad by his arm. "We'd better get out there. It will be an exciting day and I don't want to miss a minute of it."

"Yes, ma'am," he said before turning back to me. "You're coming soon?"

"Just a few minutes."

I shuddered. It was still weird to see them like this.

*And by "this," I mean happy.*

I shuffled into the bedroom my parents had assigned to me in our new capacious castle. I sighed, relieved to see David Lee Roth above my bed (a token from the parsonage). As I asked Dave if I should really wear the olive suit, it hit me: Knox and I were going to take summer school this year. There wouldn't be an Ashworth summer.

*You'll miss me, Dave, right?*

After getting dressed, I took another opportunity to watch the madness from the kitchen window. I lifted up my camera toward the new Lord's Pantry and clicked a few photos.

The twins helped white-haired ladies fresh from the beauty shop out of the new church van. *Snap-Snap.* Fat babies crawled on quilts. *Snap-Snap.* The mayor shook hands with all that passed. And Cesar and a pack of followers grilled steaks at the edge of the crowd. *Snap-Snap. Snap-Snap.* Mr. Wheeler, Mr. Randall, Mr. Gober, Judge Cagle, and several other old-timers sat in lawn chairs sipping lemonade. *Snap-Snap.* Ms. Ray hugged Boyd around the waist. *Snap-Snap.*

I heard a roar from the bleachers as Buck took a microphone and jumped out onto a makeshift stage. He introduced the town's new mascot—as I liked to tease her—Bliss LeBaron.

Bliss politely curtsied and waved. She thanked the whole crowd with her trademark exuberance before stepping up to the microphone to sing her new song about diamonds and Pink Bubble Gum snow cones. *Snap-Snap.*

I set down my camera. This town wasn't perfect by any stretch. Actually, it was quite dysfunctional most of the time. But as I watched the crowd—the same faces I saw our first day in Ashworth—I didn't see it as I did then. As I looked at the faces this time, I knew each unique story. Some of the stories were lonely. Some were tragic. Some were lovely. But they were each connected by something bigger and more beautiful than themselves.

Only one thing was missing. I had yet to see Knox.

I scanned the crowd, and it didn't take long for me to pick him out. The teenage boy who I saw loading boxes into Madame Ribbette on our first day in Ashworth. The boy with kaleidoscope eyes who had captured my heart, stood near the stage with his parents and Caleb.

My heart still pounded.

A steady stream of Ashworth citizens approached the Colvilles with hugs, tears, and smiles. Even the mayor stood in the receiving line waiting his turn to congratulate them. As the line settled down, I watched Knox survey the joyous crowd.

*I bet he's wondering where I am.*

But then, he looked toward the house and met my stare.

I waved and he smiled. He pointed toward the edge of the crowd.

*What?*

He pointed again.

Did he want me to see Ms. Brackin wearing a balloon animal hat—compliments of the church pianist? No. Ms. Ray manning the bake sale table alongside Hamilton Hughes? No. The llama that looks like Rihanna chewing on Val's purse? No.

I threw up my hands in confusion.

Knox shook his head and pointed again. Straight through the crowd.

I peered harder until I caught a glimpse of it.

As I read the unveiled sign outside the new and improved Lord's Pantry, I knew the reason why my heart pounded so heavy inside my chest. I understood too that this was the last time it would work like this. For I no longer needed signs, bells, or anyone else to tell me:

"When God winks, miracles happen."

# Acknowledgments

I would like to offer a tip of my favorite black fedora to the many people who saw me through this book.

To my friends and muses from 3-to-1 Book Club, AH-HA Club, and to the countless other friends that love me for being me—an all things 80s–loving, aerosol cheese–eating, unflinchingly honest, nerdy mom lawyer from the sticks.

To the best coworkers and bosses ever. There wouldn't be a book if you didn't make me travel. From my lookout in American Airlines seat 10A, my imagination . . . wait for it . . . took flight.

To my editors, Trey Sager, Elaine Osteen, and Marna Wohlfeld who are all better than oatmeal pies, Cheetos, and guacamole combined. 'Nuff said. (That drives you crazy, doesn't it?)

To Moonshine Cove Publishing, for your support of my vision.

To my pastor, Dr. John Fiedler, who allowed me to borrow from his inspiring sermon on Joseph.

To my family. To my parents, two people who exemplify selflessness, superhuman patience, and amazing grace. To my grandparents, testaments to the power of good stories and fried pies. To my in-laws, for your unending support. To my brother in Tokyo, whom I miss.

Most of all, to my amazing husband, Barrett, and precious daughter, Micah Rose. I'm blessed beyond measure. Thank you.

# ABOUT THE AUTHOR

Natasha Osteen lives in Dallas, Texas with her husband, daughter, and one horribly obnoxious cat. When she's not writing, she's a loud-laughing, in-the-books, know-it-all, high-strung lawyer. *So the Sign Said* is her debut novel.

A Readers Guide for

## SO THE
## SIGN SAID

# Discussion Questions

1. What were your initial theories on who changed the sign? Did that view change?

2. How does Jordan's relationship with her parents compare to the way you and your parents interact? What causes the most disagreement between you? What brings you together the most?

3. Jordan's creative outlet is photography. What is yours? Is it something you want to share with others? Why or why not?

4. Eli said, "All events occur within the natural order, not outside the natural order. Stories of the unnatural are just that, stories. They're parables, told to make a point." Do you think the author agrees? Do you?

5. This novel is filled with colorful characters. Who is your favorite? Do you know any people like these characters?

6. The author wrote this story from Jordan's perspective. How do you think it would have changed if written from Eli's or Knox's perspective?

7. Skye's death is a tragedy for which Knox feels responsible. Is it fair for him to blame himself? Who or what is responsible for Skye's death?

8. Do you have any experiences with small towns? What have you learned from those experiences? Do you prefer the big city like New York, a small town like Ashworth, or somewhere in between?

9. Jordan likes Bliss because Bliss doesn't care about "boring scandals, cliques, or malicious gossip." Are you that kind of friend?

10. At the end of the novel, Jordan looks at the town differently. Why? What has she learned?

# Interview With Natasha Osteen

1. What inspired you to write *So the Sign Said?* Boredom! I travel a lot and the first time I jumped on a plane without a book, I started writing short stories instead of watching the in-flight entertainment, *Alvin and the Chipmunks 2*.

2. Is anything in your book based on real life experiences or is it purely all imagination? A little bit of both. When I started writing, I based most of the characters on people in my life or on people sitting around me on the plane (odd, I know). As the characters developed, though, they took on a life of their own. When I close my eyes, Knox looks a lot like my husband. My best friends were my inspiration for Bliss. My hilarious friend, Richard Muñoz, became Cesar. I based Eli on my father and Boyd on my brother. Ashworth started from a little town right outside Mt. Pleasant, Texas. East New Hope and its members sprung from memories of my childhood churches: The Heights, East New Hope, Gateway, and Highland Baptist. Oh, and my father did drive the youth group down a dark scary road slowing down so a church member could jump out of the woods swinging a roaring chainsaw (explains a lot, doesn't it?).

3. Which character was the most fun to write? Which one was the most challenging? I loved writing about Bliss. She's fun, feisty,

and what every person wants in a best friend—she talks *good* about you behind your back. Knox was the most challenging character to write. It took me a long time to find his voice and understand him, but once I did, I fell in love.

4. What was your favorite chapter to write and why? I love animal slapstick so the fundraiser scene in Chapter 19 is my favorite by far. Don't ask me why but if a book or movie has rodents attacking or animals causing catastrophes, I'm rolling on the floor. It would take me days to recover from seeing a montage of the errant squirrel in *Christmas Vacation*, the raccoon attack in *Saving Silverman*, the killer bunny from *Monty Python and the Holy Grail*, and the raccoon attacking the puritan in *Furry Vengeance*.

5. While you were writing, did you ever feel as if you were one of the characters? Yes. Jordan's voice came naturally to me. So did Rachel's. They're their own characters but with a pinch of me thrown in for good measure.

6. What do you like to do for fun? I head to my grandparents' ranch. We ride four-wheelers, hike, feed cows, and I laugh when my citified husband hides under the blankets terrified when Rupert the Horse chews on our window screen in the middle of the night.

7. When you were young, did you see yourself as being an author when you "grew up"? No, I thought I'd be the second kid to befriend an alien (thanks, *E.T.*) and later I thought I'd be an astronaut. As I grew older, my expectations became more realistic: I knew I'd be a member of the President's Secret Service detail. But that's what's great about growing up—we're allowed to change. I doubt Ice-T thought he'd build an acting career around playing a cop when he was rapping for Bodycount either.

8. What do you say to the critics who say *So the Sign Said's* ending is an "unrealistic, tidy ending"? I say, "Thank you!" I wanted to give readers an escape from the sometimes lurid and depressing issues prevalent in everyday life. *So the Sign Said* is meant for readers looking for laughter, absurdity, and heroism. If you've recently changed your name to Beelzebub and you sleep in a

coffin, *So the Sign Said* probably won't be on your top ten list. As for me, if I'm going to live with characters in my head for years, I need to like them and like where they're going.

9.  Is there any particular author or book that influenced you growing up? I was seven when I started reading *The Chronicles of Narnia* by C.S. Lewis. The enchanted world of adventures and talking beasts taught me powerful life lessons that stayed with me into my adult life. Plus, in my opinion, it has one of the best last lines ever: "All their life in this world and all their adventures in Narnia had only been the cover and title page: now at last they were beginning Chapter One of the Great Story which no one on earth has read: which goes on forever: in which every chapter is better than the one before." *The Chronicles of Narnia—The Last Battle* by C.S. Lewis. I still pick up those books at least once a year.

10. If you could go back in time and tell your teenage self one thing, what would it be? Hang in there! Life is going to get really awesome, then miserable, then okay, then unbelievably heartbreaking, and then it's going to ROCK from then on. Oh and no matter how great you think you look on the first day of tenth grade, ditch the big fly-catcher bangs and the leopard print mini dress. Trust me.

# Coming Soon

MUD MILE
by Natasha Osteen

## Chapter One

**"W**e're born naked, wet, and hungry. Then things get worse."
At least that's what I overheard the Gas-N-Dogs clerk tell his acne-faced apprentice.

I guess he grew up on Mud Mile, too.

Don't get me wrong—Mud Mile isn't all bad. If you can look past the shabby trailers and red clay yards so tough that grass can't grow, there are a few redeeming qualities.

Take Mrs. Pearl, for instance. In front of her trailer she reenacts scenes from *Bambi* with plastic animal art—pink flamingoes, deer, gnomes, cats, and rabbits. Happy scenes. Not the one where Bambi's mother gets shot in the head.

And then there's Mr. and Mrs. Payne, who only live here during duck season. Before they leave, they always bring my mom, little brother, and me dishes like home-cured duck prosciutto, duck confit, and duck in pomegranate sauce—each dish made from birds they downed near the creek.

Oh, and Lucy Parker deserves a mention. Sometimes, when the whole park stinks of spoiled Spam, I stroll by Lucy's because it smells like strawberry shampoo. Practically every lady in town has been to her beauty shop, which she runs out of her doublewide. Every now and again though some country club lady drives by in her shiny SUV, and I watch her jaw drop when she first realizes the fabled salon is just some podunk trailer.

That's when I hear the clicks of their doors lock. That's when I read their lips after they see me trying to catch a whiff of strawberries: "That poor girl. Living in a place like this."

Mom thinks I'm crazy. She says that Mud Mile is way nicer than Pecan Ridge, the other trailer park on the outskirts of town. Pecan Ridge accounts for half the county's domestic violence calls—or so that's the rumor. Sure, I'm glad I don't live there, but that doesn't mean I want to live *here*.

I'm only seventeen and who knows what I'll be when I "grow up," but I know I definitely don't want to be Mrs. Pearl or Lucy Parker or even the Paynes. I'm not staying in Mud Mile—not even for duck season.

The only person that truly understands is my best friend Piper. We've lived five trailers away since we were ten. Maybe we're different in a thousand ways, but we're cross-your-heart-and-hope-to-die friends until the end.

I'm on the debate team and she's head cheerleader. I'm into calculus and she's barely passing pre-algebra. My hair is blond, eyes brown, and skin pale, and I always get a zit right on the end of my nose, which—I'll argue until my death—is much worse than full-on acne. Piper, on the other hand, has legs up to my chest, green eyes that light up a room, long honey-colored hair swirling around her at all times like a lion's mane (she goes to Lucy's trailer *a lot*), and permanently sun-kissed skin (on account of her mother being Pilipino and all).

Everyone says she's the most beautiful thing to ever come out of Mud Mile.

Only problem is, we haven't made it out yet.

Oh yeah, there's another difference between me and Piper. She likes haunted houses and I abhor them. She says haunted houses are a great reminder that Mud Mile could be worse—like if it was inhabited by flesh eating zombies.

But I'm not convinced. And after the last time, I'll never visit another haunted house for the rest of my life.

"Are you chickening out, Quinney?" Piper yelled as we waited in line.

"I bet she is," chuckled Seth. "Quittin' Quinney!"

Seth: captain of the football team, with the brain cells of a carrot. Actually, I shouldn't insult carrots like that. Anyway, he's probably one out of a hundred boys in school that desperately want to date Piper.

"I'm not chicken," I snapped, cautiously watching a demon peering through a window of the haunted house.

Every year the Rosehill Jaycees put on a haunted house in the old Masonic Temple—the one we all think is haunted anyway. It doesn't take much to scare us, but the Jaycees go all out—a valiant effort for charity, I guess.

You can always count on the same basic characters. Dr. Landry plays a deranged dentist who cackles as he rips teeth from unmedicated victims—not the best advertisement for his practice, I might suggest. Karen DeLoach runs the insane asylum, where patients scream gibberish at the top of their lungs—probably pretty similar to her job as local mayor. The town sheriff, Rick Dugan, dresses like a mummy—rumored to be from torn bed sheets from his five-cell jail (yuck). And last but not least is the crazed chainsaw-wielding lunatic that chases you out the exit door—I never stick around long enough to figure out his true identity.

But this time, as we stood near the temple doors listening to the sounds of tortured souls inside, something felt different. More ominous. Even the moon hid behind thick clouds, like it was afraid to witness the events below. I was no fortune-teller, but something bad was going to happen, I just knew it. I fidgeted in line, mapping out an exit strategy.

"Yep, she's chickening out!" Piper yelled again. "Come on, Q-Tip. I swear there's a nice love-starved freak in there that will love to get his hands on you. Awe, Sweetie! You'll finally get felt up!"

The meatheads around us roared with laughter, but they settled down when Holden Black approached.

Thank God for Holden. Timely, gorgeous Holden—even in a "Hugs Not Drugs" t-shirt. He made the meatheads nervous, further cementing my prediction that half of them would be selling vacuum cleaners by our ten-year reunion.

"You guys really doing this?" he asked.

"Of course we are." Seth puffed out his chest and ignored the lady running from the haunted house as if her hair were on fire. "I didn't know youth ministers were into this sort of thing."

"I'm an intern," Holden corrected him, "and I'm not *into* this sort of thing. I'm just a casual observer."

"Maybe you should casually observe Quinney!" Piper busted out.

As mortified as I was at Piper's outburst, I knew she couldn't help herself. There was no room for argument, Holden was "R-E-D with a little bit of H-O-T"—as Piper would say. He was a seminary student from Dallas doing an internship at the local church. And when he started, let's just say I got "religion." I made a point to attend Sunday service so I could catch "the gospel according to Hotness" (another Piperism).

Piper comes sometimes too, except mostly on Sunday nights for youth night (free pizza), Wednesday nights for youth Bible study (free potluck casseroles), and when there are special outings (with free food). But Sunday mornings I'm on my own because Piper's too busy sobering up her stepdad and his loser girlfriend.

Luckily we reached the entrance right before I died of embarrassment. Above the door, "Highway to Hell" was inscribed in glowing hot pink letters.

"This way, my pretties," a warty witch ushered us through a door. Within seconds, we were face to face with Dr. Landry and a groaning, half-alive patient. Blood, guts, and teeth were strewn everywhere. Real teeth Dr. Landry collected over the year.

*Gross.*

I gripped Holden's shoulders tightly, already petrified. But digging my nails into his soft skin gave me some mild respite. Now I'm glad I was at the tail end of our group.

Before I could daydream about why Holden smelled like butterscotch, and I started concentrating on our next destination: an extremely dark and narrow hallway. I'm a bit claustrophobic—which is ironic for someone that lives in a trailer park—so there are few things worse in my book than wandering through tight hallways of pure black.

I whispered to myself, "Baby steps! Baby steps!"

But my self-admonishments couldn't drown out the sound of Seth snickering ahead, delighted in my terror.

When we passed Mayor DeLoach she handed me a blood-stained prescription for bat's eyes. Her assistant, Sheriff Dugan, was coming undone already, long strips of cloth dangling from his arms and legs, as he moaned, "I want my Mummy."

Focusing on Holden was the only thing that helped get me through the ten-minute journey through hell.

"Hey watch it!" Seth barked.

Someone must have stepped on Seth's heel in the pile-up for the last room.

"Sorry, but you shouldn't stop short in the dark," Holden laughed.

"I didn't stop short, you—"

"This year is so lame!" Piper giggled.

But even in the darkness she couldn't fool me. I heard the quiver in her voice.

Out of nowhere, Freddy Krueger appeared in front of us.

"Then you won't mind going first will you?" Freddy Krueger asked, pointing at the door to the last room.

The door to the chainsaw guy.

"Bring it on," Piper said. She quickly tossed back her hair and punched Freddy on the arm.

"Oww," Freddy groaned. I recognized his voice—Rocky Porter. Ironically, Rocky really did live on Elm Street. He was also on the list of Piper's one hundred suitors.

"Uhhhh," he stumbled. "Okay. Here's how this works. I'm going to open this door for you one at a time. When you get to the end of the hallway, you'll find a room with six neon doors, and only one of those doors leads to the exit."

"Yeah," Piper replied. "We run around in the pitch dark trying to find the way out while some freak with a chainsaw chases us. I get it."

Piper turned to the rest of us.

"I'll go first. Then Seth, it's your turn. Chuck, you're after that. Then Holden. Then Quinney."

"Actually, I'd like to go last," Holden volunteered. He winked at me and I clumsily winked back as relief rushed over me.

"Piper, have some oxygen for me on the other side," I shouted as she started towards the entrance. "I'm sure I'll be hyperventilating."

"Your nightmare begins." Freddy Kruger grinned, and he opened the door.

Piper disappeared.

A minute later, Seth went. Then Chuck. The sound of screams and the chainsaw reverberated through the walls.

"I don't want to go," I complained, my heart pounded for all kinds of reasons.

Holden smiled. "You'll be fine!"

"You'll need more than encouragement after this nightmare," Freddy growled, urging me forward with his bladed fingers.

With a deep breath, I walked through the doorway. Behind me I heard Holden asking Freddy about which charity would receive the proceeds.

That's Holden. Always thinking about others, even in the face of a hideously deformed inbred cannibal who planned to butcher us.

I inched down the hallway until I reached the main room. It was strangely quiet. No hum of the madman's chainsaw. Except for one light bulb clinking overhead, it was dark, but I could see the six neon doors surrounding me, just as Freddy mentioned. On the right side, a pink door and a green door. On the far wall, pink and blue. On the left side, pink and yellow.

My mind raced. Where was the chainsaw guy last year? In the left corner or the right? Geez, Quinney. How do you not remember?! The left, I think. Yes, he was most definitely on the left last year.

*One. Two. Three.*

I didn't move. *Okay. Okay.*

*One. Two. Three. Go!*

I ran as fast as I could to the first door on the right, hoping he stayed true to form. At the same time my grip hit the knob, I heard the telltale yank of the cord. The chainsaw purred behind me.

The first door wouldn't open, so I quickly rushed to second. It was locked, too.

I could feel the psycho closing in, and I hurried over to the third and fourth doorknobs, but to no avail.

*Frick!*

Only two doors remained.

I feigned a step sideways, hoping to buy some time, and then booked it to the far wall, catching a glimpse of the latex monster man heading straight toward me. I found the fifth door locked—just my luck—so I knew the sixth was my ticket out. But when I pulled on the final knob, the door wouldn't open. It was stuck. Or one of the other doors was stuck!

*Which one?!*

*Go! Go! Go!*

Running in circles, I tried each door again, and again, my heart pounding and senses crazed by the smell of gasoline and the chainsaw whirring way too close to my ears.

*Why won't the doors open?!* I was completely freaking out.

Then I saw her.

*Piper.*

Piper peeked through the slightly opened blue door, laughing hysterically. I couldn't believe it. She and the meatheads held the door closed so I couldn't get out!

I decided she needed to die ASAP, whether by chainsaw or some other horrific manner, but first I had to escape.

"Run, Quinney!" Piper yelled. And I did, but unfortunately, my legs had a meltdown and suddenly I was on my back, staring at the maniac, who straddled me with the chainsaw over his head.

Part of me said, "This guy's harmless. He's a Boy Scout leader or a local politician trying to give me my money's worth." But another part of me said, "This guy is nuts. He's lost it. He's really going to tear me apart."

I froze in fear. I tried to move but my limbs refused to budge. Sweat stung my eyes and my heart raced.

"Come on, Quinney! Get up!" Piper yelled.

Grunting, I yanked myself off the floor and scrambled to the blue door.

Once I finally got outside, Piper screamed, "CR-AAA-ZY! Did you see that guy with the chainsaw on top of you?!"

"Yeah. . . I . . . caught . . . that," I stammered, trying to catch my breath. My prediction of hyperventilation actually happened.

Shortly after, Holden flew out of the exit. "What happened in there?"

"Quinney just got the piss scared out of her!" Seth said, pointing at me.

I glared at Seth before I answered for myself. "They thought it would be funny to hold the exit door shut."

Piper huffed. "We were just playing around, Quinney. You're fine now."

Holden shook his head and stood there—all tall and gorgeous with brilliant blue eyes. "Are you okay?

I felt a lump in my throat but I smiled and nodded anyway.

"What about your jacket?" he continued. "Will you be able to fix that?"

"Oh no," Piper added, her eyes wide. "Your leather jacket is totally trashed. Like you picked a fight with a lawnmower!"

*My jacket? What happened to my jacket?*

I looked down at my shoulder. A tear! I really was going to kill her now.

I'd worked at the Piggly Wiggly an entire month for that jacket, and now the shoulder was shredded! I tried not to think about those hours of counting green bean cans, bagging groceries, and cleaning the women's bathroom.

"Oh shit!" Holden yelled.

*Uh oh.*

I knew something was pretty bad if the church guy cursed. His usual pseudo-explicative was "holy manly mustache" or something silly like that. I looked down and saw the cause of his impious reaction—my sweater soaked in blood.

*Wait, what?*

In a split second, the pain hit. Raw heat surged across my shoulder and down my arm. I knew it! I've always said these places were inherently unsafe. Sure, the stupid chainsaw doesn't have a chain on it but it's still a big piece of vibrating metal! It must have nicked me on my way out the door. It wasn't deep—but it was bad enough to cause quite a stir among the local ghouls.

I truly would have enjoyed hearing the 911 call: "Yes, please send an ambulance. A man dressed as Leatherface and wearing a woman's dress injured an honor roll student with a chainsaw."

"Don't worry, Quinney," Piper said as the ambulance arrived. "I'll help you."

"Like you did in there?" I snapped.

She looked stung, but I bet it didn't hurt as much as my shoulder.

"I'm going with her," Piper informed Holden and the paramedics, who loaded me onto a stretcher.

"No," I said firmly, looking at Holden. "She's not allowed."

It wasn't until they rolled me into the ambulance that I glanced back at Piper. She stood in the midst of the meatheads watching the doors close.

Yes, I knew I'd forgive her the next day, but for the time being . . . She could go to hell.

*A portion of the proceeds
from the sale of this book will be donated to
Crossroads Community Services
to support its mission to nourish people
and power change by providing nutritious foods
to families in need.*

*For more information, go to
www.ccsdallas.org*

CPSIA information can be obtained at www.ICGtesting.com
Printed in the USA
LVOW131835120313

323909LV00008B/777/P

9 781937 327071